Tails From The Park

MAX with help from

TIM HAMMILL

Copyright © 2015 Tim Hammill

Cover Art: Deborah Graham

Book Formatting: The Story Bodyguard

All rights reserved.

ISBN: 1518770282

ISBN-13: 978-1518770289

DEDICATION

For Cissy.

TAILS FROM THE PARK

CONTENTS

AUTHOR WELCOME

Hey!

Thanks for reading *Tails from the Park*.

The stories are arranged in cycles. Some are short. Some are as long as my whiskers. I'm purring.

Pretty good for a handsome cat, right?

I've been telling these stories to my human friend, Tim Hammill. Like the great cat friend he is, he's taken the extra step to get them published just for you.

You wouldn't be here if you didn't like cats and stories. That's definitely me. A cat who tells stories. I'm working on more…with Tim, of course.

I'd really like to hear from you. Send me a message at maxtails123@gmail.com

Want to know when the next story is out? Join the Max Gang. I'll personally let you know what's going on.

http://eepurl.com/bomzvr (Just copy and paste in your browser).

Head bumps!

Max

INTRODUCTION

Long ago Max came to Tim Hammill and said, "Tell my stories."

That's how it all began.

We've had fun telling the ~~tales~~ tails. We hope you enjoy all the Max adventures and end up with your fair share of Maxitude.

TAILS FROM THE PARK

1 THE PARK

My name is Max, and I'm an American Shorthair.

I'm a white cat with a dark gray cape and a hood. To top off my look, I have a solid gray dot on my white tummy. I'm not tall for my species, but I'm attractive. Some of the people I know actually adore me. Not bad for an older feline who lost his youthful cute factor a long time ago.

That said, I possess a wonderfully chubby shape. I'm solidly built and have the most outstanding large yellow eyes. My tail is full, but not too long, and when I playfully run from my dad, that's my human dad, I bend it just so, like a furry question mark in the air, making me look…well…cute. My humans (parents) think it is all so delightful. Silly people! I weigh in at 15 pounds; I'm 12.5 inches tall at my shoulder and have excellent balance. I'm brave to a fault. Dad calls me his little scrapper, much to the chagrin of my mom. I'm extremely soft spoken and hardly ever say much.

I am the spitting image of my mother. My cat mother was an American Shorthair (ASH), too, and a real beauty. I'm very proud of her, even though I only knew her for a short time. Our genes came from either a wild Bobcat *Lynx Rufus* or maybe a European Wildcat *Felis silvestris* from the woods of middle Europe and Scotland. My siblings...and there were a lot of them...were all sort of mixed up. I was the only true Shorthair in the bunch. Not all felines can be shorthairs, you know!

I now live in this trailer park, and time stops when you're here. Well, it slows way down. The park has a wall around it, like a fort in the wilderness. It is, in fact, its own little world. The park absorbs you, holds you close, not allowing the outside in. It is hard to imagine just how little noise can be heard from the busy street just over the perimeter wall. I guess it is the nature of the park with so many sky-high trees keeping the noise at bay. They are much higher than I'd ever like to climb. If it isn't low and easy, I ain't going up it. Of course, there are the nicely curving streets and the large grassy field next to the offices and the Rec Center. It's quiet even when the local kids play quietly on the grassy field.

When first we arrived, I never went out of the house. Mom and Dad wouldn't let me. It was three whole days before I got to go out onto the deck. Maybe my parents thought I'd get lost.

Sadly, I still miss my cat mom. You see I was only a few months old when I got separated from her. I've been trying to find my way back ever since. Life was tough at first. After all, I was young and all alone on the streets. I had to live by my wits, constantly moving from shelter to shelter, always trying to find my way home.

One day in my lonely wanderings, when I was eight months old, I came upon this lady watering her lawn.

With my best sad face and blazing, lusty, yellow eyes, I cast a spell on her. She gave me a drink of cold water straight from the garden hose and took me in to meet this man, who was something of a loafer. They treated me like a king, which was good. They became my new mom and dad whom I have come to love dearly.

My dad was forever on something called a job search. He started taking things to some place called a pawnshop. In the next two years, we moved a couple of times. Mom referred to it as downsizing. We went farther and farther away from where I was born near the ocean. That's how we wound up here in the East County, living in The Park.

I remember the first day we arrived. They bundled me into this thing that they cheerfully call a cat carrier. More like a portable prison, if you ask me. She, that's my mom, always uses it to take me to that horrid person, the "Vet." He dresses in this long white coat and happily shoves implements of torture up my butt. Why do they smile at you when they do such things? It downright hurts!

On moving day, the sky was cheerfully blue. Mom was talking to me non-stop in this silly baby voice that she thinks calms me down. Actually the carrier wouldn't be so bad if she would just shut up, drive the truck, and let me sleep. I really do find riding in a car soothing.

After a short drive, we arrived at this carport thing. She parked the truck under it. My dad was already there. I could see him just over the top of the dashboard from the back seat. With military precision, Mom took the carrier...with me in it, from the truck. Dad held the back door of our new trailer open, while she raced up the short stairs and down the hallway in a blur, and arrived at the back bedroom somewhat out of breath. She softly placed the carrier down on the floor. Opening the door, she swiftly turned, smiled and waved at me. Then she exited the room, closing the door firmly behind her.

I sat there calmly waiting to see if she would come back. She didn't. I could hear noises down the hallway. Their voices seemed so close, but no one came back to see me. After I had waited some time, and knowing the drill from our other moves, I decided to leave the carrier. I stepped carefully out and into the bedroom. The bed was there, and several half-opened boxes sat on the floor. Oh! And my sandbox! Boy, was I overjoyed to see it. I crept up onto one of the boxes and gazed into my litter box, which was clean... Thanks, Mom!

When the bedroom door sharply opened it scared me half to death. I sprang to the floor from the top of the box I was standing on, making a beeline for safety under the bed. I stayed there overnight. Dad tried to coax me out, but no way. They both seemed distressed that I'd act this way, and that was good. They needed to suffer for the way they had treated me.

The days went by, and my time finally came. I slipped out of the bedroom and into the rest of the house. Mom found a fantastic spot for my sandbox, and my favorite furniture sat roughly in the same spaces as I remember them at our old house. Jumping up on the top of the couch, I made my customary three complete turns, what my mom calls "Max's round trips." The couch sits in front of an unusually large picture window where I now regularly snooze. I spend a lot of time waiting there for things to happen on what my parents call "Cat TV."

Of course, everything had changed outside. I was eager to go and explore this place they call the park. Finally, when I did get out to wander around, I discovered that my new home is rather large. It goes on for blocks and blocks. It is much bigger than any place we'd ever lived before.

It is extraordinarily large, and it's shaped like a big lopsided oval. It slopes down from the hill that is across the busy street. On the north side, a creek runs just off the property line, but it is mostly dry. Most of the units on the northwest corner are smaller and cheaper to rent. There's a tremendous number of people coming and going over there, usually on the weekends. And then there's the wildwoods…a place that is bleak and spooky.

The entire park is paved in this black stuff and has these things called speed bumps, so cars cannot drive too fast. This is good for me…being built so low to the ground I can be hard to see.

The trailer where I live with my mom and dad is number 248. It is the fifth on the right from the corner at Thatch Street, which runs around the perimeter of the park in sight of the office building with the Rec Center and pool.

The exterior of our trailer is a beige color, trimmed in a medium brown. The roof is peaked, as most of them are, but it has an extension that slants down slightly over the carport. I do love the roof; it's a really great place to sleep. There are a few bushes in the corner at the fence line, in the backyard where our property abuts our friend's, Mr. Neighbor. There's also my dad's metal shed where he keeps his motorcycle.

On the other side of the trailer is a covered deck where Mom keeps an abundance of plants, mostly palms. There are a few ferns, herbs, and a smattering of other plants. As a dutiful son, I often help her water them.

Later, I'll lie on the deck in the sun, stretching out in my most comfortable way. With my front legs stretched out, I look more like the Sphinx than the original.

Sometimes, off to the west, a trailer's open window might bring me some music. I might hear a dog bark or even some children laughing from around the corner. Then there is my most favorite of things, the sound of birds on the wing.

Later, I'll go inside, and maybe bang out some hefty ZZZs on my dad's desk. I'll curl up in a large furry ball in his inbox where Mom puts his mail, leaving him a smattering of cat hairs. Drives him crazy this does, sort of feline payback for him being so pesky to me all the time. My parents free feed me, so whenever I get hungry I wander over and power down some kibble.

Gotta keep up my strength; never know when an interloper might show up. Of course, I'd have to deal with them, being guard cat for my mom and dad. I might be small, but I am fierce.

For now…I slowly gaze out and around, taking in my abode, my vast new kingdom.

Then I ask myself: do these people really deserve a good king like me?

Purr, Purrr, Purrr…

2 THE REAL MAXTOR

OK, Tim wrote this in the third person just to preserve some humility on my part. We had an editorial discussion. I finally gave in…but just for this chapter.

Firstly, Max is super cute, a very attractive feline…

Max is an American Shorthair, but not a purebred…

He loves chocolate…[1]

He is a troublemaker big time, always getting into things that don't really concern him…

He's a white cat, with a gray cape and hood. The white runs up onto his shoulders forming a kind of two-tone effect like a nineteen forties' paint job. He has a large round gray dot on his white tummy.

---

[1] Chocolate is poisonous to cats. I made a big mistake with chocolate and suffer the consequences. Please do not feed chocolate to your cat!

When he runs and is in a good mood, he bends his tail over almost in half.

Max is 12.5 inches tall at the shoulder. He weighs in at 15 – 18 lbs., and is pear shaped when sitting up due to his chubbiness.

At the time of writing "Tails from the Park" Max was seven years old. He came to live with his human parents when he was only eight months old. He was not a stray as much as he was lost to his cat family.

Snorks… Is a sort of nasal sound that makes him sound almost "Pig-ish"…. His Dad laughingly calls Max a 'pig-in-a-cat-suit" because of Max's snorking sounds.

Has a series of Meows and Mews, Murs, Meurs, Merr-rawed, M-aw-w-r-r-r's and Maaah-raaah…However, these can mean anything. He rarely growls or hisses.

Max licks his lips when upset or anxious about something.

Max likes to think of himself as "the king of swat".

Cat TV … A place but also a refuge of sorts. It is the top of the couch in Mom and Dad's house in front of the big window. Like all of America, there is always a couch in front of a window looking out to the neighborhood.

Chuff… Or chuffing / chuffs, this is a cat thing mostly male cats do. A sort of a sneeze goes along with it.

It is used when Max needs to show disapproval of an adversary. It is very negative.

Russian Blues… Is not only a breed, as we well know, but here in the park the Blues are a horde of gangsters. They are Max's sworn enemies.

ZZZZZ / ZZZs / ZZZed etc. definitely a Max thing, it simply means he is sleeping.

T-Rex smiles… When he holds his mouth open about halfway, exposing his teeth while breathing heavily.

Lusty Eyes… He slits his eyes and stares at you until he gets his way.

Laser Eyeballs… A term his mom coined describing Max staring at her (usually to get her to let him outside). This technique is also accompanied by Max sitting in front of her so she cannot ignore him.

Nods…. He has a distinct head nod, where he throws his head and chin up instead of down.

Max's round trips…. Another Mom-ism. Max always turns three times around in a circle before he settles into a nap.

Duck position…when he lies down with his forelegs and paws tucked underneath his body. Making him look like a duck decoy.

Full Turkey.... Is just like a Duck position only with his forelegs extended out, and his rear legs swung out from his body.

Sphinx ... Is when he does his Turkey but his front forelegs are crossed at his wrists. Very regal looking indeed.

Max communicates to us via narration, he never talks directly to us or anyone as the stories are told.

Max is brave to a fault. And is often caught fighting with other cats. He has a real problem with the Russian Blues, a previously mentioned group that has invaded the park.

Max has lost a claw to fights and one to trying to get out of a pit in chapter Fuerza Bruta/Brute Force.

Max has an incredible sense of smell, allowing him to follow a human scent for miles and miles.

He is smart and can read!!! Kind of maybe, well...he thinks he can...plus, he can count... sort of.

Sadly, Max is fixed, but has a huge love for Baby, the female Calico cat. He also loves his human mom and dad.... Like all young boys he idolizes his dad.

Thinks of himself as helpful, but Max is fundamentally lazy and loves to catnap.

Children love Max and many have tried to "cat"-nap him.

Max often lies about how high he can jump. As a rule he can get himself up to a four to five foot height. However, he has been heard bragging that he can make a six to eight foot leap.

Max has two human enemies in the park...the manager and the maintenance man (who has often chased him in his golf cart).

Loves Halloween night, when he likes to lay in wait to scare the trick-or-treaters.

Loves empty boxes.

His dad plays with Max using a string then runs down the hallway so Max can pursue him.

Max has numerous toys that his mom has bought for him. His most fave is what Max calls his Santa toy. It is a Christmas tree ornament that he absconded. At times Max has imaginary battles with this toy.... calling it "The Devil Santa".

Max can see most colors with the exception of red, but this might be false.

Doesn't mind being picked up and will lay like a baby in his mom or dad's arms.

MAX

Max has a very good sense of humans who are decent. But teenagers have fooled him, therefore he is very wary of teens.

Has not killed anything since he came to live with his mom and dad.

Max does not swear, but he does have some most fave and colorful cuss words like "dog poop" which he rarely uses.

Max has a sunny and bright personality...And is eager to help and learn from the humans he comes in contact with.

Is not afraid of heights
Loves water and
Rain…
Loves to drink from a hose or faucet…. Will watch water running down a drain for hours.

Loves all trees…but is too lazy to climb tall ones.

Curiosity always gets him into trouble.

Zoned. The ability to look like he's intently listening to you, when actually he is far away. It's not unlike being hypnotized. Being in the zone is where cats go to be rid of their pesky humans.

3 MONDAY, MONDAY

Monday. Can't trust that day... or can you? It started out as a really nice one. When the first rays of sunlight came dancing through the curtains, it was like hitting the snooze button for me. I yawned, twitched a little, and had a bout of the blinkies. Time for me to get up from my fave sleeping spot, located on top of the couch looking out of 248's big window.

The sun made itself known around six thirty. Earlier it was more of a glow, which I like, too.

Because it means I've got the whole day to sleep. Most cats will power out at least eighteen hours. I don't need that much--maybe ten, no more. Like most of my feline brethren, I take it in small naps spread out over the day.

Mom came out of the master bedroom, shuffling down the hallway in her fuzzy slippers. After getting herself ready for her part time job, she'll get Dad up to go out into the world.

My dad had been on an extended job search. On Mondays, they planned out an area where dad would do his weekly hunt. But this Monday was turning out differently. Dad hadn't made it out of the bedroom when Mom opened the sliding glass door to let me out.

"OK, sweetie," she said. She calls me stupid names like that all the time. "I bet you want to go out, don't you?" She always says these "Momisms" in a squeaky voice that I just hate. I try to be a dutiful son by giving her one of my special head butts against her leg. If I feel really good, I give her a snork, that's sort of a special sound I make, drawing air up through my nose and open mouth at the same time. My dad says it reminds him that I might be a pig in a cat suit. I often don't know exactly what my dad is talking about.

I took my first steps out of our trailer and walked out onto the deck. There I struck a heroic pose like those big cats do on TV, sniffing the air for any intruders. Nothing… the coast was clear.

Mom said, "Oh, Max, what are you doing? As if, there were anything dangerous here in your own backyard. I truly wonder about you sometimes." She shook her head and smiled her wonderful mom smile. She held her robe close to her body. We walked to the opposite end of the deck, and she picked up the newspaper.

Across the street, I saw a small group of children at the bus stop. One called out to her friend who was trying to catch up. I had to turn to see her. The straggler was struggling with her backpack and was also carrying a brown bag that emitted this wonderful smell.

Fish!!! A smell I knew all too well. Unable to control myself, I was compelled to follow this young girl as she ran across the street to take her place in line with her classmates while she talked to a girlfriend.

Mom, now stood in the street, and called for me. "Max, Max, where are you?"

The doors of the bus were open and the kids marched in, no one had noticed me at all, as I walked by the girl's side. The girls sat in a seat about midway; and I, ever so quietly, jumped up, between them. I sat politely, looking straight ahead, not wanting to be rude. Finally, she looked down at me and she gave out a little "yelp." In response I "Meowed" a nice and finely crafted greeting for my new friend. She smiled and glanced away. Then finally she reached over to look at my brass nametag.

She said, "Your name is Max." At the mention of my name, my tail swished back and forth excitedly. She pointed her thumb at herself saying, "Well, Max, nice to meet you. My name is Tammy."

I had a feeling that this was important to her, so I gave her one of my nods. That's where I sort of move my head back instead of forward, bringing my chin up. This brought a huge smile across her funny little face. She must have been about ten years old. I had not seen her around or I would have remembered her sweet face with her long blonde hair and blue eyes. I couldn't see how tall she was and, to a degree, I don't care about that too much. It seems everyone is a whole lot taller than me. What struck me was her smile, which was just like my mom's. That made me feel safe.

Tammy noticed my nose flexing in and out, taking in the fish scents as I breathed. My piercing cat's eyes were locked on her brown bag. All at once she smiled broadly and said.

"I think Max wants my tuna fish sandwich." She looked over at her girlfriend and they both giggled. She opened her brown bag, reached in and pulled out a large covered thing that simply smelled divine, she unwrapped it slowly.

I sat up totally erect, with one front paw on her leg, I came in close, my nose working very fast indeed. She pulled out a chunk of white meat on her fingertip and offered it to me.

Her girlfriend, sitting next to me said. "Hold it down so the bus driver won't see you." Then she laughed into her hand.

My new friend held the big chunk out as I hooked a claw into it and ate it in two bites as some of it fell into her other hand. Then I devoured that as well. Tammy offered me more, and more still as the bus pulled away from the curb.

For the moment, I was content in the warmth of the bus, my tummy filled with fish. Children continued to enter as it stopped on its route. The last was a big kid, who carried a large box covered in plastic wrap. It smelled bad, but my sense of smell had been disturbed by my tuna fish breakfast.

Bobby was this kid's name and he wanted to sit in our seat. He made a big deal out of us sitting in his spot, but Tammy defended all of us, then explaining that I was her "Show and Tell" project. The big kid had to sit in the very back row with his large square box on his lap. The bus turned up the park's main street that led past the office and rec center. As I looked out the window, the light was snapping past the trees up in the branches, I could just make out some of the park's squirrels, dancing and flittering about, making their horrible squirrel noises in their horrible squirrel voices. Someday I'll get me one of those beasts. Until we moved here I had never seen a squirrel.

As we traveled, the rhythm of the bus gave weight to my eyelids. Curling up into a ball next to Tammy, I drifted off to sleep. I was laying down some good ZZZs, when Tammy woke me up, with a gentle nudge from her elbow. I looked up to see her funny face and her girlfriend.

"Come on, Max. You need to get up…we're at school."

The girls giggled as I got to my paws and stretched my back in an arch. Tammy was busy pulling out a bunch of books from her backpack. I sat and watched her when the big kid in the back reached over and tried to grab me. Screaming, the girls fought him off. He went out the back door saying he'd tell on her and he'd get me yet.

The crowd of children was thinning out. Tammy opened up her backpack for me to climb in. Her girlfriend's face beamed in laughter, "He will never get in there, you dope," she said. Tammy smiled holding back a giggle. "OK, Max. Time for us to go, so in you get."

If there is one thing about me, it is the fact that I am very curious. So I stuck my head closer to the opening of the backpack and sniffed at it. I gotta tell ya, it was really inviting.

A huge voice came from the front of the bus, "Come on girls, you'll be late for class."

With that, the voice got up out of the driver's seat and started to walk down the aisle picking up candy wrappers and other trash. I glanced up to see his enormous body fill the aisle of the bus. Without a second thought, I scooted inside the backpack. Tammy pulled the drawstring of the pack closed with a quick snap of her wrist.

I felt comfy and safe inside this nylon cocoon. Actually I could see through it. I could make out Tammy's shape as she stood up in the aisle. She pulled the pack up and over her shoulder. My body settled into it at the absolute bottom.

As we walked along, I could hear voices all around me. Some of my fur must have been sticking out of the pack because someone pulled on it. This got a pretty big 'meow' from me. The hallway echoed in laughter. Then we went up a flight of stairs, my body bouncing inside her backpack as we went. Tammy stopped. I could just make out a doorway. She stepped inside and swung the pack off her shoulders, placing me gently on the floor. I struggled to get my nose out of the top, but the drawstring had been tied too tight. I settled down and waited… again falling asleep.

Later in the day, the trip home was really just the reverse of the trip to school. But, this time, I was saying, 'goodbye' to a lot of new friends. On our street, Tammy got off the bus, still carrying me in the pack. She stopped in front of the trailer across the street from my parents'. She was trying to make up her mind about something.

As she approached our trailer, I stirred inside my nylon cocoon. She walked up the stairs. At the top, she took the pack off of her shoulder, set me on the deck, and then knocked on the screen door.

On the third knock, the screen door opened. My mom looked down at Tammy, "Yes?" she said.

I could see Mom through the webbing and let out a little "meur." (That is a little throaty, soft sort of sound…not quite a "meow.") She must have heard me because she looked around just as my new schoolmate introduced herself.

Tammy's youthful voice lifted up towards my mom, who now looked down at the backpack. "Hi." The youngster said with a smile, "My name is Tammy I live down the street over on Paloma."

"OK. Did you hear something?" my mom asked.

"Like what?" The youngster replied.

"I don't really know. It sounded like…."

"Like Max," replied an excited Tammy.

At the sound of my name, I let out another "meur". Tammy knelt over to untie the top of the pack as she continued. "I've got your cat, Max. He came with me to school." After she opened the pack, she reached in and lifted me out. Eagerly I extended a paw out toward my mom. My new classmate kept on talking as Mom held out her hands and took me. She kissed me all over my head bone. Yuck, I thought and I shook my head vigorously.

Mom held me up in front of her. She gazed straight into my eyes and said, "I've been looking for you all day long, mister, but you've been at school with Tammy." She sighed, and smiled that Mom smile.

Tammy told her all about how I got on the bus and rode to school with her, and how all of her girlfriends giggled and petted me. And her teacher giving me (I mean us) first prize for something called "Show and Tell." She related how I sat real still during her presentation about our ride to school on the bus to the class. I waited with baited breath, dreading the next words to come out of Tammy's mouth, but she only stood there and smiled a little sheepishly.

This is what she didn't tell my mom.

As I sat on Tammy's desk at school, I could smell it and hear it quite clearly. It was surrounded by lots of Tammy's classmates all "o-o-hing and a-a-hing" over it. In fact Bobby held not a box, but a cage, in his arms just a few feet away. In it was this incredible squirrel, all red and fluffy. But that didn't stop me from leaping off of Tammy's desk. I scurried around kids' feet and tried my best to grab at the beast through the wire sides of the cage. This bit of cat frenzy made all the kids in the class squeal and laugh. Tammy had to pry me from the cage as I howled and hissed at her much to everyone's delight.

And for a few moments this was all it was going to be, a stand off of sorts. Bobby, the owner of the squirrel and a much bigger kid, started to yell at Tammy about me. He waved his arms around; as he did the cage slipped out of his grasp and fell to the floor. The oversized door sprung open and for a second the squirrel and I locked eyes. I twisted and turned in Tammy's arms pushing against her body to get free, but she held me tight. It wasn't until Bobby turned and shoved her that she loosened her grip and I jumped to the floor. Immediately the squirrel took off in a bid to escape me.

I took off after the runaway squirrel out of the classroom and down the hallway. At the end was an open window with branches of a tree within leaping distance. A big bell went off and lots of children started to spill into the hall. We dodged them with no great effort, me on one side and the squirrel on the other. Then I drifted over into the middle only to have the squirrel leap over me as he darted to the other side, or was it my side?

The end of the hallway was getting closer and closer. I came within a few inches of my prey, but he was just too quick. We made two more passes when suddenly the last of the classrooms emptied and even more children came running out. Three stopped in front of us, Mr. Speedy (and he was, too) dodged to the left. I slipped past a small kid's feet and slid along the wall on our right. My eyes were glued on him as he streaked to the safety of that open window, now only a few feet away.

It was now or never... I dropped down as low as my body would allow and dug deep for more strength. With the wall as a brace I leaped up to the window casing. The squirrel did exactly the same, but he seemed to fly over it, and past me.

The last I saw of the squirrel he had made this incredible and effortless leap into the tree and was gone. On the other hand, being unrestrained, I tumbled across the window casing and for a fraction of a second I could look straight down to the ground; I was very high up indeed.

I held out both paws and with claws extended I snagged something, as I slid to the edge. Whatever it was, it was a white color and it chipped off as I slipped over the edge of the window. My whole body seemed to swing right to left, and then back again. The chips had stopped flying as did my movement, at least my downward movement.

My legs ached and I thought my claws were going to tear out. I looked around for a way out, but really the only thing I could do was to let go and drop to the ground and hope for the best.

I let out a huge "Meow." No one came to my rescue. My mind drifted to Baby, an acquaintance of mine, that I might not ever see again, or my Mom. Next time I should mind her and stop what I'm doing before I get into trouble, like hanging out of school windows dangling way too high off the ground.

As I looked up Tammy's head popped into my view from the depths of the window. With a smile on her funny face, she reached down to grab me by one paw and with her other hand she snagged me by my other leg and pulled me back through the window and into her arms. She squished me almost to death, my eyes bugged out of my head bone. But I didn't care and licked her on her face over and over again.

I've never been so happy to see a child before, ever!

She got me back to her desk, again much to everyone's delight. Well, everyone but the teacher. There was a big meeting at the back of the classroom between the teacher and a man in a dark suit about sending Tammy and me home.

Tammy swore me to secrecy saying, "Now Max, we won't worry your mom with the squirrel adventure. It will be our secret…OK?"

Tammy reminded me of a time long ago, of a secret of my own, when as a kitten, I lived in the house by the ocean with my cat mom and my cat family. One morning a fresh-faced little girl came out of the house into the backyard where our entire litter of kittens were chasing after flies and eating the wavy tall grass. Upon seeing this little girl, my siblings all scattered amongst the bushes and into the big cardboard box that served as a playpen for us.

The girl came across the grass with this enormous grin on her face, sort of stumbling as she ran toward me. Bravely, I stood motionless in the yard. Squealing with delight, she tried to pick me up, but she didn't have the strength to hold onto me. After a few attempts, she got tired of this and simply sat down in front of me. Feeling playful, I stood on her legs and rubbed my cheeks against her face. As a kitten, I was just learning…I'd seen my cat mom do this with the people who lived in the big house. And everyone seemed so happy with her. The little girl let out this wonderful laugh. Over her shoulder, I could see a tall woman at the back door of the house. She smiled too. Overwhelmed with excitement I jumped, in my kitten's fashion, up toward the little girl's face. She screamed in terror then fell over to one side. Witnessing this, the woman yelled something and ran toward us. She had a dishtowel in her hand that she snapped at me. The tip of the towel caught my hindquarters and it stung mightily, too. I ran to the safety of the bushes in the yard, with my rear leg throbbing in pain.

Tammy's young voice snapped me back from the past. She was asking if she had done anything wrong by taking me to school. If not, then maybe she could come over and play with me in the future. Mom thought about this as she let me slip through her fingers and drop onto the deck with a thud. I guess I should lose some weight. I walked over to Tammy and rubbed my entire body up against her leg. Looking up, I could see my mom smile down at me. The moment seemed to hang for some time, as the past and the present revolved around in my mind. Expectantly, both Tammy and I watched her.

"Sure you can," my mom replied.

"Great," Tammy said. Then, she bent down to pet me.

Mom stepped back into our trailer. As she held the screen door open, she said, "Come on Max. Your big day with Tammy is over."

Before leaving, Tammy opened one of her books and took out a white piece of paper with a blue ribbon attached to it. Offering it to my mom, she explained, "This is Max's award from my teacher. It's yours. Everyone in the class applauded when my teacher called out his name and I went up and got it," she said, her voice filled with pride. Still smiling, she repacked her books and waved goodbye. We both watched as she walked away down the street.

Tammy would come to visit often in the next months and I'd see her from time to time on the big grassy field where all the kids play. She would come over to me, wherever I was, and stroke and pet me. Then one day she and her parents moved away from the park. But that wasn't to happen for a long time, there were too be many adventures and mysteries yet to come with my new friend.

My mom looked down at me saying, "No one's going to believe this…and a blue ribbon, too."

I headed off towards the couch. As I climbed up to my perch, Mom placed the piece of paper with the ribbon on the dining room table. She laughed out loud and turned into the kitchen. I made my customary three turns to get comfy, what my mom calls "Max's round trips." I settled into my most favorite spot to knock off some ZZZs before dinner.

Mom was right. It had been a full day. ZZZs.

P.S. They are still looking for that pesky squirrel, too.

4 NOT FADE AWAY

I lay deep in sleep in the warmth of the sun. There, in the early morning light, the Roly-Poly man came around the corner in his chug-chug truck. Suddenly I heard little footsteps coming across the deck. I rose like a lion. On seeing them, I sat to be polite. First the white one spoke, oh so sweetly. She was followed by another, all, in black. They fluttered their wings when it occurred to me that they might be feline tricksters, and merely here for fun? Or could they just be bums? Who could have so quickly taken to flight?

But instead they had found it easier just to… not fade away.

This dream was still vivid in my mind when I awoke. My chest thumped and for a second it was hard to catch my breath. Rolling lazily over in the tall grass, I gazed up into the morning sun, my vision filled with glaring white light.

I stood, but was a little shaky. I yawned, and then had a good stretch, first my front legs one after the other. I thought I heard something coming from the deck—the sound of tiny footfalls padding along. No one appeared, so I assumed I was the only creature here in the back yard. Slowly the dream came back to me, which is odd, because I can't remember most of my dreams, at least not entirely. But this one, though vivid and clear, made no sense to me.

The dream aside, the day was new and wonderful. I walked up the stairs and onto the deck to check out what was happening here, at our end of the park.

Across the street, my mom's friend, Victoria, was up. Broom in hand, she had already swept off her driveway. We'd had a week of strong winds and there was a lot of debris on the streets and all over the park grounds. Of course, the big field, that's where all the kids played, was speckled with leaves and branches. Victoria waved at me as I drew back yet another big yawn.

With a final blink, blink I started my day.

In back of me, the sliding glass door opened and my mom stepped out. She also yawned big as she made her way to retrieve the newspaper that lay at the bottom of the stairs. She waved at Victoria and wished her well; the two women walked to the middle of the street where they spoke something called "gossip."

I slipped unnoticed past the railing, and then silently dropped to the ground. In the corner of my eye, and from above, a flash of white appeared. Startled, I stopped in my tracks and followed the white flash as it darted through the air many feet off the ground. Behind me, one of my mom's hanging plants spun around and around. A black streak swooped low just missing me. I crouched in the front garden then sprinted to the middle of the street keeping low, my nerves on edge.

I glanced over at Mom and Victoria as they continued to talk. For the moment, all was quiet. Oddly they kept swatting at the air all around them as if bees or something were attacking. Thinking this odd even for the park, I forced myself to simmer down and waited cautiously.

From around the corner came the familiar sound of the mailman in his little chug-chug truck. Such a funny man! Of course, he liked me and took me on his adventures delivering his mail. So when he pulled up alongside my mom and Victoria, I simply walked over and stepped up into his truck. I hopped up to the big bag he had filled with letters and settled in. Off we drove. Then he reached over to grab for more mail when he accidentally grabbed me.

He knew immediately what this furry thing was and exclaimed, "Hey, Max, where you been there, sport?"

I nodded and gave my friend a big snork. He smiled and we continued on down the street delivering mail to all in the park. At old Mrs. Anderson's, he had to get out to take her a large box which he got from the back of the truck. He struggled with the box because his big tummy got in the way. Maybe that's how he got his nickname "The Roly-Poly Man."

Mrs. Anderson was watering her front lawn. The two of them talked as the cool spray drifted across the yard, and into the truck and me. I closed my eyes and lifted my face to the spray letting the water touch my whiskers and make them all dripping wet. When I opened my eyes a streak of black jetted across the truck's windshield. I sat up alert...and arched my back (it makes us cats look bigger to a foe, you know). To my amazement, a small white chubby kitten sat in the street beside the mail truck. She (I seemed to sense she was a she) sat looking sweet and calm, then she nodded to me. I took a step toward her when a pair of upside down pointy black ears appeared at the top of the windshield. More of these ears and the top of a furry head came into view. Finally, a kitten's face with flashing yellow eyes stared back. The appearance of these chubby little imps stunned me.

Meanwhile, Mrs. Anderson and The Roly-Poly Man parted; they waved and he walked briskly back to the truck. Beguiled, and being way too curious for my own good, I decided to leave the mailman to his rounds and stepped out of the truck, exiting on the driver's side. As he boarded The Roly-Poly man bent over, he ruffled the hairs on top of my head bone and said. "See ya, Max. Have a good day."

The truck drove off on its chug-chug way, swallowed up by the morning's light. This left me alone in the street. Well, maybe not exactly. Why hadn't he seen them as well, I wondered? As the truck pulled away the black one disappeared behind it. Then he reappeared from the other side only now in midair...he had wings; he was flying!

Immediately, I understood those white and black flashes and streaks earlier.

The kittens moved over in front of me, she, the white one, was very dainty and polite, even lady-like. Her blue eyes were soft and peaceful, her smile tranquil. She sat calmly then stretched out these magnificent white wings from behind her. She almost levitated off the blacktop. He, on the other hand, was something else. Impatiently he tapped his little foot, err paw...as he stood in front of me. His forelegs crossed over his chest that made him look comical but stern. Their features were as fine as I had ever seen on any cat, kitten or adult.

Excitedly, her tail switched back and forth like all cats do. That's when he did a bad, bad thing. He side stepped over to her and stomped on the tip of her tail.

The smile never left her face as she pulled her tail out from under his rear paw. Only then did she shoot him a stern look of her own.

He's a troublemaker, I thought. Later I would learn what an understatement that was.

"We're your angels, Max, and we are here to help you whenever you wish," she said sweetly.

Oh, boy! As if I didn't have enough troubles…now I have angels.

5 BABY

Today I thought I'd spend time outside; but first, I have to get Mom to open the door and let me out.

How do I do that you ask? Why, laser eyeballs. I sit a few feet from her, with all my poise and natural grace, and stare at her intently. It works every time. Lately, she's been scouring the newspaper for a job. Not for her but for my dad. So it takes a little longer than usual, but in the end I get outside, as I pass through the door I often give her one of my best snorks, which she always likes.

Outside, I test the air to see if there were any unwanted guests. If there were, I'd immediately chase them off which I truly love to do. Today there were no skunks, possums, raccoons or any felines who were lost. Some of those freeloaders like spending time lounging in the tall grass I call flage. On our deck, my mom has a bunch of palms and lots of ferns on tables, which is good for me, lots of places to hide. From behind these pots, I lay in wait for my dad so I can ambush him. I'd do my wiggle-butt for traction and launch myself out wrapping my front paws around his ankles. Then I scamper off, with my tail bent half way over.

As fun as my parents can be, sometimes it's good to get away from them. On these occasions, I go see Baby.

Baby is a beautiful calico that lately I've lavished a lot of personal attention on. Her coat is a mottled brown, tan and black on her all white body that is way off the charts. She's new to the park and I've been helping her get used to the place with all of its wild ways. Most importantly, I have shown her who not to carouse around with. It's hard to believe, but there is a bunch of unsavory Russians here. Yep, Russian Blues. We've no idea where they all came from, but the other day I found a couple of these wannabe badasses lurking around and was challenged to defend my territory. It was a mad scramble of teeth and claws. I managed to draw blood on the biggest one. The second one took off. I just let them both go, because I'm not as fast, I am more stocky and muscular, and totally fierce.

I needed to inform Baby about this important bit of cat news. I stood in front of her sliding glass door waiting for her mom to come and open the door so I could sneak in. I saw my Baby on the couch. As she rose up, she stretched. Makes me a little faint just to think of it. She is sooo beautiful. She finally got off the furniture and sashayed over to sit in front of me. She nodded hello. Then we stared at each other through the glass door for the longest time.

I wanted to tell her about those horrible Russians. The story would end, of course, in the description of me, the hero.

At that moment, a yellow cab pulled up to Baby's trailer. Out of the rear door stepped Baby's mom, bag in hand. She looked sort of sad as she walked up the steps. I sat up giving her my best T-Rex smile, opening my mouth and wrinkling my nose. Then I glanced over at Baby to see if she was checking me out. Yep, she was smiling too. Baby's mom bent over and scratched me on the back of my head so I gave her a couple of snorks. She smiled that sad smile, took out her keys and opened the door.

Quickly, I slipped in between her ankles just before she stepped into the house. Sneaky, huh?

Baby followed her mom over to the couch in the living room. The room looks just like ours only painted green. The drapes are long and good for scratching. The couch is older, lots of carving on the arms and legs. I walked straight over and rubbed up against the nearest leg, leaving my scent on it. Just to drive Baby crazy later.

On a low table next to the couch, the phone rang. Baby's mom picked it up and said "Hello." Baby hopped up on the couch and waited patiently beside her mom, her long tail switched back and forth. I moved to where Baby's tail dangled over the edge of the couch. She turned and looked at me as I softly bit her tail. She responded by hitting me on my head with her paw. I dropped her tail and took off down the hallway, with Baby in hot pursuit. We ran into her mom's bedroom where I hid under a bedside table. She couldn't see me from the middle of the room, and then I darted out. That's when she tackled me and we tumbled over and over.

Coming up fast, I almost had her by the scruff of her neck when she bolted to the right. She collided with the table on which another telephone sat. The receiver got knocked off the cradle and the handset fell to the floor between us. We could hear her mom's voice clearly. Together Baby and I leaned in to hear what was being said. The voice on the phone was low. It sounded like the other person had been crying. Baby's mom said that she'd heard the news about her sister and had been waiting for a call, anxious for an update.

They spoke like this was a secret, her sister being sick. Both agreed it would be a big help if Baby's mom could move back to this place called Detroit to help take care of her sister. The low voice informed Baby's mom that the sooner she got back there the better. They finally agreed on a date to pack and vacate her trailer. Then the low voice asked what she was going to do with Baby. They talked about something called an animal shelter.

The voices said goodbye. Baby's mom hung up. The buzzing of the phone was the only noise in the room. Soon Baby's mom stood beside us. She bent down and picked up Baby, cradling her like an infant. Lovingly holding Baby, she sobbed.

I felt like an intruder at this moment so I walked down the hallway to the kitchen and out the open sliding glass door. Outside, the evening sky had turned dark. Angry clouds filled the horizon.

I didn't see Baby for some time and truly missed her. A few days later I walked over to her trailer. There was an awful Russian blue by her back door. I slowed down. He stood his ground and stared at me. I came to a stop and took a low posture, my ears laying back. I took a quick look over my shoulder to see if any others were in back of me. When I turned back to face him he, was gone.

I strolled up to the glass door. Baby was there rubbing against it and purring the sweetest purr I'd ever heard. I nodded in my most cavalier way and rubbed myself against the glass as well. This was getting us nowhere.

Looking around I noticed there was an open window with a wire screen over it. The problem was, it was too high and there was no place for me to land.

I needed to think about this. As if on cue, Baby appeared in this window.

A plan came to me.

I sprang up with all my might but fell short of the window. I tried again. This time, my paws hit the screen. Incredibly it moved. I tried again. I extended my claws, but I couldn't hold on. When I landed on the ground I felt a pain in one of my fore claws. Blood trickled in between the pads of my left paw. I ignored the pain and once again flung myself up at the window. With Baby pushing from the inside and my fifteen pounds pulling from outside, the screen finally separated from the window.

We fell to the ground. I blinked at Baby. The two of us took off toward my place running as fast as we could.

Back on my deck Baby licked my wound and nuzzled me. It was fantastic. But what could we do next? Could she stay with us? My mom and dad would have something to say about that.

As we sat pondering these questions, the answer drove up and parked in our carport. My mom was home. As Mom approached and caught sight of my bloody paw, she screamed and scooped me up. I tried to wiggle out of her grasp, but she managed to hold onto me.

Baby gazed up at us.

Mom jerked the slider open and in she went, but the door slid shut before Baby could get in. I meowed my most desperate meow. Mom no doubt thought I was being a wuss.

Mom cooed, "Oh you poor thing, so much blood, you are such a little trouble maker." Followed by. "Tonight I'm going to keep you in for your own good." With that announcement, she turned and finally noticed Baby. "Who's your little friend, Max? She sure is a pretty one."

Mom kissed me on my head bone, and then took me into the bathroom.

Faintly I could hear Baby's sad meows calling me, from the deck.

Mom didn't let me out that night. I think she knew something was up. In the morning, she gave me extra fresh water and food before she left for work. My dad was out of town so I'd be locked in with no way to get out to be with Baby. Later when Baby did show up we talked a bit through the glass door, using our special language of meows and mews. She'd slept outside our trailer all by herself, listening to her mom call for her late into the night.

Then I remembered the hole in our bathroom floor: If you pulled the corner of the carpet back you could look down and see the underside of our trailer. Maybe she could squeeze through the hole and into the house. Excitedly I ran to the glass door and told her my plan. Like a shot, Baby took off. From outside I heard her as she started to dig a hole under the trailer skirts. I pulled back the rug and a streak of light poured onto the ground below, showing her where to go. In a minute, her paw reached out of the darkness from below.

Looking down, I saw her yellow eyes peering back at me; her purrs filled my ears and my head. Reaching over with my paw we touched. I was transfixed.

More problems. First, she could only get her muzzle through the hole and more importantly, she hadn't eaten in at least a day. I bolted to the kitchen and my food bowl. I pushed it with my nose across the slick kitchen floor. At the rug, the going got tougher and slower. After only a couple of feet the bowl stopped. I'd gone as far as I could go by just pushing it. And I was still only halfway there. I sat and thought about what to do next.

Baby's paw dropped back down the hole and out of sight. She must have been terribly hungry and utterly exhausted. *Think, Max, think.* I was going mad with no plan B. The minutes painfully ticked by when I saw her nose and part of her muzzle again come up through the hole in the floor. Instantly I knew what to do.

Springing to my paws, I scooped up a few pieces of dry food from my bowl, and carefully walked back to the bathroom. There I dropped small amounts of dry food to her through the opening. She ate it hungrily.

So far, so good. At least she was safe and close to me. After a while she indicated she was full. There was water out on the deck, and I knew she could smell it OK.

Our next problem: what was going to happen with her mom and what was this shelter thing?

The answers would have to wait because we both fell asleep. I had never felt so complete in my life.

Dad returned that night, which kept Mom occupied. I stayed away from the bathroom so as not to draw attention to Baby. Later I overheard Mom talking to her girlfriend, saying she thought she heard a child whimpering in the night. The sound seemed to come from under the trailer, she said.

In the morning, Mom announced that she was going to investigate the sounds from last night. My dad told her to be careful, the metal skirts surrounding the trailer might be sharp. Then he left on his job search. Armed with a flashlight, my mom walked out of the door to find the source of that noise she had heard the night before. I tried to go out with her, but she used her foot to hold me back. I leaped up onto the forbidden kitchen counter and watched Mom's progress.

She found the hole pretty quickly. Surprisingly it was quite large and I found myself filled with pride at Baby's feat. Mom easily pulled back the metal skirt and exposed the underbelly of the trailer with its forest of jack stands and plumbing. Cautiously she bent over, and then she stuck the flashlight into the opening. Then two things happened; Mom spotted me shouting. "Max, you get off that counter, you bad cat."

"Sticks and stones, Mom," I thought.

And Baby flew out from under the trailer. She was up and over the backyard fence in a flash. Mom turned just in time to see that magnificent tail disappear. I heard her whisper, "So, it was her."

Returning to the house, she picked me up off the counter and said. "I had a feeling you were involved in this mystery." She continued, "Seems you have a friend there, buddy."

"Yes, OK?" I thought, "but where did Baby go?"

Mom left for work and again she locked me in. All day long I lay beside the rug and the hole in the floor waiting to see if Baby would return. I must have fallen asleep because the next thing I heard was the kitchen door opening. My mom walked in with her work stuff and a missing cat poster in her hand with Baby's picture on it.

Mom walked into the bathroom, bent down and pulled the piece of rug back exposing the hole. Looking down, she could see directly into the underside of the trailer. She must have remembered it, too.

I stood up, my eyes still blinking from my catnap. Just then Baby's paw appeared. Mom gasped, then laughed and said. "So that's where you've been." I bent over and nuzzled the side of my face on Baby's paw and looked up at my mom.

Standing up, she took the poster and as she walked through the kitchen she grabbed a handful of my cat food. She left through the sliding glass door. In a few moments, Baby's paw disappeared. I ran into the kitchen and jumped back up onto the counter just in time to glimpse Mom with Baby in her arms, leaving through the back gate. Sadness swept over me. I hunkered down and waited.

Night fell. People coming home from work flipped on their outside lights. Our end of the park slowly came alive. Then I heard footsteps on the deck. The glass door opened and my mom stepped in. She was holding her arms against herself saying, "Damn it's cold." She turned and opened the door wider. To my surprise, in walked Baby's mom with Baby in her arms. She let Baby slide down out of her arms onto the floor. I jumped onto the floor to stand beside Baby. The two women talked. Baby's mom asked my mom if she intended to fix something, saying that it would have to be done pretty soon. I didn't understand what they were talking about. Then they both turned and intently looked at me. But that didn't matter, Baby was here.

I crawled up to where Baby was sitting and submitted to her by laying on my side. She responded by licking my head bone and rubbing her cheek against mine. The women looked down from their imposing height. My mom asked. "Did you know about this?"

Baby's mom replied. "No, I had no clue." They smiled at each other, and then hugged as new friends do before saying goodbye.

As she left, Baby's mom was softly crying.

And my life would never be the same.

6 BLACK DOG

It's as if he'd stepped out of a dark novel on a bad night in the driving rain. He had that look about him: an aura of evil. This beast was black from his scarred head to the tip of that long, thick tail. His mouth hung open, emitting a constant stream of drool. As he walked he dropped his massive head low, sniffing the ground for a scent of something to hunt, to kill and eat...something like me.

We'd all taken to calling him Black Dog as if it were a title of sorts. Mean and dangerous, he must have weighted in at 150 pounds. A Labrador mix with a lot of Rottweiler in him, he would be a handful for anyone. And the tik, tik, tik, tapping of his long claws on the blacktop was eerie... especially at night.

He appeared at odd times, there was no way to know when he'd show up. But he always came from the south, his scent drifting ahead of him. Most cats at my end of the park were all keeping close to home because of him. I'd taken to lounging on the deck, keeping one eye on the street and the other on Baby...just in case.

So I wasn't surprised one late afternoon when Black Dog silently strode into view, slack-jawed, drooling, and looking mean. He'd silently come from in between two trailers down the street. I knew he was hunting. He was snorting now and again with that nasty, drooly grin on his dog's face. To make matters even more intriguing, the park's maintenance man appeared in his golf cart from the opposite direction. Both stopped suddenly and stared at each other. I've had several run-ins with the maintenance man in the past, all of which ended in my being blamed for lots of damage that, in fact, I was not responsible for. Well, at least not all of it. I knew this man had a bunch of tricks up his sleeve and didn't play fair when it came to transient animals drifting through 'his' park. Maintenance Man got out of his vehicle, a long pole in his hand. A looped rope was at the other end.

Suspicious, Black Dog moved sideways. His ears twitched. A menacing growl emanated from deep in his throat. As a rule, I try my best to leave all dogs alone. But even I can't trust myself from doing some sort of mischief, to these beasts whenever I can get away with it. My Good Angel felt sorry for him; even my Bad Angel said I should pass this one up. So I decided to let it go and watch these two morons fight one another. But then I heard a voice come from a small box sitting on the seat in the golf cart. The voice belonged to the Park Manager (who disliked me as much as Maintenance Man did). The black box screamed, "Do you have him? Well…do you?"

Maintenance Man reached for the box, pushing a button on its side, he yelled into it. "Not yet, I'm…"

Black Dog chose this moment to lunge at the loop of rope on the end of the pole. He grasped it in his meaty jaws and pulled on it, hard. Maintenance Man was yanked away from his golf cart, his left arm extended as far as it could go. He tripped and stumbled across the blacktop, toward Black Dog. Deep growls filled the street as Black Dog pulled Maintenance Man, who had now fallen onto the street, dragging him farther and farther away. Maintenance Man struggled to his feet and pulled the pole back. For a moment, it was a standoff.

Curiosity came over me. I wanted to see what was up with this black box; the one Park Manager was hiding in. Good Angel warned me not to be so nosy… Bad Angel agreed. He said with a wink, "You might get hurt." A dare is a dare even coming from a cat angel. Stepping off the railing, I dropped to the deck. An easy leap from there brought me to the street and the golf cart. In a second, I was standing over the black box. The Park Manager was still yelling instructions to Maintenance Man on how to apprehend Black Dog.

Trying to steady himself, Maintenance Man grabbed the windshield brace on the golf cart. His adversary made one last effort to pull him away. Then the looped rope broke in two. For a moment it looked like this heavyweight bout had ended in a draw. Well not exactly. Tricky Maintenance Man lifted the pole over his head, and brought it down hard, missing his opponent by inches. Black Dog simply placed a huge paw on the pole, making it immobile. Barking furiously, the massive canine bit the pole and wrenched it with ease from Maintenance Man's hands. Then the mighty beast thrashed the pole from side to side in victory.

A little shaken, Maintenance Man reached over for the black box but grabbed me instead. Not surprisingly, my Bad Angel flew away in a hurry. With a howl I lashed out at Maintenance Man scratching and clawing his hand and arm. He recoiled and yelled in pain. I had but a second to make my escape. I stood with my front paws on the backrest, which turned out to be a mistake. With my bare back exposed, he was able to grab me by the extra fold of skin over my spine. In pain, I let out another howl as he pulled me off of the seat and held me up over his head with a look of triumph on his face. But it only lasted for a second, because when he looked down he was staring straight into the dark eyes of Black Dog.

In an instant, Black Dog reared up to his full height and snapped at Maintenance Man's arm. The massive dog missed, but his weight pushed his adversary over. Halfway down to the ground Maintenance Man's grasp on me loosened and I fell out of his hand and onto the street with a painful thump. Dazed, I rolled over onto my side to see him running down the street yelling something about a mad dog. While I was trying to get up, the shadow of Black Dog swept over me. He stood astride where I lay. Terrified, I looked up at him. He opened his mouth, huge amounts of dog drool hung down inches above me. Yuck.

I thought "Oh! Max you poor slob, this is it," and closed my eyes, awaiting my fate.

I could feel his breath on me. Then his teeth grabbed the scruff of my neck and, ever so carefully, he raised me up. Just as carefully he walked back up the steps of our house and placed me softly on the deck. The next part I hate to admit…but he started to lick me from head to tail.

Mom chose that moment to come home. The sight of me lying on my side all soggy with dog slime and with my enormous rescuer standing guard over me, must have given her pause. She stopped at the bottom of the steps. Black Dog came up on all fours and menacingly leaned forward, again a deep growl coming from deep in his throat. Mom stepped back, dropping her work things on the pavers. I think she must have been scared, but it didn't show on her face. For a few seconds my new buddy watched her intently. I let her know I was OK by giving out a nice "Mah-rour-r-r-r." Then incredibly, this gigantic beast whimpered as he sniffed the air over the deck railing. On alert, his ears rapidly twitched from side to side.

From the south came a whistle, then what sounded like a young boy's voice called out a name that I'd not heard before. Barking, and dancing from side to side, Black Dog knocked over a couple of my Mom's plants, immediately his thick tail wagged when two people, a woman and a young boy, appeared in the street in front of our trailer.

My mom slowly turned toward the street, a slight smile on her face. She waved, haltingly at them. Black Dog bounded from the deck with a happy look on his battered dog's face, he flew past my mom and almost knocked over the middle aged woman who was holding a dog leash and collar in her hand. He lovingly licked and nuzzled both of them. I watched this family reunion with keen interest.

I'm going to have a little talk with my Bad Angel, soon.

Still nervous, my mom sat on the steps and began talking in jerky sentences, finally asking the woman where they had come from. No doubt she felt relieved at being liberated from the danger of this giant dog, who now appeared to have an owner.

The woman introduced herself as Val and her son, Robert. They also lived in the park. They had to leave their dog at home alone in the daytime until Robert returned from school to let him out for a run. Today they were both late, so Black Dog had simply let himself out. Val was aware of the complaints about their dog and his occasional fights and wanderings in the park. She'd not said anything to the park manager about owning a dog because they hadn't paid extra money to have one in their rental.

During this conversation, I'd taken up a spot next to my mom, nuzzling her side as she listened to our new friend. I leaned on her, as I was still a little groggy from being man and dog handled.

In a moment of truth, Val told my mom how she'd wished she'd gotten Black Dog fixed to keep him at home and not out fighting with the neighborhood dogs. Now she feared he was too old.

After a pause she said, "It's getting late and we don't need to be here when the maintenance man comes back for this thing." She indicated the golf cart still parked in the street, the radio crackling out its interesting sounds. My mom's new friend took the leash and collar and slipped it over Black Dog's head; he looked at her with love and devotion. Robert clapped his hands, and took the leash from his mother then the two of them ran off down the street. Val said good-bye to my mom.

While Mom petted me in silence, she gazed thoughtfully beyond the now empty street. We sat there for a long time. Later during dinner, when my dad asked her what had happened that day, curiously she replied:

"Nothing."

7 RED SAILS

Saturday is supposed to be a good day, a nice day. It should be a relaxing day, not unlike all of my days. So I was terribly put out when my parents woke me up early out of a sound sleep. I mean, how rude! Besides, my mom had kept me in last night and there was no food in the bowl.

Mom kept going on and on about how she refuses to have what happened to that woman's Black Dog happen to me. She got up from the table. "Do you want any more coffee?" As she passed by the refrigerator she exclaimed, "Oh, damn. Look how late it is, you've got to go if you want to see the V-E-T today."

Unconcerned, I yawned and stretched out to my full length. As Dad disappeared into the laundry room he replied, "You mean you don't want Max tom-catting around at night getting into fights and being a tough guy?" I closed my eyes and heard him rummaging around above the washer-dryer in the laundry room near the back door. "What is he up to?" I asked myself in-between yawns.

"Yeah, right!" Said Mom. "Let's put it this way. If you don't take him, you wouldn't be tom-catting around me either." The noises from the laundry room became louder. "You had better hurry… It's quarter till and the doctor doesn't wait around for anyone, especially on Saturdays."

Now on full alert, I opened my eyes and licked the top of my nose…a cat thing. In seconds, that dreaded cat carrier came into view. Dad was going to take me where?

The drive to the vet's was unnerving at first. I had just started to relax when he stopped the truck, opened the rear door, and took the carrier out. He did this "click-click" noise he thinks I like. I hissed back at him. He didn't fool me…I knew this horrible place was the veterinarian.

We went into the waiting room that was painted a sickly green color. He placed me in the carrier on the floor next to a chair. He talked in hushed tones with the receptionist, who sat behind a large piece of glass. She was a young girl of twenty or so. She smiled at me. I instantly hated her, too. Dad came back and sat in the chair. He stuck his fingers through the vents of the carrier trying to scratch me behind my ears, but there was nothing he could do to ease my suspicions. After a while, I heard the girl call out my name.

Dad picked me up and we went through a door into a small white room. Inside, all those doctor smells engulfed me. At the sight of the silver table, I started to panic…licking my lips repeatedly, another cat thing. Dad placed the carrier and me on the table. The doctor entered. He had a small head but was very tall and thin. He looked odd in his white coat. In one swift movement he opened the carrier's door reached in and pulled me out.

I can usually break away from most people. But these doctor devils have a way of holding your front paws and rear legs so you can't move. I looked at my dad and hit him with my most heart-wrenching "Meow." He just stood there and looked around at the shelves and stuff…everywhere but at me.

That's when I felt the sting in my hindquarters. It was fast, I'll give him that. It was also extremely hot. A groan escaped from me, and then things got fuzzy and dim as if the lights in the room were going out. I slipped away into the fastest and bestest catnap I've ever had…thanks, Dad.

From a secret place in my cat's mind, I remembered a night not long ago. I came upon this old trailer, maybe early 80's with a shoddy paint job, a sort of neon two-tone. "What was so interesting?"

Well, it isn't the guy who rides that humongous black motorcycle. It was his dogs.

One night I crept along their backyard fence just out of reach. Being so close to them drives them totally nuts. I love teasing them like this. From the ground these giant dogs watched me closely. Both snarled and growled viciously at me. I walked on slowly paw over paw being as careful as I could. The bigger of the two lunged at me while the smaller one barked loudly, its voice reverberating in the small backyard. The fence moved back then sprang forward, almost launching me into the air. Maybe this wasn't such a great idea after all.

The biggest dog fell against a trashcan, which made an incredible racket. The other dog snapped at my tail. Both barked their ugly sounding dog barks over and over again.

Just then, an outside light came on over the sliding glass door. A man's body filled the, now open, doorway. I dropped down to the ground as one of the dogs came at me. The man's husky voice rang out. "April. Howard. Shut-up."

Backing up in-between the trashcans I took a swat at the beast and caught him on his nose.

He yelped in pain. I made a mad dash through the open doorway of the trailer and slid across the floor ending up in the kitchen.

From between the guy's legs came the smaller of the two dogs. Snarling, the beast slid into the room. She fell and rolled onto her back, careening out of control across the kitchen. I leaped onto the kitchen counter. Immediately, he jumped up at me.

I swatted him. The man grabbed, then pulled, her toward the open door. With his foot, he kept the other dog, the bigger of the two, the male, out of the trailer. Then he shoved both out. At this point, thankfully, he slammed the glass door shut.

I paced back and forth on the kitchen counter, my paw red in his dog's blood. He smiled at me, took a paper towel from the roll and wiped my paw clean. "Hey! Hey! Badass, you've got some big balls there. You came pretty close to getting hurt." I didn't understand exactly what he meant, but his voice was calm so I allowed him to continue to touch me.

The dogs were at the back door still snarling showing their white fangs, their noses pressed against the glass glaring at me. The man walked off, saying. "You've got them pretty wound up… better to give 'em some time to calm down. I'm going in here and watch some TV if you'd like to join me."

The dogs had kinda lost interest in me. One left and the other stretched out with his big, gross, furry back pressed against the glass.

I took a chance and slid down off the counter and hit the floor with a loud plop. I heard my host laugh from the living room. When I peeked around the corner, I saw him on the couch with his feet up on a long low table. A small cup in his hand, the smell told me it was coffee. I looked around the kitchen…no dog food on the floor, so the dogs don't come in here.

There was no table in the dining room like at my house. Instead, there was this large black motorcycle that looked just like my dad's. Harley something or other was printed on the tank. I stood up on my hind legs to get a better look at its top. When I glanced over I saw the man look at me. He smiled, and then quickly looked away.

Slowly, I made my way to the couch and hopped up on it next to him. He didn't move. I sidestepped closer to him. We sat like this for some time, but eventually he reached over and petted me. Reading my tag, he said, "So your name is Max. It's a good strong name for a ballsy guy like you. I'm Jonathan." He took my right paw into his beefy hand and shook it, "Glad to meet you, Max."

All of a sudden, through the open windows at the side of the trailer a roaring, vibrating sound filled the room. The noise hurt my ears and I could see some of my host's possessions rattle and shake from the force of the sound waves. Jonathan's coffee cup literally bounced in its saucer. Jonathan stood and went to the window. He looked through the blinds. "Not to worry…it's only a few friends, but I'm going to let you out anyways."

He picked me up and we moved to the back door, and then he dropped me onto the stairs. "You can come back anytime, Max," Jonathan said. Then he quickly shut the door.

I trotted down the stairs, avoiding Jonathan's rather loud, late night guests and made my way to the street and home. The moon was shining down and a helpful light breeze moved me along. Off to my right I heard the flutter of large wings and feathers. I slipped under a bush as a massive owl flew into my view and down the middle of the street...it was an awesome thing to see, this glowing mass of white and gray, gliding silently along a few feet off the blacktop. Being a careful beastie, I waited there for a minute, and then ever so cautiously headed to our trailer.

The next few weeks were quiet in the park; nothing out of the ordinary except the weather had gotten warmer. At night, I heard AC units running. People who don't have air conditioners just leave their windows open and let their electric fans blow.

It was on a night like this, a real hot one, that I left the comfort of our house. I sat down under the only street lamp at the end of our block, when my eyes fell on Jonathan's trailer. A light came on in the back. Excellent, someone I can visit. I trotted off, eager to let Jonathan see me.

Now only a few yards away from his house, I heard a mighty noise coming from close by. I picked up my pace and ran up his driveway. I slipped in beside his car and waited.

At the bend in the street, headlights streaked across the trailers, shadows jumped from the trees and the white light exposed all my cat friends, their eyes alive and glowing from their hiding places.

I could feel a rumble in my chest as the sound waves flowed toward me, inches above the ground.

In a second, three motorcycles pulled up in front of Jonathan's trailer. There was so much noise that I hunkered down with my front paws over my ears. My body vibrated from all that power. The three men planted their feet on the blacktop and suddenly all was quiet. The only sound was that odd "tink, tink" noise that hot metal makes as it cools.

A light over the back porch came on and the door swung open, revealing a bare-chested Jonathan. Seeing my chance, I bolted out from my hiding place and was past him before he could react. I made the sharp turn at the hallway that led into the living room and crawled under the couch. All I heard were muffled voices from outside.

The voices grew louder, followed by the heavy clump of boots hitting the floorboards. The trailer shifted as a thousand pounds of men walked into the living room. I could just make out the black boots of three men, followed by Jonathan's bare feet. The black boots came toward me, turned as the owners sat down on the couch. The springs sagged under their weight. I could see Jonathan's feet stroll across the rug and stand in the middle of the room. If I stayed here I'd be crushed so I dug my claws into the rug and bolted out from under the couch. I circled around Jonathan's legs and looked up at him.

His face wore a look of concern. From the other side of the room I heard a large voice say, "What the hell, JR, you the local pound?" Laughter came from the couch.

Jonathan replied, "Not likely…this is Max. He visits me from time to time." He bent over and scratched my head vigorously. I gave him a good snork and sat down close to him and glared at the three men with my striking yellow eyes.

"Let's cut the crap…we came here to talk to you about business not F-ing cats!" The tone of this voice worried me. From my angle, all I could see were dark grease spots on dirt-splattered jeans. I strained my neck, extending it so I could see more of the man on the couch who was threatening my friend. A beard covered most of his face. His dark eyes were little slits and his long, stringy, black hair hung down well past his shoulders. All of his attire was black. He wore a vest with a bunch of patches on it, as did the others.

Jonathan didn't move, so neither did I. For a few seconds, the only sound in the room was the electric floor fan. Its gears slipped, making this strange sound as it rotated from side to side, as if the thing couldn't make up its mind on what to do.

Jonathan said, "Wait here." He turned and left the room leaving me alone with the bikers, so I put on my fiercest face and stood my ground. When he returned, held in his hand was one of those black vests. He handed it to the man who was standing. They all looked a little embarrassed. Standing Man took the vest. He said, "Here, TC, you hold onto this." He tossed it to the man sitting on the far end of the couch.

That's when I saw it, as it wiggled and waggled.

The Sitting Man said aloud, "What about the other business?"

Jonathan replied, "You're not getting my bike…f-you!"

Standing Man said, "Oh no, we were only told to lift your ink."

Before anyone could say another word I squatted down low on the rug and took up a pounce position.

That's when, TC the man at the end of the couch, said, "What the f is up with your crazy cat, Jonathan?" They all looked at me. I could hear snickers from them as I tensed for attack.

The Sitting Man said, "Shit, man, look at him stare at you, TC!"

"What the…" Alarm shot across TC's face as I started my attack. At the edge of the rug, my legs sprung forward as he jerked his head up. I aimed at his beard. It must have been a foot long and had a knot at the end. A dozen or so hairs formed the tip. When he spoke the end of it wiggled and waggled.

As I flew up past TC's knees I heard Jonathan yell, "Max-x-x."

An astonished TC leaned back and moved his right arm to block my flight. With my yellow eyes flashing, all fifteen plus pounds of me crashed onto his chest. With my paws open… the prize was within my grasp.

He tried to wriggle off the couch but only succeeded in slipping onto his back. The wispy hair was now mine. I stood on TC's stomach and batted that dastardly hank of hair back and forth, spitting at it as it wiggled, which drove me into a deeper frenzy.

TC stood up. I fell to the couch and spun around, looking for my quarry. My frenzy over…I started to relax. Standing Man, with tears falling from his eyes, had doubled over slapping his thigh. The Sitting Man was holding his stomach, roaring with a belly laugh.

By this time, I had regained my stoic feline composure. Sitting down on the couch I watched as the men quieted down. A change had come over them… even TC smiled. Standing Man snapped his fingers. The Sitting Man picked up the vest and the group made its way to the back door. Still laughing, Standing Man said, "Don't worry, you're OK by us."

In a serious tone Jonathan asked, "And my ink?"

Standing Man replied, "Your tattoo can stay where it is."

TC slipped by them saying, "That cat is F-ing dangerous, man."

Still laughing, Standing Man said to Jonathan, "That cat saved your ass, sport. He's got balls that one." With a wink and a smile he left.

Outside the electric starters ground over in unison the Harleys came alive. The engines roared as they all left into the night.

The vet was nowhere to be seen. I realized I was in the backseat of dad's truck. We drove for a while and finally arrived at home. The dinner table was set and the TV was talking. Once inside, I slowly crawled up onto the lower part of the couch...for some reason, I can't make the leap up to the top of it. So I lay down right there on the cushions and fell asleep. There in my catnap dreams, I'm chasing something, but I never quite catch it. I also had a strong urge to eat red meat, maybe a bird or even a large bug or two. So incredibly yummy.

During the evening, my mom became super excited; a band had appeared in this old movie she was watching. A piano began to plink out a tune. Mom pulled my dad up and out of his favorite chair. They do this thing they call dancing. She held him as they spun slowly around, lovingly smiling at each other. Together they hummed along with a squawky saxophone that had now joined the piano.

My mom wistfully sang, "Red sails in the sunset, way out on the sea, oh carry my loved one..." It made Dad smile...really big.

Then the most unexpected thing happened. Dad dipped Mom. She laughed saying, "Honey, your back...remember your back!"

He replied slyly, "Well, you know there is another great exercise for a man's lower back." She laughed her mom laugh, as he straightened her up. Sure enough as if on cue...he groaned aloud. His hand slipped down to his lower back as he limped towards his chair.

"Oh, honey, does it hurt? Are you in pain?" Mom asked as she helped him.

Pain! What do they know of pain? For some reason I can't curl up it hurts so bad. My lower pelvis aches and my balls throb. That stupid song repeats over and over again in my mind. Finally as I start to nod off a fuzzy black hole appears in front of me. I fell in it as everything else faded away into the all-forgiving blackness. From the depths of my memory and far, far away, I heard a voice, a distorted voice, it's Standing Man's voice. It declared. "He's got balls that one."

Hear that Dad.... I've got balls.

Zzzz...

8 NOWHERE MAN

The fog lay like a shroud over the park. It was early morning, still halfway dark outside.

Across the street from us was Victoria's trailer. She was one of my Mom's friends, who just loves to garden. She was especially fond of the bush that grew in front of her trailer. I love it, too... but just to hide under. On long nights, it is always a good spot for me and my thoughts. Catnap dreams, that's what I call 'em. This bush didn't keep me warm but the fog was wet and any place I could find to keep me reasonably dry was a good place to hunker down and wait for the sun.

After a while, I needed to stretch, so I crawled out, making sure I missed as few of the big drops of dew as I could. At the edge of the blacktop, I reached forward with my front legs and then pulled my weight against my back legs. Then I topped off my stretch with a big-g-g yawn.

My Good Angel came bounding out from under Victoria's trailer all chipper and alert. I had no idea where my Bad Angel was. More than likely he was still asleep somewhere. An odd sound came from the west end of our street. At first there was only the crunching of rocks and dirt like the noise large men make when they walk up our driveway. The sound got louder, but all I could see was the gray fog slowly drifting about. At times like this the fog adds an extra bit of protection for beasties like me. A kind of friend, who won't let you down. Because it never makes you promises, and, therefore, will never break its word to you.

A shape seemed to appear then disappear in the wisps of fog, all the while getting closer and closer. It looked more like a black shadow than a man. I felt no danger. But it made me curious. So I sat and waited. Good Angel sat beside me she shook her head bone about as little flicks of dew fell upon me in the grayish hue. She stretched her back and fluttered her otherworldly wings. She brought up a hind leg to scratch her left ear, which made me smile.

We saw a man. His beard was long. He wore an odd hat, all crumpled and dirty and a bulky gray overcoat. The coat swung in back of him as he briskly walked along in the cold. He was dirty and smelled strange. I thought he was a traveling man who had spent the night in the dried-up riverbed to the north of the park. It seems these days there are more and more of these fellows coming up out of the thickets down there. They wander through the park on their way to somewhere…or nowhere.

My dad often tells my mom not to talk to any of them. Hobo's is what he calls 'em. But that doesn't hold any sand for me because I'm a guy who can take care of himself.

When he saw me his face erupted into a big friendly smile, not unlike a lot of them who do this wandering thing.

This fella stopped a few feet from me and snapped his fingers together like my Dad does when he wants me to pay attention. At the sharp sound he made, a startled

Good Angel darted off into the fog leaving a swirl of discarded space in the wall of foggy atmosphere that marched in its way down the middle of the street and beyond.

I thought it odd that he took no notice of her and her abrupt departure. But maybe he had other things on his mind.

I looked up, waiting to see what he would do. Off in the distance, a car engine started up. The noise echoed from trailer to trailer, making him cringe. But it didn't stop him from speaking to me. "Hello, little buddy. Boy, it's a cold one this morning."

Not wishing to be rude, I nodded and flashed him an extra nice T-Rex smile. He stooped down and politely held out his hand, first the back of his fingers and then his palm. I sniffed at his hand and allowed him to pet me on the top of my head bone. He then stroked my back all the way down to my tail, which I liked tremendously. I sensed that he liked me, too, and he was about to pet me again when the lights went on in Victoria's kitchen.

He froze in place, not moving a muscle. A look of concern swept over his face. His eyes narrowed as he brought his hand back to his body and then quickly under his coat. He looked like he was groping for something.

Seconds ticked by. I wondered why he was so afraid. Suddenly he stood up and strode away. The fog enveloped him as he became a shadow again. Before he disappeared, he turned and waved, leaving me with my solitary thoughts. From out of nowhere Good Angel reappeared hovering just above the ground. Our thoughts seemed to meet and mingle; she hung her head and looked so sad; a tiny tear slipped out of the corner of her eye, perfect crystalline and pure it plummeted to the blacktop below.

From across the street, I heard our sliding glass door open and my Mom's voice call out, "Max, come on in…Max, honey." She does go on like this whenever I've been out all night. Not to fear, I had my angels with me. I strolled across the street, moving slowly in the cold. The warmth of our house was merely a few paces away, but my thoughts were with the man, the hobo, that wanderer. You see, I know something of what he's living through.

As a fellow traveler I, too, wandered but unlike him, I got lucky.

9 ALL BUICKS GREAT AND SMALL

You could hear the argument from far away… people were yelling at my old friend Mr. S and they were loud, too. The hood of his 1955 Buick Roadmaster was up, nearby stood a couple of young men stripped to the waist, their bodies all covered in colorful tattoos. One of the fellas got into the Buick and left the door open. For me, this was really inviting. I envisioned myself stretched out at the back window on that space they call a rear deck.

These young guys were desperately trying to start the old Buick. They worked on some wires under the dash but the Buick's motor only ground slowly, over and over.

A very large woman screamed at Mr. S about wasting her time. Something about her and her sons coming. "…all the way down here to look at this piece of crap lead-sled." My, my, such language.

With that, my curiosity finally got the better of me. I jumped up onto the front fender where one of the young guys was yelling about a dead battery. I stood there when he angrily pushed me away. I lost my balance and fell to the ground.

I heard Mr. S say. "Don't be messing with that cat or you'll deal with me, son."

Quickly I scooted under the Roadmaster, to come out on the other side. It was then I saw the young guys start to go after Mr. S. The one at the hood slammed it down and said, "That fur ball…I'll kill it if it comes near me." The second young guy got out from inside the car. He and his very large mom came right up to the stairs where Mr. S was standing. The argument grew in intensity getting much louder than before.

Meanwhile, the door of that warm car stood open… just for me. I scampered inside as the Very Large Mom shoved her finger into Mr. S's chest. He shoved her back, whereupon she stumbled into one of her sons. Together, they fell against the Buick's door, slamming it shut.

Inside the car, I sat on the front seat unnoticed. I wanted to get a better look at what was going on with Mr. S. I stood up to get a better view from over the steering wheel and leaned to my right. That's when I spotted this stick thing jutting out just under the steering wheel. This stick would be a neat thing to stand on, all nice and shiny. With my front paws, I balanced my fifteen pounds on it. All of a sudden it moved down making this 'clunk clunk' sound. I looked over the dash and directly into Mr. S's eyes. He stopped arguing with the fat mom. Alarmed, he shouted, "Max!"

One of her sons, the one with the tattoos, lunged toward the driver's door handle. He slipped and fell as the car moved backward. Very Large Mom screamed and Mr. S grabbed his chest as the Roadmaster rolled down the driveway and into the street. Hitting a bump, the large car bounced and I fell onto the front seat.

After all this excitement I decided to make my way to the rear deck for my nap. I hopped up onto the top of the front seat and from there jumped to the rear deck. It's so roomy… and with a great view too. The sight of all the trailers going by as we rolled down the hill was really neat.

Mr. S leaned against the mom how sweet. I could also see the two fellas running after the Buick waving their hands. "Maybe they're not so bad after all," I thought.

The car came onto level ground and slowed almost to a stop. Then another bump in the road sent the Roadmaster and me into Teddy's trailer at the bottom of the hill. We grazed the rear porch, sideswiping the length of it. Not to worry, the outside of Teddy's home was a real eyesore.

Now, with regard to the history of the park, Teddy's trailer is a rarity. Not only did he own his trailer, but also the land it sat on. Full ownership seldom happens in this little bit of American Mobile Estate Heaven. Teddy had the unit not only remodeled but lengthened, expanding the rear bedroom at a right angle to form a long L shape. Later he raised the ceiling up to make it even more custom, but he never got it painted. The outside remained the original Winnebago color of neon green mist on the lower body, a white stripe and powder blue top.

The Roadmaster had come to a complete stop a few feet in front of a car with a big star in the grille. It was now time for smart cats to flee. I made my way to the open window on the driver's side. Placing my paws on the door I leaped out, to land on the steps of Teddy's rear porch.

Donna, Teddy's older sister, threw open the door and leaned out exclaiming, "What the hell is going on out here?" I stepped in, unnoticed, and heard someone singing out of a black box that Teddy plays all the time. "We skipped the light fandango, Turned cartwheels 'cross the floor." The black box sort of rattled and vibrated as it spoke. The young guys were now at the Roadmaster. They screamed and yelled excitedly at Donna. The men then started shoving and punching each other. I peeked around the corner and saw Teddy. He stood in the middle of his sparsely decorated living room holding a smelly glass in his hand.

Donna walked in. He asked her, "What was that?" Before she could answer him, he saw me at the end of the hallway. His face lit up. "Max, little buddy, what's up?" He likes to call me his 'little buddy' a lot. I nodded to him in acknowledgement. He smiled that big Teddy smile that I love.

Thinking everything was perfect, I strolled in with my tail straight up in the air like I owned the place. In a way I do. I walked right up to my old friend and gave him a sincere head butt to his leg. Teddy grinned at me and bent over. In turn, I gave my friend a snork and topped off my greeting with one of my famous T-Rex smiles.

Donna stood next to him and with her foot she nudged me away from Teddy.

"What...you got another fleabag mooching off of you, Theodore?"

My pride ruffled, I crossed the living room floor to the couch in front of the custom window that Teddy had installed. Donna stood there, her arms crossed. She spoke sternly, "You might think I'm crazy, but I'm not. You had six weeks to get this trailer into shape so we could flip it. Times up, tomorrow..." She cut her words short. Turning on her heel she stomped out of the room. As she passed me she pointed and said. "And you, you fleabag, one of these days I'll catch you alone... then I'll..." She cut her threat short, then walked out through the door and into the street.

Teddy and I locked eyes. In his calm voice he said, "She'll simmer down. You wait and see." He took a sip of his drink.

We could hear Donna screaming at the young men, who were unsuccessfully trying to start the Roadmaster. A huge argument started between them. The Buick was blocking her car, the one with the star in the grille.

While we were listening to this, Teddy smiled and said. "I know what you're thinking, but I'm not going out there… no way."

It was time to let these humans settle their differences on their own. I made my usual circling motion to get the maximum softness out of the cushion and settled in for my afternoon nap. Thirty seconds later, I was out for the count…Zzzz.

I must have been asleep for some time because when I woke it was dark. I got up, stretched and made my way to the side door looking for Teddy.

His property is in the shape of a big triangle. Sided by three streets, the lot is an island. The add-on trailer forms a secluded courtyard of sorts. Teddy built an eight-foot wall that runs along the front and back street, with a large gate in the back for easy access. Inside there are a few tall trees in a far corner. That's where I usually get in. On the outside is an oleander bush. Its low branches are just right for me to climb up on and from there I can make the short leap over the wall. There is a shallow pool in the middle of the yard. I think they call it a play pool. I've seen Teddy playing in it many times, always at night with different girls, who like me a lot, showering me with oodles of attention. Around the yard are plants of every kind…queen palms, ferns. It really looks like a jungle in there.

Often I help Teddy water the plants. Sometimes, he'll playfully spray me with the hose, from which I escape with ease. Water fascinates me. It is the coolest thing there is, water. I can sit and watch it for hours.

Leaning from around the door, I noticed Teddy sitting on the steps by the pool. Donna was there too.

"What do you want from me?" he asked his sister.

She sat next to him on the step hanging her head like there was a lot of bad news with her name on it. There was no reply from her. The seconds ticked by.

Moving across the yard, I sat beside his shoes. He still didn't acknowledge me. Normally he gives me lots of attention, always saying things like, 'good boy' and stuff like that.

Teddy faced his sister while I moved to a new position in front of him. He had a grim look on his face. My friend started to say something but stopped. I reached out and tapped his leg with my paw, but he wouldn't look down.

"What's 'a matter, Theodore, cat got your tongue?" She smiled at her little joke.

"I don't know what to say about selling the trailer…" Teddy said, and looked up at the darkened sky.

An exasperated Donna replied, "Just sign the papers. You know…here's a second chance, for me! I'm not asking too much, am I, Teddy?"

Teddy shrugged.

She just sat there smoking, letting the ash build up. Gray smoke swirled around her head.

Blue moonlight filled the garden. A mist hung over the pool, the palms swayed as a gust of wind swept in, ruffling the fur on the back of my neck. Boy, do I love this garden! Donna gazed at Teddy, watching him as he struggled with his thoughts. She said, "Look, you need to buck up and do this for us."

Teddy looked around the garden before he answered, "I'll be gone for a long time. Will you be able…"

"Able? To do what? Who knows? Let's not worry about that now, Teddy. You need to get ready for them in the morning. It'll be a long day." She dropped her cigarette stub onto the ground and stepped on it.

"Yes"…was all he said.

I wondered if Teddy was going away somewhere. Finally, he saw me, he smiled and scooped me up in his arms. When he scratched my chin I let out a long, low purr. "Do you know that this little guy is my best and only friend here at the park…has been since the day I moved in?" He continued scratching my neck and behind my ears.

Donna came over and reached out as if to pet me. I gave her hand a swat. Not hard, but she didn't see it coming. She jerked her hand back and laughed, then Teddy started to laugh as well as he let me drop to the ground.

"Come on, I'll help you get packed, Okay?" she said. With that, they walked off toward the sliding glass door.

I followed at a short distance, curious about what they were doing. They were all the way down the hallway as I came around the corner. By the time I got into Teddy's bedroom he had placed a few shirts and things into a black bag. They finished packing in silence. At the doorway, Teddy hugged her. Tears welled up in his eyes. Seeing me, Teddy bent over and scratched my ears and I gave him a couple of snorks.

"Maybe you should take a picture," she said, sarcastically.

The suggestion made Teddy's face light up. "Yes, that's it, just the thing to do."

He pulled his cell phone out of his pocket and handed it to her. She took the cell and pointed at us, saying, "I don't think your friend here likes me much."

Teddy made a click, click sound and he picked me up. I butted my head against his and the flash went off. He hugged me and let me slip out of his arms and onto the floor. I felt his fingertips slide across my body as I descended.

I looked over my shoulder; he smiled and waved at me. "Bye, Max."

They disappeared through the gate that led to the side street.

I heard Donna say, "They're not going to let you keep a cell phone, you know."

Teddy replied, "True…we can stop on the way and get some prints made."

There was the sound of a couple of car doors. A second later Teddy's Mercedes started up, the headlights arcing into the night sky as the car quietly drove off.

In the distance, I heard my dad whistling for me. I ran to a friendly tree and with a little help from a low-lying branch, I easily went up and over the wall. Dad was waiting for me at the sliding door. I scooted inside and I gave him a snork… humans like my snorks, a lot.

"Where have you been, you little troublemaker?" he asked as he shut and locked the door.

I had a bite to eat, and then curled up in a ball on the arm of the couch and ZZZed out.

Hours later the morning light filtered in through the curtains. Mom walked into the room, holding the newspaper in her hand. Dropping it on the dining room table, she went to the kitchen. When Dad entered the room, he kissed her on the neck, making her squeal in delight. I uncurled and stretched out my front legs. Dad waved at me saying, "Morning, Max." He opened the paper and read in silence. All of a sudden he exclaimed, "Wow, that guy…you know down the street. He lives in that ugly old Winnebago. Damn, what's his name?"

Mom replied, "Oh, Theodore something, Max's friend. What about him?"

Dad answered, chewing on a piece of toast, "Well, he surrendered himself to the Marshalls last night. He is starting a twenty-year sentence for embezzling money from the company he worked for."

Mom looked down at the table and said. "Oh! That is so sad." Bored, I rolled over and went back to sleep.

Later that day, a large moving van pulled up to Teddy's. A bunch of men took Teddy's furniture out and stacked it in the back of the van. I saw my most favorite couch get put inside so I crept into the open van slowly. Out of nowhere someone grabbed me from behind holding me by the scruff of my neck.

Mean Donna hissed at me, "I told you I'd catch you sometime, you flea bag. I've no idea what my brother saw in you." She flung me down the loading ramp. "Now, scat!"

Landing on all fours, I glared back at her and gave her an angry hiss in return, then turned to leave. At times like this it's best to just break even.

Time passed and Teddy's garden became overgrown with weeds. People came in and took plants from the garden, saying that they needed to be rescued. The pool turned green and a million bugs took over the yard. That's when I stopped going over. After that, I would just lie on the top of the wall and watch the kids from around the park break out the windows, making Teddy's property a mess.

One day, the guys with the tattoos showed up and tried one more time to get Mr. S's (remember Mr. S?) Buick started, but it wouldn't start. They worked hard at it, too. One of the guys kept saying, "Give, Baby, give," as the old starter motor ground down the new battery they brought, eventually killing it dead. They then pushed it over by the back gate leaving it where Teddy's 450SL should have been parked.

A few weeks later a wrecking crew tore down what was left of Teddy's trailer. In just a few hours, they loaded the remains of it onto a huge flatbed truck and hauled it away.

This made me afraid that Teddy wouldn't be able to find his way home from wherever he was. I hope he hadn't left because I did something bad.

But I'll keep an eye out for my friend, just in case he ever needs my help.

10 THE FORTUNE TELLER

"Went to the fortune teller to get my fortune read. I didn't know what to tell her. I had this dizzy feeling inside my head." So goes the song, now let me tell you about the park's fortuneteller. Her name is Gail and she lives in space #167. The place is not terribly spooky considering what she does; as a matter of fact it looks quite normal. There is always a line of folks out her door and into the street, sometimes even causing minor traffic jams. Believe it or not, the occasional fistfight even breaks out between really mad customers trying to get in to see her.

As busy as she is, she always makes time for me. I'm a fascinating and ongoing study for her and her witch girlfriends. They think I am a particularly delightful subject for their spells. Almost like a "Familiar Spirit."

The street she lives on is the only one not named in the park. For some strange reason, the builders never got around to it. One reason could be that it runs through the middle of the park and Gail says that the middle is where the best sensitivity resides. And that power held those men at bay, just waiting for a lovely West Witch like Gail (though Gail is a White Witch) to come along and claim the abode and the street. Power or not, this location is where the contractors placed their really large office trailer, an enormous triple wide.

After the park opened, Gail's place was, for a while, a model for potential buyers to look at the wonders of mobile estate living. Gail came upon it one weekend and immediately cast a spell on it. The manager at the time doesn't remember selling it to her but on the following Monday, pink slip in hand; she moved in and started her witches' business in earnest.

There are only a few trailers on this short street and all are surrounded by tall trees with massive trunks. These cone things fall from their branches all the time, which makes it dangerous for guys like me to walk underneath them. Owls like to perch from time to time on the large, thick branches, and these friendly trees are full of squirrels too. All in all, an unusually active street, this short one filled with trees, witches and animals.

On the outside, her trailer doesn't look any different than the hundreds of others, but at night it comes into its own. An eerie color seems to hang in the air around it. It's one that I've never seen on any other trailer. A hue that welcomes, it makes you smile as you enter the yard. Sometimes it even changes as if it were a big aluminum chameleon of sorts. After leaving, no one can agree on what color exactly they had seen. Around the front yard a line of bushes acts as a sentry, guarding her abode and all in it. The sound of slender branches lazily moving back and forth enhance the feeling of tranquility. In times past, people have burst into spontaneous readings of poetry quoting works that they didn't even know. For instance "when words stood as tall as trees and hailed as kings amongst kings for themselves and yes even humans."

That said, it's what happens on the inside of Gail's that is so spooky. For it was her cards that we all came to see. She had been teasing me for weeks to do a reading.

My journey to Gail's trailer was unexpectedly quick. That was because I had brought along my Good and Bad Angels and they whisked me along at a fast pace. I don't bring them with me often. Sometimes they just show up and at least one of them will always get me into a lot of trouble.

All of a sudden I found myself standing in the road at Gail's front yard. The lights were on and music softly crept across the lawn. 'Could be a party', I said to myself. My Good Angel thought I should come back another day. My fun-loving, Bad Angel didn't agree and wanted me to burst in and join the festivities. Always curious about musical notes and with Bad Angel egging me on, I followed the trail back up the stairs. I sat down on the porch and looked up just as the front door opened. There stood one of Gail's witch girlfriends who looked down at me and exclaimed, "So, who is this I wonder?" she laughed, "A little one that brings littler ones with him," she looked directly at my angels, then turned to call her hostess to the door.

Gail opened the screen door and asked me ever so nicely, "Sir, would you care to enter?" The offer was so warmly extended…how could I refuse? She held onto the door as I strolled in. Slipping her foot into the doorjamb, she kept Good and Bad Angels from entering. "I only offer Max the hospitality of my home tonight; you two have to stay out."

Once inside, Gail bowed in a polite curtsey, her full skirt flaring out in a circle. She dressed as she always does, looking every inch the gypsy fortuneteller. She introduced me to all that were in attendance. There was Pam, who I already knew, and Clare, a visitor from another town, and lastly a young girl hardly old enough to be out late at night. She was a red-haired, brown eyed vixen whose name was Susie. Gail clapped her hands and said, "Coven, I am pleased to introduce you all to my friend, Max." With that she swept her hand in a large motion starting from Pam and ending with me. They all came forward to look me squarely in the eye. Bending over, Pam felt my wet nose and declared it just right for a good luck charm, a special charm for her troublesome and unlucky Mah Jong pieces.

How? Could cat snot bring luck to anything, I thought.

Sensing my apprehension but undaunted Pam sat down on the Persian rug. She held out her hands palms up toward the ceiling. There a little fog appeared all of a sudden. She mumbled a bunch of words as I reached for the fog, when immediately I felt a hand grasp my nose. Looking at her hand so close, my eyes quickly crossed. Pam smiled, kissed me on my head bone, stood up…actually more like she levitated, and drifted over to an overstuffed sofa, sat down and produced a small empty bottle. She placed her finger along the edge. It filled up to the rim with a clear fluid; she capped it and slid it into a pocket in her full skirt.

Then she said, "Well, now, what are we going to do with him, I wonder?"

They turned to look at me, still sitting on the floor trying to uncross my eyes. They all waited for Gail to announce what was up for the Maxtor.

"Ladies," Gail said slyly, "I was thinking that it might be fun for us to have a cat that can talk."

The room went silent. Gail cast her gaze around, and finally said. "What are we, a coven of true witches or a band of lame ducks?"

No sooner had she uttered these words than they all burst into an excited verbal exchange. I tried to follow, but it was just too much for me. In the end they thought the talking cat was a little too ambitious, and agreed that they should start with a basic Tarot card reading. In fact, the reading is what brought me here tonight anyway. Gail looked at me and winked. She then walked over to her well-stocked library and started to search for a book.

The four of us sat in a circle on the floor. Pam took up the task of my reading while Susie held me on her lap. She spread the cards out in a sweeping movement that was so quick I almost didn't see it happen. I gazed at them and "Meowed" letting Pam know something was amiss.

A startled Pam asked, "Have I done something wrong, young gentleman?"

"Maybe it's the cards. Are they too close together?" suggested Susie.

Clare added, "Don't help him too much. It will interfere with his reading."

"Ah ha! You might be right," answered Pam, "let us just move them apart a little. You do realize that this is the first time I've ever read for a feline. Things will no doubt be a little different."

Once they were all in agreement, then in concert, their fingers moved deftly over the cards. I swear that they barely touched them. It was almost as if the cards moved by themselves. Satisfied, Pam nodded to me, her head of steel gray hair bobbed as she spoke. "All right we can now begin, young sir." With that, her eyes sparkled as she smiled at me.

Looking down, the cards all appeared to be the same. It was my nose that had me searching from left to right. Finally, I sniffed at one card close to my right paw. The girls squealed in delight. Unlike the other cards it slid out and into Pam's hand. She turned it over and announced "The Queen of Pentacles, ladies! He will have an interesting past, this one will." The room was electric with excitement.

I looked over my shoulder to find Gail with a large, old dusty book in her hands. Her reading glasses were drawn down to the tip of her nose. She grinned at me then went back to studying her book.

So it went. Pam asked me to concentrate and pick two more cards. I selected the Two of Cups, and lastly the Three of Pentacles. One card kept sliding out slightly. Pam kept pushing it back into the swept deck. "Oh no, not you and not tonight," she exclaimed, waving her finger to make her point to the wayward card.

Pam opened a book that lay at her side and declared my reading a success. She started to give us all the results. "The Queen of Pentacles informs us that I 'am in fact charming and a romance, is headed my way. I'm magnificent and have immense generosity."

The girls all nodded and whispered excitedly to each other. Pam continued. "The Two of Cups says that I'm filled with love, passion, and friendship. Three of Pentacles said I can apply my knowledge and skills to great advantage. Oh! And that I'm noble and will have great renown and glory."

The rest of the night spun by me in a whirl, everyone was having so much fun. Clare appeared with a tray of tall glasses filled with a red beverage. No matter how much they all drank, the glasses seemed always to be full. They toasted me as a first for their coven and offered congratulations on my most wonderful reading. Finally, a happy Gail stood over us with a handful of powder that she threw into the air above our heads. The room went white in a flash. The other women stopped as if they had become frozen. Gail's voice spun around and around the small gathering, as if her words were chasing one another.

"I hope I get this right," Gail said under her breath.

"Come witches to the circle drawn and bring the cat within, we ask permission to take a hair and summon Lady Bast. Make this, your minion, err, cat! Like as us that we might hear his voice, and to know and understand him. Lady, allow him to understand these words we know, to share his wisdom and ours. We ask this for the good of all and harm of none."

The room grew dim and then fell into darkness. I stumbled out of the triple wide to get some air, my head filled with a dizziness I'd never had to deal with before. On the front porch, I sat to catch my breath. High up in the big tree across the street hid an enormous owl. There amongst the low branches he craned his neck to check me out. We gazed at each other for some time before Gail's voice drifted out of the front door. Her words, "Max, come on in the house, honey!" were literally visible to me floating in the air.

Startled I walked under them, surprised at their litheness and collective beauty. They drifted on the wind as if only I could see them. However, I was wrong. My companion, the owl, immediately swooped down to street level. He flapped his mighty wings a couple of times and streaked toward me and my words. My Good Angel covered her eyes as my Bad Angel hid behind the open screen door. I stood up in a vain attempt to protect my beautiful words. I was totally prepared to do battle with this nocturnal, ghostly giant. He came in fast to blindside the floating 'm'. He held out a huge claw and before I could reach out to him, his talon sheared through the letter and broke it apart, the entire phrase, now slashed, faded away.

Later, my trip home started at the top of those stairs. Good Angel, wings beating, stayed close to me, all sad eyes at the loss of my words. Bad Angel sat at the top of the porch acting out what I should have done to the owl, blow by blow. In a peak of anger I side-kicked the little troublemaker into the bushes below the porch and then I walked down and into the street. We had walked a short distance when Susie stepped out of the doorway. She waved at us and then she seemed to shrink. By the time she reached the bottom step, a fox appeared in her place and bounded off into the darkness.

How I got home from there I simply do not know, but in the morning I awoke on top of the couch. Baby was down the hall looking around the door into my parents' bedroom. I could hear voices and laughter. Oddly, a haze drifted down to the floor from my mom's big bed. It parted to make its way around Baby, swirling along as if it didn't have a care in the world. As it went, letters started to appear on the floor and walls. Just multi-colored words. They moved around slowly all by themselves with no apparent destination.

My mom's voice lifted up and out of the room, it traveled down the hallway and into my ears. My interest was racing as I stepped off the couch and walked toward Baby, who became surrounded by all those letters and words. She gazed at them, not knowing what they were or what to do about them. All of a sudden Baby swatted at a lazy looking comma that quickly darted away. But I knew that this was Gail's witchy-work here for me to see.

Mom laughed, "Well whaddaya think, is it good or not." More mom laughter "And you better tell me the truth, buster, or I'll get you big time."

My mom has a way with her words, you know.

The bed rocked a little, as Dad's bare legs popped out from under the covers. When they both spoke more words filled the air in the bedroom and streamed into the hallway.

"Please! Tell me again what you wrote last night, won't you?" he pleaded.

Mom's voice rang clear as I strolled into the bedroom. I strained my neck to see what was going on in their bed.

In reply she said, "It happened late last night after everyone had gone to sleep. I heard this scratching at the kitchen door…it was Max." Her voice trailed off a bit. "Honey, he looked horrible, like he had experienced something awful." I started to jump up on the bed when my dad turned to see me on the floor.

"Hold that thought while I get this beastie out of here." He swung his bare legs over the edge of the bed and scooped me up in his hands and tossed me out of the room. Then he shut the door. Baby sidled up to me as more words continued to flow under the door.

"So what happened?" he asked. "By the way, I do like what you wrote. It makes me seem so special."

"Well, it came to me, a little later after Max came in. They were like a kind of seamless parade of words. It was as if I could see them all around me."

There was a bit of subdued laughter and what sounded like what my mom does to me on my head bone, what she calls smooching. It got harder to make out what they said and the new words came out in a jumble. All of sudden the bed knocked hard against the wall, followed by a lot of laughter.

"Watch it, there Mister. You'll have to make an honest woman of me if you keep this up."

A short time later I could hear my dad, out of breath, and said, "Where were we? Oh! Yes, you called me charming and said romance was headed my way. I'm magnificent and have immense generosity. I'm filled with love, passion, and friendship. And I can apply my knowledge and skills to great advantage. And lastly I'm noble, and will have great renown and glory. The last twenty minutes attest to that."

"Don't be vulgar, old man." Mom replied.

Dad started laughing, barely catching his breath, "So now you have become a fortune teller."

"And you made me a promise there, buddy." Mom replied.

Baby lost interest, turned and walked down the hallway into the kitchen. Dad spoke up still laughing. "Ok, ok, I'll do it. Just don't make me laugh." His voice lifted melodically. As he sang, the words all in sequence slipped under the door to appear on the floor and this is how they read.

"Now I'm happy fella well, I'm married to the fortune teller. We're happy as we can be, and I get my fortune told for free."

"Mmm bop, bep, bop yeah!"

11 THE EARTH MOVED UNDER MY PAWS

Dad had gotten it into his head that he was going to walk me on a leash like a dog. No way was this is going to happen. When he put the harness on me and attached the leash, I sat and waited. He stood off like he expected me to come to him. I took a step forward and then did this trick that I just loved to do. I simply fell over onto my side.

Dad sat down on the edge of the couch and looked at me very forlornly. Part of me, a very small part, felt sorry for him. But this leash thing was a bad idea. He called out to my mom, as he looked at me, "Max will not take to the leash." He sighed. "He just falls over on his side."

Blame it on my Bad Angel, Dad. Since my angels have been around I've been getting into lots more trouble than normal.

Mom's distant voice answered him. "Well, you know how he is. If it's not his idea, it's not going to happen." She paused for a moment. Outside it seemed so still. No birds chirped and there wasn't any wind to speak of. "Why don't you take Max and some of your job resumes and drop them off at a few places. It will do both of you good to get out of the house."

Dad had just unleashed me when it happened. The trailer shook from side to side and did this dippity thing. The walls moved in and out. There was a loud rumbling noise. I was in mid-stride when I felt the quake. Now, you see when large trucks (mostly brown ones) go over the speed bumps outside our home, we always feel some shaking. So at first I thought this was just a truck, nothing more. But it was bigger, much bigger and with more movement. A loud crack came with the dippity movement. The sound came from all around us, which was just as unnerving.

Dad went nuts. He took off down the hallway screaming, "That's an earthquake!"

I tried to sit, but everything around me was in motion. The chairs at the dinner table started dancing. Everything on the table slid to one side and fell off one by one. The pictures on the walls were swinging. The front door screen buckled and flew open.

At this point I got a little concerned.

The new flat screen television shook on its stand. DVDs spilled from a cabinet that stood beside me. A lamp on the cabinet fell over onto Dad's humongous overstuffed chair. When it fell, the light bulb popped.

Then as quickly as the shaking started, it stopped.

That's when Mom came down the hallway saying, "I know it's an earthquake! I can feel it, can't I?"

Dad was right behind her carrying a bunch of stuff in his arms. He was panicking and screaming, "Okay, okay let's all get outside." He looked over at me and said "Come on, Max, outside. Where's Baby…where's Baby, Max?"

Like I'm going to answer him. *Silly human.* I thought.

"She's over here by the door, dummy," Mom replied.

She opened the sliding screen door and Baby took off like a shot. I was in the midst of stretching when the second jolt hit. It was a big one, too. It almost knocked Mom off her feet. She fell into that director's chair she keeps by the door. As Dad reached out for her, he dropped all the things in his hands. The dining room chandelier swung wildly from side to side.

That's when I made a beeline to the open front door. Outside, I made a hard turn on the deck and launched myself through the air into the safety of open space. I landed on the blacktop unscathed. My knees had buckled and I stumbled. Then the earth moved under my paws again. A bunch of new cracks opened up in the street right in front of me. I swung to my right and focused on the perimeter wall in back of the trailers across the street.

I took dead aim at the middle one, the dark brown one next to Victoria's where the Henderson's lived. Mr. and Mrs. H were running out of their trailer, their arms filled with boxes and stuff. I scrambled up onto their barbecue in the backyard and used my forward momentum to leap up to the top of the eight-foot-high perimeter wall. Balancing on top, I was preparing to jump when I felt something beside me. It was Baby. Without looking at me, she leaped to the ground and in an instant she was outside the park.

The wall began to sway so I dropped to the ground and dashed after her. The two of us ran down the narrow trail along the outside of the wall. I looked back to see a part of it literally topple over. A large hole appeared. At least they won't be able to blame that one on me. Baby and I picked up our speed when all of a sudden the ground under us dropped away. Above us the trees swayed, almost twisting around in their home the ground. Some large branches waved as if saying h-e-l-l-o. One came darn close and for a second I thought that we might be in danger, but it only swept over our heads waving its goodbye. There was a loud noise as it hit the ground inches in back of us.

We finally stopped falling and came back to earth. Or did the earth come back to us? We ran past the main creek and came to the RV parking lot. There we took cover under an abandoned camper with a blue stripe. There was another surge in the ground and then all was still.

We hunkered down and waited. The sun was out, the sky was blue and the trees in this part of the park were all extremely leafy, they looked sedate even. The stillness was shocking. It was almost as if the quake had not happened. But these marvelous trees entertained us as they softly sang their bushy song and swayed ever so slightly as dollops of light moved around on the ground. The sun worshiper in me wanted to crawl out of here and catch some rays. Baby read my thoughts and held out a paw letting me know to stay still.

Shortly afterward, a whole bunch of critters marched past us. Some moved slowly and others were really picking them up and laying them down, as my dad says. At that moment, it seemed like everyone in the river basin was going from where they were to a new place somewhere else. A few squirrels scampered past. One stopped and quizzically looked at us. Baby gave him a spirited hiss-s-s-s and he wisely moved on. A possum fell out of a tree and waddled under a bush down the trail. Two horses, both with empty saddles, trotted by. Together they whinnied and neighed at us. They looked concerned about their long-gone passengers. Feeling much safer here under the van, I let my eyes close and drifted off to sleep.

Suddenly I was running down an alley not knowing where I was going. My legs hurt, mainly because they were so short and I'd been running such a long way. Running hadn't made me tired since I was a kitten, so I must have been a kitten in my dream. The grass on either side was tall enough for me to hide in. I stopped, looked around and crawled into the flange. I just knew my cat mom would find me. I lay down in the grass and waited.

Off in the distance I could hear a dog barking loudly. All I knew was, for now, I was safe. The sun beat down on me, and blink, blink I fell asleep.

When I awoke, it was totally dark and getting cold. So I stepped out and looked around. The alley was empty. Nobody was here that I could see.

Nothing smelled familiar either. No scent of my cat mom and nothing looked the same. I meowed and meowed but no one called back. I sat down, forlorn, and for the first time ever, I felt all alone.

Later I made my way slowly out of the alley and onto the street. Lights were on in many of the houses close to me.

As a litter of kittens, we were never let into the house. The backyard had a tall fence around it, and being so small, we never saw over it. The dog attack had driven me through a small break in the fence. If only I could find my way back to the yard…and my family.

I can't remember ever having been picked up by anyone other than my cat mom. What humans could do for me I didn't know, or where to find one of these puzzling creatures. Maybe in the houses that were all around me? Could I find a human in those houses? Bewildered and afraid, I sat at the deserted intersection not knowing what to do. I saw a house close by and made my way to a big bush in the yard and slept under it. The night was cold, and not having my littermates to keep me warm, I slept poorly.

The next day I awoke to the soft "mews" of another cat. I slipped out from under the bush, which brought me to a short white wall that ran the length of the house. I climbed up one of the bushes bigger branches to the top of the wall and then to the edge where the sounds of the other cat came from. There in the backyard of the house was an orange tabby cat. He appeared to be a little older. Standing up against the wall, he sniffed at me. It was then that I caught the scent of food.

Hunger made me hurry down the side of the wall, almost falling on top of the tabby as I run toward that wonderful smell.

At the back door of the house, sitting beside a rug, was a bowl filled with this stinky stuff I can only describe as heavenly. I dove right in, devouring as much as I could. About halfway through this meal, the door rattled. Through the lower glass pane, a pair of black shoes and white socks appeared. Startled, I backed away from the bowl. The door opened and Shoes 'n' Socks stepped out shuffling onto the rug. I had fallen off the rear porch onto my butt, as the shoes said "… and who are you, little one?" The voice was soft and I wasn't afraid. Her body was round and fragile looking, her face was small and so far away it was difficult for me to see her. My first thought was to run, then the tabby made up my mind for me as he pushed against me. Because I was so small he easily knocked me over. I got to my paws and ran off to the safety of the nearest bush, the tabby in hot pursuit, swatting at my tail.

From under the bush, I watched as the door reopened. Shoes 'n' Socks brought out another bowl filled with water. The door closed. After a period of time, I made my way back to the porch to drink the cool, clear liquid. For a cat to drink properly you bend very small parts of your tongue to capture the cool water as you draw it up and into your mouth. I hadn't done it many times before and it was a little daunting.

Later that night I curled up around my bush and slept better, having a full tummy. My new friend, the tabby, was nowhere in sight. He must have been inside the house.

The next day dawned bright and I awoke early. There, sitting on the porch, were two bowls filled to the brim with food and water. For a long time, they were there every day. Shoes 'n' Socks never tried to pick me up, even when she introduced me to hands and arms. Most days I would play with the Tabby, but whenever Shoes 'n' Socks came out, our play would stop and he would run over to her, rubbing up against her leg. Her voice would coo out these melodic words like "When will he come over to say hello Smokey?" From that time on, she always called him Smokey… Well, she also called him "Kitty, kitty, kitty." But she never gave me a name and she never allowed me into her house. From outside the backdoor windows, I'd watch as she played with Smokey in her home, just the two of them.

I was growing daily and getting stronger, too. Then one day after what seemed like a long time, she didn't come out. Hunger drove me from the safety of the yard to the scary world outside to seek food. I had been away only a few days. When I came back, the house was empty; Shoes 'n' Socks and Smokey were gone. I waited a couple of days before drifting off myself, wandering down lonely and sometimes dangerous alleys, into new neighborhoods, always looking for my cat mom and my family.

This was the start of my life on the street. Always moving, never staying long in any one place. Always looking for my cat mom and my family, and always alone.

When I awoke from the dream, I was by myself and overcome by panic. Where was Baby? I had to find her! I trotted down the trail searching for her. At the RV entrance that led into the park, I saw her some distance ahead of me. I picked up my pace immediately. Apparently she heard me because she took off running through the gate, straight at a boy on a bicycle. He was talking to a young girl who held a bunch of school books in her arms. The girl pointed at Baby, who had slowed down to a walk. Baby strolled up to them and politely begged for attention. The girl bent down to pet her. I was only a few feet away when the boy tried to kick Baby with his foot. My painful experience with people as a kitten came to mind, I became enraged, and decided to act. I dove straight toward him with my ears pinned down in total anger. He was straddling his bike, so I zoomed in on the closest undefended body part... his leg. Claws extended, I lunged.

Making contact with his knee, I dug in. First one paw high up on his thigh and the other low just behind his leg. For good measure I sank my fangs through his jeans and into his kneecap. My fifteen pounds of body weight ensured his pain.

The girl squealed and moved away. At first, the boy didn't know what to do. He tried to grab me by the scruff of my neck. I clenched harder with my claws. He fell off the bike and onto the ground, shaking his leg. Pain racked his face. When he started to scoot backward, I let go. I turned, chuffed at him and took off down the street after Baby.

As I ran, I dug into the small cracks of the blacktop with my rear paws and pushed as hard as I could. Reaching out, I pulled in with my front paws and threw myself forward. Baby had already covered a lot of distance down the street. She was quick. Her tail switched back and forth some twenty feet away, taunting me. Again digging deep, I pushed off, using my rear claws on the blacktop. I grimaced as I propelled myself toward her.

I had closed part of the distance as we flew past the point where our adventure had begun earlier that day. Baby was still ahead and was now at the intersection of the two busiest streets in the park, Thatch and Magnolia. She made an effortless right hand turn onto Magnolia. Her body was so light it seemed to move like magic. Then she poured it on…her tail switched easily in the vortex behind her.

Lowering my head, I leaned into the turn, but my extra weight carried me into a wider arc and I lost some forward momentum. Again, I dug into the blacktop with my claws and pulled even harder. I was gaining…just a few more strides I'd be upon her. I pulled with my front paws and brought my rear legs up, I stretched out my full length, for a second I was airborne, past space and into my own time.

She moved as if she were a blur. My speed caused my ears to pin back and my eyes to tear. Automatically, my inner eyelid slipped down. I was a little unsure, but I shifted my weight. It was now that I made my bid to first catch and then to pass her. I was closing fast when she drifted off to her left onto the large open grassy field where the park kids play ball. She hit a soft spot in the grass. Her rear claws dug into the ground, throwing up a tuft of grass back at me. I had to duck my head, it was that close.

Her tail swung into my vision. The sight of her body was amazing and wonderful. The muscles under her skin stood out, making her fur ripple. Her neck stretched as her rear legs pushed farther out. Her limbs crossed over as she left the ground. For a fraction of a second, we were both flying free of this earth.

Like magnets halfway across the field, we drifted together. I reached inward, with all my might and pulled even harder. At long last, my superior strength was showing. Baby lifted her pretty head, her nostrils flared to fill her lungs with air. My chest expanded, too, as we ran together. She brushed against my shoulder as I came up beside her. We took a stride in sync. At that point I passed her, then slowed so she could stay with me.

Together, in a blur, we pushed our legs out. And, together, we crossed them over, filling our lungs, pulling hard, our bodies stretching out to their full lengths, together. Holding our heads up high and out...together.

And together, our paws never touched the ground.

12 PETE AND REPEAT

We were outside on the driveway, on a fantastical sunny day. Birds flitted around and bees were collecting pollen from the little yellow flowers planted in a nice row along the driveway. Dad had just finished washing and drying the truck. I was lying on the hood basking in the warmth of the sun, letting its rays beat into my bones. The thought came to me that this could be a good time to mark some excellent Z's, but the best-laid plans of felines often go awry.

A young girl was visiting from down the street. She helped Dad wash the truck. He hadn't talked much because the youngster was such a chatterbox. Talk, talk, talk...she never shut up. How could I get any sleep?

She kept asking my dad the same question over and over again, and he kept answering her, "Repeat." Then very quickly she'd say back to him.

"Pete and repeat were sitting in a boat, Pete fell out. Who was left?"

"Pete and repeat were sitting in a boat, Pete fell out. Who was left?"

But why was my dad asking over and over again for her to repeat it?

"Pete and repeat were sitting in a boat, Pete fell out. Who was left?"

"Pete and repeat were sitting in a boat, Pete fell out. Who was left?"

Who cares? This is silly. I stretched out to my full length, rolling over a bit to expose the gray dot on my tummy to the sun.

I was close to drifting off when the answer finally crossed my cat's mind, "Ooh, ooh, I know who it is. I know! I know!"

13 KA-BING

Last Friday night was a night to remember. I'm lucky to be around to tell the story.

Next door lives a young girl, named Melissa, who is single and has a boyfriend, named Stan.

They were having a mild disagreement about a party she wanted to attend. He wanted to stay in with her. I'm sure the night would have started with a romp in the hot tub. She, on the other hand, thought that was a bad idea. If he wanted to get in the tub, he could do it alone.

They sounded a lot like my mom and dad. Speaking of my dad, he was in the kitchen washing dishes. The window was open. He listened closely as they argued. Mom drifted by, slapped him on the butt saying, "You don't need to eavesdrop on her, you dirty old man." With that, she closed the window and left the room. Dad followed her but not before opening the sliding glass door and letting me out of the house.

Our outside lights had gone dark and my parents were in their bedroom watching TV. I was on the deck at the front steps huddled down in my best turkey pose (that's where I sit duck-like but pop my legs out on my sides). Indeed, I was looking great, scanning my kingdom. I had not a care in the world, or at least that's what I thought.

It wasn't long before Melissa's boyfriend, opened the back door. He stepped out and slammed it so hard that the dining room windows rattled. He screamed at her, "See if I come back, bitch." He got into his truck, started it up, and left. His rear tires screeched as he drove away. A few minutes later, she came out, got into her little car and left as well.

That all happened around 8 o'clock. I settled in for another little nap before midnight. That's the hour when I usually go out on patrol. I don't go far at night and not after a long catnap because I wake up sort of slow. It's better to have your wits about you when you're out there in the dark. It was a nice night, not too cold. A slight breeze had picked up from the north. The sky was clear and filled with stars. Oh, and the moon was out, and as big as it gets this time of year.

First, I should tell you about this wonderful talent I have. Dad dubbed it "Ka-Bing". As you probably know, most felines have good jumping skills. What you don't know is that mine are really great…off the charts even. My best of the best is Ka-Bing. I create a lot of tension in my rear legs as I sit. When the time is right, I launch myself straight up as if zooming into space. With a bit of focus, I can scale our six-foot backyard fence without much trouble. Impressive, yeah!

This ability had served me well in the past. It had allowed me to escape from wild animals, dogs, and even very mad people.

I awoke as a car came around the corner at the end of the block. It was Melissa. She pulled into the carport and opened her car door. Laughing, she made her way to the back steps. In a second, the passenger side opened and a large man got out and followed her. There were whispers and giggles as she tried to get her house keys out of her bag. They managed to get the door open and together they stumbled into her house.

A moment later, I heard the hot tub come on, then the bubbles, followed by a big splash, then a little one.

It was then well past one in the morning and I was behind in my patrol duties. I got up to walk down the steps. Suddenly Stan's truck pulled up. He opened the door, and then quietly crept down the walkway to the rear of the property. I could see him standing on his tiptoes at the rear gate.

Feeling that something interesting was about to happen, I crept along the deck till I got to my mom's favorite blue Adirondack chair. I made my way noiselessly up onto the back of the chair to get a good view of Melissa's rear gate. With one paw on the chair and the other on a hanging Boston fern, I stretched out my neck. I could see the boyfriend clearly as he opened the gate. The hinges were rusty and squealed as it opened.

Then...silence... not a word or a sound.

Suddenly, the night exploded in angry incoherent voices. Melissa came out first, wrapped in a large beach towel. Her long wet hair swung around her, as she ran toward the back door.

Then, Stan came out from the backyard. Right on his heels was Melissa's guest wearing only his wet underwear. Meanwhile, on the steps, Melissa was shaking her fist saying, "You're not my boss" and "I told you to go...now go!"

Stan was about to reply when the other guy shoved him, forcing him to turn around. Both men threw their blows at the exact same moment. Sadly, Stan missed, but the other guy landed his punch square on Stan's chin. Stan reeled back, falling onto the hood of Melissa's car with a loud clunk. This set off her car alarm making even more noise.

Houselights flicked on up and down the street. A dog barked in the distance. Behind me I heard our sliding glass door open. Dad stepped out, in his robe.

With a big yawn, he said to me, "What's up, Max?"

Like I needed to tell him. He knew what was up. Our rear porch light lit up both of the yards.

Dad and Melissa locked eyes across the small side yard.

"Look, you simple bastard, you woke everyone up," she screamed at Stan, clutching the towel tighter to her chest. She stormed off through the gate into the backyard, pushing her new friend off to one side as she went past him.

"I can not believe this is happening." In a few seconds the lights came on in her trailer.

Minutes ticked by finally the car alarm stopped, the back door swung open, revealing Melissa clad in an afghan wrap. Her hair now combed but still dripping wet. She stood there, and glared at her boyfriend.

Stan hung his head sheepishly and said in a quiet voice. "I'm sorry."

For a moment they both looked really adult. Behind Melissa a figure appeared...it was the other guy. Fully dressed, he managed to slip past her and walked quickly down the steps.

At the edge of the driveway, he called out "Nice to have met you.

Stan muttered, "What a jerk."

All of a sudden, the street was lit with two sets of headlights and flashers. Someone had called the sheriffs. The deputies came from opposite directions, and stopped in front of Melissa's trailer, both held flashlights, which they used to scan the backyards.

Dad had walked over to the front of our deck at the top of the steps. I sat beside him. A big voice asked Dad, "Did you call for assistance, sir?" A flashlight's beam struck my dad, illuminating him.

I couldn't see Melissa's guest. He had melted away into the night.

To the officer's question, Dad replied "No!"

From across the yard, Melissa yelled at my dad, "So it was you who called the cops."

The first officer said, "Now, Miss, let's hold it down."

It was about then that I heard the first sound that bothered me. It came out of the back seat of the second squad car...sort of a shuffling, whining noise...no, not a noise... a voice.

There in the back seat I saw the outline of the biggest dog I'd ever seen. My blood ran cold. I moved closer to my dad, fear gripped me to my core.

Dad's soothing fingers touched the back of my neck. His voice said, "Its okay, little buddy. I'm here."

Melissa was yelling something at the top of her lungs. The squad car's rear door opened, and the K9 officer said, "I'll have a look around in the back with Luke. Maybe there's another party-goer we missed."

When the Luke's paws hit the blacktop his head came down as my ears snapped forward. I scooted backward behind my dad's leg. Dad's hand hovered above me when the Shepherd lunged straight at us. The cop, who held its leash, hadn't attached it yet. For a fraction of a second, everything stood still. Did I say everything? Well, everything but me. I turned and made a beeline to the middle of the deck.

My heart pounded in my ears. The Shepherd's pointed ears were just visible over the top step. I had maybe two seconds before total disaster would be upon me. In between our deck and Melissa's carport cover was a line of lemon trees. I drew myself down into a coiled position, building tension in my rear legs. I felt the deck rumble with the jolt of one hundred and thirty pounds of mean police dog, the policeman's voice grumbled, "Shit! My first day with this dog and all hell breaks loose."

Now was my time to act.

I made the leap to the metal handrail then Ka-Binged, very gracefully I must say, straight up to the nearest tree branch just as the Shepherd snapped at my tail…I always forget about my tail.

I wrapped my front paws around the branch. My hind legs dangled like a monkey's. It wasn't going to hold me for very long either. I made myself as comfortable as I could, and looked down at my antagonist.

He jumped up at me, but his weight carried him over the handrail and onto the ground below. Meanwhile, his handler was trying to get around Stan's truck, while the other officer had his hands full with Melissa and her boyfriend. The police dog took a second leap at me, but he fell short. Feeling safe, and tired of his antics I leaned down as much as I dared. I'm sure he thought I'd made a mistake. He barked a couple of times and made another attempt at me.

As he rose he seemed to move in slow motion. With his teeth bared his dogface was getting closer and closer and getting bigger, too. His front paws moved as if he were swimming. Being the local king of swat I took dead aim on his nose, which stood out for the offing. My claws were extended to the point where they hurt, I cut loose and swatted my target with all my might. My index claw made contact as he came up. I watched as the claw sank in deep, really, really deep.

Dad's voice rang out, "Max-x-x!"

As the dog fell away, blood spray filled the air as if it came out of the garden hose. He was yelping before he hit the ground. A bit of flesh fell from the tip of my claw as it retracted.

The cop who held Melissa and her boyfriend turned and hurried to help Luke. The K9 officer finally made it past the truck and wrapped a cloth around my victim's bleeding nose and carried him to the back of the police car.

Meanwhile, my dad was underneath my perch. Holding out his arms saying, "Damn it, Max, you'd better come down, buddy."

Just then Mom yelled franticly. "Oh no, what's happened to Max?" She was standing in the doorway in her robe. The other cop came from behind Dad with his gun out and aimed it at me.

The Officer exclaimed, "Hey, Boss do I shoot the cat or what?"

Mom pointed at the cop and screamed. My dad turned. He saw the gun and acted. He pushed the cop who fell onto the side of Melissa's trailer.

He exclaimed, "Don't you move...either one of you. That's an order." Then he stomped off to his patrol car. He began yelling into the radio thing. I was getting used to my high perch and thought I should come up here more often. That's when the officer came back. He stood in front of my dad and pulled handcuffs out of his belt, "You, sir, are under arrest." And then he cuffed him.

Mom got excited all over again as Dad meekly protested. Dad yelled out to Mom, "Call a bail bondsman and tell him where I am."

At this point, the officer said, "You won't be arraigned until Monday morning, fella." He snickered "You're gonna have a fun weekend, sport."

Mom disappeared into the house.

In a few moments, a third patrol car appeared and two more cops got out. The arresting officer turned to speak to these two new policemen.

The three cops finished their conversation and as a group, walked over to just under the tree. One had a blanket. He stood directly under me. The other two stood on either side of the tree. "This was not looking good!" I thought.

I looked over to my dad in the back of the squad car he yelled.

"Run, Max, run."

That was my cue for me to get out of this tree. I started to shimmy backward as the branch swayed. In hindsight, moving was a big mistake. The two policemen had begun to shake the tree wildly, and in a few seconds, I lost my grip and fell like a furry rock and dropped into the blanket below. I was trapped.

I had the sensation of movement. Then caught the scent of my dad, and calmed down a bit. To let him know I was there, I let out an "M-aw-w-r-r-r." Not a mournful call mind you, but just a "hey" meow.

The patrol car started, there was that ever-present radio noise and then I heard my mom's fading voice, "I'll bail you out, boys, I promise."

Then Dad spoke up from the back seat, "What am I being charged with, officer?"

"Assault, sir."

The officer who held me asked, "How's the dog doing?"

"Well, he has one busted up nose, that's a fact."

The man holding me laughed and said, "So how are you going to write this up? It's going to be a little tricky."

"As far as I'm concerned they both attacked us…him and his f-in' beast." The driver said.

"You should have called animal control. Where are you going to keep him?"

"Him who?" replied the driver.

"Him, the cat," said the other cop. "Maybe you should have thought this one through better."

From the back seat, I heard my dad laugh under his breath.

We came to a stop and the officer holding me got out of the car. I could see through the worn spot in the fabric, there was a glass door and these long green walls on the ceiling were lights in long tubes. As we entered this room there was a burst of applause.

"All right, all right," said the officer who held me.

Finally, I was placed on a hard surface as the blanket fell off me. I found myself alone in a small room with a big window. Many smiling faces peered in at me.

Just behind these men stood my dad, there was one officer, The Sarge, who spoke to him. After a few minutes, they took Dad away. I sniffed the air and knew he was still close by. Tired I took my usual two and a half turns to settled down, and fell asleep.

Sometime later I woke to find two female officers staring down at me through the glass. They smiled at me and one even waved. The knob on the door jiggled a bit and then one of the girls said, "If he's under arrest shouldn't he be fingerprinted, Sarge?" This was followed by peals of feminine laughter.

I hopped off the bed and sat just inside of the door up against the wall so they wouldn't see me. The lock disengaged and the door started to swing open. I backed up carefully, still sitting on my rear legs, the part that my mom calls my 'rabbit's footies.'

The door had opened a scant six inches. My hasty plan might work, but it would be close. I lowered and tensed myself, moving up to the narrow opening. I could see a shadow spilling into the cell from the doorway. Tucking my tail between my rear legs, I bolted through the doorway and was outside in the hall before anyone could react.

Behind me were at least half a dozen officers including the two women I'd seen in the window. Above me was The Sarge. He was a huge tall man, powerfully built with a rugged face who did not look very pleased that I was loose in his building. In a flash I took off down the long narrow hallway.

That's when I heard a voice say, "Max." It was almost a whisper. The voice was my dad's. I skidded to a stop and meowed. He was sitting in a small room with bars all around it. I sat at the bars, which I could have walked through easily enough.

Dad reached out and scooped me up into his arms. I gave him a head butt to his forehead. "I'm so sorry this had to happen to you, Max," he said sadly.

Happily, I gave him a snork and he smiled.

By this time, The Sarge was at the bars. He said to my dad. "Ok, this shouldn't be happening....I'll take him."

"Where? To the pound to be put down?" Dad's voice was rising as he choked back tears. "It's more your fault than his. Your cop lost control of his dog."

The Sarge's grip was strong, but he didn't hurt me so I submitted. "He assaulted my officer, sir! Now just give him over to me."

"What officer? That was a dog that took off after my cat." Dad was getting more and more angry.

The two female officers joined our group. One reached over and easily took me out of the Sarge's hands. The girls were cooing and making those girly noises I like. One of them said aloud, "Sarge, we've got unfinished paperwork on him." The Sarge nodded.

As they left, with me, I heard the Sarge say, "Yes, the police dog will be okay. He's got four stitches."

The girls took me to a new part of the building and into another small room, placing me down on a counter with a bunch of forms and smelly black inky stuff.

"This is going to be so funny," said the blonde with the nice smile.

"We'd better hurry!" replied the short dark-haired girl.

"Here, you clip the hairs between his pads and be real careful. We don't want to hurt this precious little guy, do we?" The blonde nuzzled me in back of my ears where it's so soft. She rolled me onto my side. The short dark-haired officer carefully turned my right paw over and started clipping. In no time, the long hairs were carefully cut back almost down to the web.

The blonde then pulled out an ink pad from a small drawer and inked my paw. Ever so carefully, they pressed my paw over a piece of paper, first one pad at a time then the whole paw. Finished and trying to contain their laughter, they carefully cleaned the ink from me.

While the dark-haired one held me, the blonde did some writing on the paper. She bent over and kissed me on the head saying, "You, Max, have just been paw printed." They then burst out into laughter.

The Sarge stood in the doorway glaring, "What's this?" He asked.

"It's just a joke, Sarge. He hadn't been printed so we thought..." She smiled at me lovingly.

Sarge barked an order. Immediately both officers came to full attention. The dark-haired officer dropped me to the floor and I darted off down the hallway. In a few minutes, I walked into a large room filled with chairs. Way off in one corner lying beside a desk was Luke, the police dog. He had a bandage wrapped around his nose. My entrance had gotten his full attention so his nose still worked. He didn't rise up, he didn't bark. But he did start to whimper at the sight of me.

I ignored him, the big baby…and started to investigate the room. Behind me, I heard some voices and then Dad's "Max come on, little buddy, time to go."

I took off toward my dad, my tail bent over in my playful manner. He reached down, and picked me up. Sarge was there and both of the female officers, too. The Sarge shook my dad's hand. While the female officers petted me softly everyone seemed so pleased. The girls said, "Oh, you're so cute," and "You come back and visit us soon," followed by even more giggles.

As we walked along, other officers were walking in with lots of cop stuff in their hands.

As we passed, I heard one of them say, "Hey, that must be that cat that got arrested earlier tonight."

Another one said, "That's who all the press is waiting for outside."

We walked out of the last room and found ourselves before a glass wall with a couple of large glass doors. There was a bunch of people standing outside. Some had cameras and others were talking wildly into these funny stick things, which they held out to us.

Dad saw Mom at once. She stood next to a man with a nice suit like I see on TV. She waved at us wildly.

We stepped out into the cool night's air with only a few feet between the crowd and us. Mom and the man in the suit came up to us. She planted a kissed on Dad's cheek and said, "I love you, I love both of you. I was so worried." I yawned as she scratched my ears. "The press thinks this is a big story for some reason. You know…human interest." She said with her wonderful Mom smile.

103

"Well, maybe we should show off for them a little," Dad said, looking at me. He smiled. "It's you they really want to see…right, tough guy?" Holding me under my butt with one hand and cradling me with his other, he raised me up over his head as far as he could. I ascended slowly. I cast my eyes over their heads and into the night's sky that seemed to explode with white light from their cameras. The press (they don't look so pressed to me) yelled things at me like "Oh, get that" and "Isn't this great." They called my name "Max", "Max", "over here, Max". I yawned again. They all smiled, "Oh, oh, get that," followed by more white-light flashes.

I looked down at Mom and Dad as the man in the suit leaned over to Dad. He raised his voice to be heard over the din. "I think they'll drop the charges after this." He motioned out toward the press. "Tomorrow's papers will be full of you guys." He smiled and waved, "Maybe even some TV time too."

Mom grinned really big and hugged Dad.

The wind picked up to bring me a feast of smells. I'd never been this far away from the park before. Everything seemed so new. More new press people were running over and the old press pressed in. But my dad never wavered as he held me up, not a bit. He said, "About time we caught a break."

It had been a long, curious night. I was looking forward to getting home so I could catch some serious ZZZs.

14 HEIDI FANG

The reporter on our TV kept saying the same thing. 'Heidi is missing.' Everyone wanted to know where she had she gone? That was the big question on everyone's mind. From the International Mexican border to Orange County, "Where is Heidi?" was the headline.

The reported told us all about her...Heidi is a Savannah cat. That's a hybrid, not that I have a lot of knowledge of such fancy breeds, they don't travel in the same circles as a guy like me. Heidi's descendants were Servals which are African wild cats. They were crossbred with domestic Siamese. The end result is one big, really tall and lean beautiful animal, called Savannahs.

On that fateful day, I was snoozing on the couch and I happened to look up to see Heidi's image on the screen. Her owner had several minutes of video showing her cat running through their house. She stood about eighteen inches to the shoulder and tipped the scales at twenty-four pounds. Long and leggy, her hindquarters were higher then her shoulders, making her look as if she were on the prowl all the time. Her coloring was a cool brown with whitish under-markings. Her head was taller than wide. Her eyes had a wide boomerang shape with a hooded brow. A black "tear-streak" mark ran from the corner of her eyes down the sides of her fat puffy nose. There were short black stripes and spots on her hindquarters. In a certain light, they might even look golden. Then there were her, gigantic, seriously pointed ears.

Boy, did I like her look! The reporter had gone all the way up into the east county to do an interview with Heidi's mom who, understandably, was broken up about her disappearance. Beyond the fact that Heidi was a wonderful animal to look at and that her family would miss her, she was worth a lot of money too, like up to ten grand.

I jumped off the couch and sat down directly in front of the TV. Most of the time these programs simply put me to sleep, but not today! The pictures of Heidi had me mesmerized. My attention didn't go unnoticed either. Baby sat close by, watching me intently.

The reporter went on to explain that Heidi had escaped through an open door. Then into the San Diego hinterland. When the news was over, I turned around and caught Baby staring at me. I could have sworn that her eyes had turned green. I didn't have any idea why she would be mad. Sometimes it's a whole lot easier not to confront her, so I slunk away toward the open back door.

Outside, I found a place to lie in the sun. I stretched and rolled around on the ground a bit.

Suddenly, over the back gate I saw a blur of spots in the shadows. I came upright and waited.

Nothing...

I crept into the tall grass which I call the flage. Then I saw it again, a blur of brown spots. The spots were creeping along to my left, moving toward the street. A second later, the spots became clearer. Under the cover of a Mexican palm, they stopped. From the shadows, a golden feline limb stretched out into the sunlight. I rose up an inch and my gaze locked onto a pair of yellow eyes...cat's eyes.

Over my shoulder, I saw my mom as she waved at me and then shut the sliding glass door.

My tail slowly switched back and forth, and for the longest time, nothing happened. Then that leg touched the ground and a bit of weight was put onto it. When stretched out, the spots were more elongated, making them look like stripes...black on brown with hints of gold.

A gust of wind lifted the palm frond, and I got a good look at her for the first time. My eyes grew large almost bulging out of my head. Man, she was beautiful, simply a stunner. We were now maybe eight feet away from each other. She took another step. As she came out of the shadows the grass crunched under her weight. Hey, I've seen some leggy gals before but whoa...she was something else!

I heard something in back of me. Mom? No, it was Baby staring me down from the kitchen. She was looking through the sliding glass door and meowing over and over again. What was I to do? I mean nothing had happened yet. So what was Baby all bent out of shape about?

That's when Heidi bumped into me.... Quickly, I stood up as tall as I could and swung my right forepaw over her shoulder. I grabbed her with my teeth at the scruff of her neck and brought her down. Back in the kitchen, Baby was going ballistic. I stood off from this newcomer switching my tail from side to side really fast. She just lay there. Then she put out her paw to me.

Oh, boy! This was going to be tough.

The kitchen door opened, and I heard my mom step out onto the deck. I could also hear the tap, tap, tap of Baby's claws. She huddled behind Mom, not coming out from behind mom's shoes.

"Max, what have you got there?" Mom asked her voice a little surprised.

I let my guest up and she sprang to her paws, running around me in circles.

Mom squealed with delight, "Max has got a girlfriend. Max has got a girlfriend" She sat down on the top step, clapped her hands together and smiled at our guest. Baby looked from behind Mom as she wiggled her fingers at Heidi (she thinks that works on me, too). Our guest stopped. Her head bobbed up and down on her long neck as she walked over to my mom who reached down and looked at her collar. I hadn't noticed a collar before! "Well, your tag says your name is Heidi." With a huge smile, mom said, "I'm so pleased to meet you, Heidi." She pointed over to me, "I think you've already met Max." Heidi sat down by mom's feet. "My but you are very tall aren't you? Max, did you notice how tall she is?"

Did I notice? I shook my head and fell over onto my side with a thud.

"I have an idea, now don't anyone move." Mom stood and said, "I'll be right back." She went into the kitchen. I was looking around for Baby when mom returned. She had a bowl of Science Diet in her hand. 'That's My Science Diet, Mom!' She placed the bowl on the deck in front of Heidi, who made a dash to the bowl and greedily gulped down the food. In seconds, the bowl was empty.

"Oh, you poor thing, you were starved weren't you?" Mom smiled and walked back into the house. "Let's find out more about you, young lady." Incredibly, Heidi followed her inside the house as Mom shut the screen door in back of her.

"Now wait a minute. That's my house!"

I stood up and walked over to the kitchen door. Luckily the screen was only partially closed, I managed to open a space big enough to force my ample body through it. Mom was in Dad's office, in front of the computer and sitting next to her on the desk was Heidi. Mom looked over at our guest, "There you are…you're a Savannah." On the computer screen, there was a picture of a cat that was very tall and looked 100% like our guest. I placed my paw on my mom's chair, she shooed me away saying. "Please, Max don't be so needy."

That's ok…I'll just wait until Dad gets home. I thought.

Some time later, a truck pulled up, and Dad got out.

I was on the couch, way up on top. My attention was divided between cat TV and Heidi who was now snooping all through the house. She was into everything; Mom had to get her out of the cupboards where she keeps the family dishes and twice out of a closet.

Mom was getting tired of lifting this twenty-four-pound cat around, and the "aren't…you beautiful…" thing was now wearing thin. At least it was for me.

Dad walked in through the back door. Meanwhile across the kitchen, Mom had opened the sliding glass door to let me out. I stepped outside and sat down on the deck. Just then I was knocked over by our guest. Heidi flew off the deck and onto the grass.

Mom tried to tell Dad about Heidi, starting with "Oh, you'll never believe what Max brought home, Honey." Dad stood at the sliding glass door watching us playing on the grass. Mom continued, "Isn't she great…she's a Savannah cat," and on and on. Dad had not said a word until Mom got to the part where she saw our guest's name tag.

Dad interrupted her. "Heidi, her name is Heidi, right?"

She stopped in mid-sentence her mouth open, "Well, how did you know that?"

He stepped out of the door slowly. "It's been on the radio all day. This cat went missing from her home two nights ago, and not that far away from here either. Half the park is out looking for this one, it could be her there is a reward of five thousand dollars to get her back." Mom stood beside him with her mouth open.

The moment Dad stepped out; Heidi took off, as in gone. I turned and caught a glimpse of her tail fly over the back gate with a foot of air between. I ran off after her...she might need me.

The park's version of an alley is the space behind the trailers. Some of those alleys go straight through to a street. At the back gate, there's a shallow depression that I've dug out to accommodate my new girthiness. On the left, there is a short path of grass that leads to the street. That's our alley. I ducked under the gate and wiggled my way to the other side, then off to my left and down the grassy path and into the street. It was really the only direction she could have gone, but I didn't see her anywhere.

A loud voice came from the intersection thirty or so feet away, where a bunch of teenagers were looking through the bushes of an older trailer. There seemed to be people everywhere. One of the teens, a fat one, yelled, "Look, there she is." The dummy thought I was Heidi and began running toward me. I've always made it a rule that if anyone yells at me in the street I run first and make sense of it later. This was one of those times.

In front of me, the street curved around. There was only one trailer at the intersection. It sat against the wall that surrounds the park. Old Mrs. Anderson lives there with its jumble of bushes. It was a perfect place to lose pesky teens. Mrs. Anderson never takes care of her yard, she just waters it. It's all overgrown on the sides with rose bushes, and in the back it's a jungle of tropical plants.

The fat teen was getting closer to me, and they were all yelling, "Here…she's over here." I waited until the last second. When he got to within ten feet of me, he slowed down. He probably thought that he'd just bend over and scoop me up. When he got real close, I bolted toward Mrs. Anderson's trailer. In seconds, I made the short run into her side yard. To my horror, another kid was standing in the exact place where I planned to make my escape. This second kid was bigger, older, and in much better shape than the chubby one that I had left huffing and puffing in the street.

There was a lot more yelling from all the kids as the bigger one lunged at me. I broke to my left, almost getting snagged by a rose bush. I had to reroute under the lower limbs of this bush and was forced to slow way down. That's when a third teen showed up. He literally crashed through the line of rose bushes that must have been four feet tall, screaming as he fell to the ground. I made a hasty stop. Just in time, too, because the big teen almost stepped on my tail. Oh, how I envied Japanese bobcats and their short tails. He reached out wiggling his fat fingers around trying to grab me. Heidi flew through the air to my rescue, and all but stood on the kid's face. The three teens were now all in a muddled heap, desperately trying to grab either one of us.

I made my way across the backyard, with Heidi beside me, dodging palms and all kinds of tropical plants. At that moment, a very mad Mrs. Anderson opened her back door and threw a pail of water on the pile of screaming teenaged boys in her backyard. She yelled, "I told you kids to stay out of my yard." With Mrs. Anderson's voice ringing in my ears, Heidi and I got to the side fence. I aimed at the center board of the fence and hoped no one had found or fixed my secret exit. I slowed my pace and adjusted my aim. I tucked in a bit and pointed my right shoulder at my target. I hit it firmly, and it swung out. I stepped through the hole and into the next yard. Heidi was right behind me, but we weren't home free yet.

In front of us were two young girls sunbathing. Behind us, the chubby teen was trying to get through my secret swinging board, but he had gotten stuck. There was a screeching sound as that section of fence gave way and the teens fell into the girl's yard. The air filled with shrieks from the girls and shouting from the boys. Meanwhile old Mrs. Anderson, now armed with her garden hose, squirted all of them with water through what was left of her fence.

Heidi and I had picked up our pace. I made a left turn at the far side of the yard and made a dash to the street and safety…or, so I thought. In front of us stood my dad, feet parted and arms akimbo. I lowered my haunches and slowed to a stop. He glared down at me. I just knew he was going to be mad. I sat at his feet and cringed while licking my lips repeatedly, a cat thing.

When he spoke his voice wasn't angry at all. "Max, who's your friend here?" He pointed to Heidi who was behind me. I flashed my best T-rex smile at Dad and switched my tail back and forth as I "Meowed." To her credit, Heidi then came up and sat down beside me. We must have been a sight sitting side by side. She looked even taller sitting than standing, something to do with her sloped shoulders.

"You must be 'Heidi', right?" Dad asked in a friendly tone. At the mention of her name, she pranced sideways and nodded. She flicked her tail as if saying, 'Yep, that's me.' Smiling, Dad bent over and picked her up in his arms. He turned and walked toward our trailer saying, "Come on Max, I'm sure all that noise over there somehow involves you."

The racket had died down a little, but I kept a look out over my shoulder, you know, like a rear guard. We walked the short distance back home. Upon arrival, I came face to face with Baby. Oops! I had forgotten about Baby. Oh, dog poop! I was in for it now!!!

Opening the door, Mom said, "Where was she? I was so worried."

Dad looked down, "She was with him," nodding disapprovingly at me.

"Oh!" was all my mom said. She cast a look on me, followed by "Max!!! You trouble maker…you."

Dad handed Heidi over to Mom, who lovingly stroked the huge feline. "Oh, yes, there you are. My, my, you are a heavy one."

Mom let Heidi slide to the floor saying, "There you go, sweetie." Heidi started exploring again walking slowly through the kitchen and into the dining room. I just sat waiting for someone to yell at me.

Dad asked, "Okay, we've got her. Now what?"

Standing a few feet away in the kitchen Mom said, "Hmm…we should look at the news tonight. They'll know how to go about it."

"Is that how you found out about her…watching the news"? Dad queried.

Looking a little crestfallen Mom replied. "Well, no. Actually Max was playing with her in the backyard. Yes! It was Max who found her first," a big smile on her face.

"Are you sure, it wasn't from the TV?" Dad asked, trying to lock eyes with her. He took a step back and continued. "Okay, it was Max who found her. But how did you know about her? And now how do we get her back to her owners and collect the reward?"

Mom cleared her throat and looking sheepishly she replied, "Ahhh! The reward?" Mom watched Heidi who was wandering around the room looking at all the same things she had looked at earlier in the day.

"Well, let's talk about this in the bedroom. I need a shower. What's for dinner?" His voice faded down the hallway. Dad always asks that same questions every day.

"Oh, I have to show you the new shampoo I bought for you, honey."

I was alone with Heidi and Baby...Gulp!

That's when I felt Baby's eyes on me...drilling holes into my body from across the kitchen from under the dining room table. This needed action now! A plan started to form in my mind.

I walked over to the basket where my toys are stashed. I took the devil Santa out and started to bat it around, going from a single paw then to two, taking swipes at it with equal amounts of force. Quickly I moved it out into the middle of the room, backing off and fiercely hissing and snarling at it. I came in real low and pounced on it. With the Santa in my mouth, I looked up expecting to see Baby and Heidi watching. But alas, no, neither was there.

Mom walked by with Heidi in her arms, she was scratching the huge cat around her ears. Dad was standing in the doorway putting on a new shirt, "Turn on the TV and let's see what the news has to say.

Mom found the remote, switched on the TV and said, "What if she isn't the same cat? I mean it could just be a mistake." She nuzzled into Heidi's ear murmuring softly. "Maybe we could keep her."

Oh yeah: that would work out really good for me. I thought.

The news came on. And sure enough, there was an alert. "Where is Heidi?" was emblazoned across the TV screen. A newscaster was updating us all about the lost Savannah. He informed us that Heidi had one little flaw: one of her teeth, a cusped was longer than the others. It jutted out and looked odd. From that moment on, to me she became 'Heidi Fang.' Aside from this small flaw she was normal for her breed. And the reward was mentioned again.

Dad had come down the hallway and stood behind Mom when he said "Open her mouth...lets take a look."

Mom looked somewhat puzzled. "What?"

Dad replied, "Her tooth, Silly."

Mom stepped away from him clutching Heidi closer to her chest. With a sigh, she answered him, "You don't have to...I've already looked. It's her, and there is a phone number on the tag around her neck."

I was sad and happy at the same time. It was like winning the Lotto my dad plays all the time. You know, you've won, and that's great...but you've won and that's not so great. Not so great because nothing will ever be the same again.

At that moment, I knew Dad was going to make the call. He went over to the phone and punched in the number as he walked down the hall. Mom took Heidi to my food bowl. "I'll bet you're still hungry." With that, she placed Heidi on the floor in front of my bowl. I left the table and moved silently to the edge of the kitchen floor where Mom and I admired Heidi as she ate. "Max, keep an eye on her while I check on your father. Ok, sweetie?"

Time slipped by as Heidi ate in silence. Because she was so tall, she had to dip her head straight down into the bowl. Her tail curled around her body; she made such a beautiful sight. I took one step toward her when she looked over her shoulder and hissed at me. She then turned and munched away, on my food! I backed off returning to the safety of the dining room table.

From down the hall I heard, "We are going to make some bucks, Honey. Where's Max?" Dad came into the dining room and picked up Heidi into his arms. He bent over to look under the table through the tangled forest of furniture legs; his big face filled my view.

"Hey, Max, little buddy…you are The Man." Just then the phone rang. Mom picked it up, listened and said, "Oh yes, we're here. Sure we can come out…just honk your horn, we'll come out to you. Yes…248…that's right." She hung up the phone and threw her arms up into the air as Dad spun around with Heidi still in his arms. In a few seconds, a pair of headlights lit up the curtains, and a deep throated and expensive honk filled the night. I lifted my head and caught a glimpse of Heidi. Our gazes locked for a fraction of a second and then she, my mom, and my dad all walked out the back door.

Time always seems to move more slowly when you're helpless. For me, this was one of those times. There was nothing I could do about this situation, so I simply had to wait. It seems as if I have to wait on humans for lots of things, to let me in or let me out or charge up my food bowl or for them to just go away.

Eventually, the back door reopened, and my parents had come back in. Mom held a piece of paper up over her head exclaiming, "Oh, what we can do with this money? Just think of it… all this money for us!" Well, at least they were having a good time.

But now I knew I had to make amends to someone else so…

I searched and found Baby not far away in the living room. I lay down in front of her, submitting. I tried to find a kind place in the depths of her eyes. "Let me in, Baby. I know it's tough sometimes to accept my selfish male ways." I took a deep breath and offered her my head...nothing. I reached out a paw, opening my claws to let her know that I was totally submitting. Again, nothing. I was stunned; this was serious!

Baby merely looked off somewhere in the distance, which isn't that easy because our trailer isn't terribly big. How does she do that? I wondered.

Mom and Dad were standing in the hallway, but they were too wrapped up in their world to notice me. Dad leaned against the wall and let out a sigh. Mom turned her face into the crook of his neck. She whispered those words that I've not heard from either one of them for some time, "I love you." They did look happy. I'll say that for them. They both glanced over to us in the middle of the living room. My mom waved her fingers at me and leaned her head against Dad's chest.

For some strange reason, the happier our humans are, by extension the happier we are, or should be. However, at this moment I was sad because Heidi was gone. And Baby was very upset with me. Well, Baby...she'll come around. If there is one thing I know about her it is that she just needs time.

After all, it is simply impossible for anyone to stay mad at me for very long...

15 THE BURGLAR

For some time, a local stray from down in the river basin had been making forays into the park. My park. I'd only seen him from a distance. He was bigger than most with a mottled, dirty white coat, and an irregular stripe of black across his face, like a mask. Everyone had taken to calling him "The Burglar," which fit him big time!

Of all the things an interloper could do in my territory, the absolute worst thing was to mark it with his scent. This was my personal space and I claimed a lot of it in my corner of the park. Here, in our little world, we cats maintained a live-and-let-live lifestyle. When it came to me, I marked my territory and enforced it as well.

It was a gray and dingy morning. I thought I would stay inside and be warm just lying around the house, but alas, it was not to be.

When Mom opened the curtains in the front room she exclaimed, "Oh! Honey, there is that big cat. The one that looks like he has a mask on." She pointed toward Victoria's house across the street. My Dad went to the door and stood there for a moment, his hand on the doorknob. Seconds ticked by as he slowly opened the door and stepped outside.

I was on top of the entertainment center where it is extremely high. High is good because my parents are always looking for me under things. I dropped down onto the doorsill and slipped out before the screen door had shut. I snuck around my Dad's legs as he turned to answer Mom when she yelled, "Damn that cat. Honey, Max just got out and he's on the deck."

I went around the corner and stood at the top of the steps. At that moment Victoria, a broom in her hand, was swinging at my new nemesis. She almost got him, too! But he dodged all of her attempts and looked terribly upset with her. Winded, Victoria dropped the broom to the ground. Thinking she was finished, he crossed over to the street. As he did, Victoria made one last mighty effort and swung her broom at him in a wide arc, inches above the concrete. If she had connected with him he would have left in a hurry.

Not this alley cat…no way. He stood his ground, ears pinned back and with a deep hiss, he turned. In the blink of an eye, he leaped onto the broom and swatted at Victoria's legs. She screamed and fell backward onto her back steps. Taking his time, my foe turned and strolled away from her as if he owned the place. At the corner of her trailer, he backed up to the wall and let loose his scent. Now this beast had gone too far!

But, from The Burglar's point of view, going "too far" was exactly his intent. Like all bullies, he always pushes to see who will and who won't push back.

Mom poked her head out of the doorway. Dad spoke up, asking, "Are you okay, Victoria?"

As Mom pushed Dad to the steps, she yelled out "Do something!"

It's OK, Mom. I thought I could take care of this bad boy myself, and jumped from the deck onto the blacktop.

As I dashed across the street, The Burglar looked me straight in the eye. His eyes were dark, maybe even black, and showed no emotion as he reared up. I could see the muscles in his hind legs bulging out. His scraggily tail switched back and forth, slowly, not expending too much energy. He was saving himself for the battle to come.

He was old and twenty pounds at least. His head was gigantic, much bigger than I'd realized. And with that swipe of black fur across his face, it made him look dangerous – no EVIL.

Because I had to cross the street, to confront him, I had lost some control over the fight already. It was a poor choice on my part, for when we made contact in the end, I knew his greater weight would tell. My only chance was to meet him as soon as I could and that meant in the air.

My claws made that tippity tappity sound on the blacktop, the fur on my tail extended out like one of my mom's cleaning brushes. My ears were pinned back. I let out a deep savage "Moarhhhh" (that's my fighting howl) to let him know it was me he had to deal with. I left the ground and soared through the air, claws extended. The burglar had now risen up to his full height. He leaped, too, and met me about three feet off the ground.

We hit each other with a loud bone-crushing thump. All at once we were a turning, snarling, blur of gray and white fur. You probably couldn't distinguish where one of us started and where the other left off.

Suddenly it was hard to breathe and, to make matters worse, this beast stunk. The odor was like the alley cat he truly was. We hit the ground hard, he on his back and me hovering over him. Both of us were desperately trying to make contact with the soft flesh of the other's neck. From behind me, I heard a movement. I could feel a human hand on my back and the sensation of being jerked away from my foe.

Dad to the rescue!

But this fight was only getting started. In an instant, Dad dropped me as both of us fell to the ground, a stream of blood running down Dad's arm, which had The Burglar hanging onto him.

I got to my feet, err paws, and attacked the Burglar from behind. I flung myself onto his back, my claws slashed into his sides. I drew aim midway up his back and sank my teeth into his spine. A colossal howl came from him as he rolled away from me. Turning, he met me head on. He lunged but missed his mark. When his head started to slip past my nose, I bared my teeth and grabbed his cheek. I pulled in the opposite direction, bringing him down.

I could feel him give as we dropped to the blacktop. Now, with only seconds from total victory, I heard my mom's and Victoria's voices and felt that broom hitting both of us. In a fraction of a second, I made a tough decision and opened my mouth to let the Burglar go. He was up on his paws in a heartbeat; spun around, looked at me and "chuffed" before he darted off down the street.

I started to get up on my paws to pursue him, but was stopped by my mom, who had again brought that broom down. With bristles in my face, she had pinned me to the blacktop. She bent over and grabbed me by the scruff of my neck. Then she stood up with me hanging like a large furry question mark in the air. Mom tucked me into her arms, no doubt for my own safety. She even hissed at The Burglar as he slowed down to a walk before disappearing around a trailer at the end of the street.

Victoria helped my dad to his feet and proclaimed that his wound wasn't that bad. Dad grimaced as he started to walk towards home with Mom. I looked up and saw my other adversary, "The Ghost," sitting across the street at Melissa's back door intently watching me. How will I ever live this down?

All I could think of was, "Ah, Mom, I could've handled him all by myself."

16 FUERZA BRUTA – BRUTE FORCE

I awoke to a wonderful morning.

Mom was already up and she had opened the blinds for cat TV by the couch. The sky was a brilliant blue with a hint of wispy clouds. Dad was getting the last few minutes of sleep before going out on his daily job search. The other night he announced that he might help a friend in his handyman business, working strictly for cash.

I strolled toward the back door, stretching as I went. Mom let me out. I moved slowly through the sliding glass door, letting the chilly early morning breeze sweep over me. I sniffed at the last of the night's smells. There wasn't a hint of anything hostile. My family was safe. That's the first thing I do every morning; check for any threats or intruders. Mom and Dad don't know I do this for them. It's a kind of 'guard cat' thing that I perform *pro bono*.

Mom told me to play nice, then she shut the door. *Play nice? Oh, Mom, please.* This is going to be a great day for catnaps.

The backyard had plenty of tall grass. I was enjoying a nice roll in what I call 'flage', tall wispy grass, when I caught sight of a big juicy green grasshopper. We locked eyes. He took off with me bounding along behind him.

Until I came to the gate. Dad built this, it's made from a half section of wooden lattice easy for grasshoppers to pop through. For chubby felines, it's not so simple.

This left me with my first decision of the day--under or over it? I launched myself up and over in this marvelous 'ka-bing' jump that landed me onto the big wooden spool on the other side.

Luckily, Mr. Grasshopper was still in my sights. I dove at him. To my chagrin, he leaped ahead of me. I chased him down the grass alley then quickly across the street, swatting at him as I went. Finally, I tagged the hopper and flipped onto my side. But I had a loose grip on him, at best, and he wriggled out of it.

Imagine the sheer balls of this little insect, as he jumped off my paw, and landed a good eight feet away. Being green made him easy to track because he stood out against the blacktop. I spotted him just a foot away from the next trailer, an old abandoned one with an overgrown front lawn of dried yellow grass.

Somewhere between the overhang of the trailer and the blue sky, he disappeared. I made a last ditch effort to grab him, and threw myself up into the air, furiously swatting at where I thought he was. Gravity got me and I came down with a thud. Alas, I realized my grasshopper was gone.

That's when I saw it, the big yellow, standing maybe twenty feet away. How could I have missed it before? It was huge, a monster. I'd guess it was thirty feet long and fifteen feet high and it was yellow. How did it get here? Something this big I would have noticed and heard. I found what looked like steps, so up I went. At the top was a floor that was made out of worn down metal, with imprints of muddy men's shoes everywhere. There was a broken and torn up leather seat, and these big sticks were on either side of the chair. I climbed out onto the front and stood on top of what looked like the hood of my Dad's truck. Before I could investigate any farther, I heard voices. Men speaking in a language that I have heard from time to time in the park. The words were spoken really fast, and interspersed with English.

"Did you turn everything off like I told you, Dude?"

"Sí, Patron. I did."

"What about the water? You know…we'll break some pipes. We always do with these old single-wides."

"Sí, I know. Yo sabe. Am I going to drive the dozer today?" he asked eagerly.

The two men were dressed in dark work clothes with a vest of yellow stripes. Each had on a helmet, just like the color of the monster. I jumped from the hood to the tracks and was on the ground in a second. I took cover to watch. One of the men climbed up the same steps I had, all the while talking to his companion.

I moved deeper into the bush, finally making contact with the trailer's skirt. A second later, the yellow monster came alive. It jerked and started to shake. The ground trembled. I panicked and forced my body in between a bulging piece of the metal skirting that surrounds all of the trailers in the park. I plunged into the underworld darkness beneath the old single-wide, a safe place to hide until the yellow monster went away.

But instead of going away, the noise grew louder.

I crept over and found a break in the metal skirting so I could watch the monster. One of the men sat up in the monster's chair. The other was on the ground talking to him and waving his arms around. Shaking and shuddering, the yellow monster backed off the grass and onto the street. I thought that maybe they were going to take the monster for a walk and leave. Boy, did I get that wrong!

This unit had lots of jack stands under it because it was so old. Off to one side a couple of large water pipes jutted up from out of the ground then up and into the floor. Like under all other trailers, the ground was flat and hard. But there was one difference, a big hole in the ground near the street. It must have been ten feet across. Why was it there? I didn't have a clue.

It dawned on me, with no other breaks in the skirting, I'd have to leave by the same hole. The yellow monster was creaking and clanking along as streaks of light from small holes blinked on and off. It stopped halfway across the front of the trailer, sounding as if it would fall apart. It turned and lunged at me.

The monster hit the trailer and it shook wildly above me. I could hear wood popping as the single-wide swayed. Then it was hit again. And again the old trailer lifted up into the air and fell back onto its jack stands.

I was trapped.

I could hear one of the men walking around inside the single wide, yelling at the driver. I heard a ripping noise and a crash as something heavy fell to the floor followed by the sound of breaking glass.

"Come on, hit it again…harder."

He must have been in standing in the street. I quickly ran to the front corner. As I went streaking past, I saw a few jack stands that had fallen over and, in the middle, some that had buckled with the shifting weight. The area under the trailer now seemed smaller. Dust was everywhere.

Again the trailer shook and more jack stands moved while others bent.

I heard the sound of a man's boots. I forced my paw through a small break in the metal skirting. It pinched me terribly, but I wiggled it furiously and howled trying to get his attention.

He started talking again saying, "Fuerza bruta, man." Then "I'll do it." Through a hole in the skirts I could see him as he climbed up the monster's steps.

"Move over. The walls have to come down all the way or the roof won't fall."

The yellow monster screamed as it moved forward. I'd pulled my paw out of the skirting when the machine hit. But this time the monster kept moving forward, lifting the trailer as it went. Daylight filled the underworld, but there was so much dust I couldn't see where to go. The crashing noises were deafening.

Above me the floor sank down. Then I remembered the hole in the ground. Terrified, I crawled along, feeling my way with my front paws in the dark and dust until I found it. I dragged myself over the rim and tumbled down to the bottom.

The machine stopped. Its horrible noises were replaced by the ting, ting of cooling hot metal. Their voices drifted away. The last words I heard were something about lunch, and that it would be easy to demolish it now that the roof was down.

Then over the rim came a boil of dust. It descended down the steep sides of the hole like a living thing. There was enough light that came from the breaks in the floor to see it, but only faintly. I was about to shut my eyes to keep out the dust when I noticed that it stopped halfway down. A wisp of it slipped over what looked like a ledge. If I could make it to that ledge, I might be able to climb up and out.

The ground down here was softer so I stood up on my hind legs and started to scratch at the steep walls but earth kept falling in. I'd have to jump.

As a rule I can jump a five or six-foot fence easily. I gathered myself and flew up toward the ledge. I almost got my paws to the edge, but fell back down to the bottom of the hole.

One more try, I said to myself. All the while the trailer was settling.

With all my might, I coiled like a steel spring and shaking with tension, I "ka-binged" up to the ledge. I felt my paws go over the rim as I dug my rear claws into the soft earth below me. Holding on, I took a deep breath, got to my elbows (yes, cats have elbows) and brought my rear paws farther up, one at a time until I was safely onto the ledge.

Totally exhausted and filthy dirty, I lay on my side to rest. I tried to keep my eyes open but couldn't. The last thought I had was of that damned grasshopper…I hope to meet him again someday. Then blink, blink and I was gone…asleep.

"Images danced in my mind. It was a journey into my past. It was lonely on the street. One day I came upon a large vacant lot. There were a bunch of holes in the ground with pieces of wood lying across them. Young boys were hiding from one another under these. At times, they would jump out and attack each other with rocks and sticks, while loudly yelling and shouting. I thought if I could join in one of them might take me to their home but it was not to be. A few who did see me threw rocks at me. One hit me on my side and the boys all laughed and jumped around.

I hid in some of the holes at night, but these were large and very cold. In the early morning a couple of people would bring their dogs to run in the lot. They found me easily enough. Most of the time I'd back into the hole as far as I could, and swat at the dog's paws or their noses. I was still so young and inexperienced that it was hard to connect with them. After a while, the humans would call to the dogs by name and they'd run back to them. It was pure magic that the mere mention of a name could stop a hunting instinct so acute as those dogs had.

It must be wonderful to have a name. I told myself that someday I'd have one, too. But where would I get one and who would give it to me?

I have to say that getting food wasn't so easy either. The time I spent in the vacant lot left me exhausted and hungry. Hunting is natural for felines but there is a learning curve. After a few false starts, I finally scored a lizard and had it for lunch. After chasing it for a long time, I snagged it and was about to devour it when its tail came off. The lizard then ran away. Some days, I ate. Others I wasn't so lucky. I drank out of nasty gutters in the street and often almost got run over by cars.

The pickings were getting slim around here so I decided to move on. Across the street was a parking lot with a lot of cars going in and out. One morning, a new smell was in the air. It came from across the street from a car parked by itself. The street was empty so I dashed to the far side and was under this metal guardrail and into the lot. I must have startled the driver because this thing in his hand fell out onto the black top. He yelled at me then and quickly drove away.

I walked slowly up to the thing he'd dropped. It smelled odd but good. I sat in front of it and warily pulled it out of its thin paper skin. Hunger made me take the skin into my mouth. It tasted terrible and getting it out of my mouth was difficult.

With the paper skin off, it smelled so good. Without a second thought I sank my teeth into it. My jawbone hurt as I closed my mouth around it. Tears welled up in my eyelids. All of a sudden, I became aware of being vulnerable here in this parking lot. Frantically, I dragged my prize backwards trying to pry a piece of it off as I went. From under the guardrail a couple of squirrels appeared. They chirped and then sprang at full speed toward me. In a second they were biting and pulling at the other end of my meal. I managed to tear off a large hunk and marched off to finish my best dinner ever.

Beyond the guard rail, where the cold wind came from, was this huge body of blue, water. One day I explored all the way down to the end where it dropped off into the water. I crept to the edge and with my paw I dipped it into the water. I drew my paw up and licked it. The taste was horrid, making my mouth pucker. It wasn't a nice taste. This water thing was very confusing.

 When it got colder the cars stopped coming. Days went by and my hunger was less acute, more like a mild annoyance. I needed to leave this place beside the big blue water. Where was I to go? I lifted my head and "meowed" in my loneliness as I watched the bright sun burn itself out in the big blue water. I swore I'd search for my cat mom and my family.

The images faded, while the meows from my dream vibrated off the floor of the trailer over my head. I awoke with a start not knowing where I was. As sleep slowly left me, I remembered the hole. I reached up real high and clawed out a big pawful of dirt and small rocks. After a while, my claws and pads were aching. There was one odd shaped rock that refused to come out. Hooking a claw into a crack, I pulled and pulled. Finally it gave way but it almost took my claw out with it. I was bleeding and the pain was terrible, but I continued. Finally the first hole was finished. I reached out and pulled myself up to a long rock that stuck out far enough and was big enough for me to stand on.

It was a start…

My paw was throbbing but I picked up my pace, digging faster, getting closer to the rim and safety. From nowhere a bulge in the wall appeared…it started to crumble. I heard it before I saw it…water.

First, it was a slow trickle. Then it got bigger. Finally, it burst. Clumps of dirt and rock flew out in all directions. Pressure driven, the water was turning the far wall into mud. The spray drenched me. The bottom of the hole was soon filling with dirty water and it was getting closer. I clung to this slippery slope as small rocks pulled out easily, almost to the touch. I stood and pulled myself up to the rim but slid back down to the ledge.

To my horror, the spray had made the ledge even smaller. Soon it gave way, sending me tumbling down to the bottom of the hole and into the water. I had to paddle furiously to stay afloat.

Again I thought I was doomed. Then I heard voices. The workers were back. I gathered my strength and let loose with a howl.

"Did you hear something?" One of the guys asked.

"Hear what?" was the reply. I let out another howl. This one I was sure they heard.

"Come on, you must have heard that, Jefe?"

"Ok, let's get the bulldozer's blade under the corner, we'll lift it up and have a look. Damn this is taking way too long." He sounded angry.

The water had now lifted me up and over the ledge. There was nothing I could do but swim. I paddled around in circles as the hole filled.

From outside, the yellow monster came back to life. I thought, this is it…I'm going to die. The yellow monster hates me cause I walked on it.

When the jolt came this time, it was very different. The corner leaned in; the whole trailer moved a few inches away from the street. Then from out of the side of the hole I saw a terrifying thing, large menacing animal teeth dripping water and mud.

Terrified, I let out my loudest howl yet.

A voice said, "Wait--wait I heard something funny." Through a crack in the skirts I caught a glimpse of a man's face. A crevice was draining the hole near the trailer's skirt and the underside of the trailer's floor. Mud was slipping back into the hole as more water kept filling it up. The man let out a yell as dirty water swirled around his feet.

"We got a water break, man!" He said angrily.

I drifted toward the crevice that was dumping water out and onto the street. As I got closer to it the skull of that animal stood out from the mud and rocks, a bit of white and black fur was attached to it. I was looking at one of the park's skunks. As fast as it appeared, the body with its skull and horrible grin fell into the water with me and was taken away into the crevice. The skunk's remains acted like a broom and swept it out. Immediately the volume of water picked up and drew me closer to the crevice.

The flow of water pulled me backward across the hole and into the crevice. I think my tail was outside, it felt lighter somehow and I could flick it around. My butt would be next as it started to slip out of the crevice.

Then, I realized I was stuck in the crevice. Water now swept over me in a torrent. I couldn't see. My eyes filled with dirt and I'd swallowed a lot of water. I took my last gasp of air as rushing water covered me. My body had formed a plug and my lungs were bursting.

Suddenly, I felt strong hands, like my dad's, around my ribs. I was lifted high into the air. Once outside, I coughed and gagged as big fingers worked my stomach. Water jetted out of my mouth. I looked up and blinked. Above me were bright sunlight and the blue sky.

A hefty voice asked me, "Hey, Cat, how you doing?"

Dazed, I looked over at a brown face with a short beard. He had sparkling brown eyes that twinkled at me and his smile was as bright as the sun.

When I sneezed, he laughed. Then carefully placed me on the ground. The torrent of water from under the trailer was now just a trickle. As I watched, it came to a stop, forming a harmless brown puddle in the middle of the street.

"What you got there, man?" a voice asked as the other worker came from around the corner of the almost flattened trailer, a large pipe wrench in his hand. "Looks like a drowned cat."

They started to talk very fast in that language I didn't understand. They laughed and stomped their boots. As I coughed up even more water.

I shook off as much water from my body as I could then, limping on my bad paw, made my way back home, leaving a trail of blood as I went.

I crawled under the gate and into our backyard. Mom was on the deck. She took one look at me and screamed. Dad rushed out and picked me up. Mom had a towel in her hand and began wiping me down.

"Oh, dear! He is filthy." She took me, saying sternly, "Max, what happened to you?"

Dad reached out and took my paw in his hand. He turned it over to inspect it, as I let out a loud, "Maaah-raaah."

Mom said, "Oh my, he's cut!" She clutched me to her chest almost to the point that I couldn't breathe.

I looked up into her eyes and let out another pitiful, "Maaah-raaah."

Lifting my good paw to her face, she kissed it and smiled meekly.

"What do you think happened?" Mom asked dad as he looked down at the ground. I knew he'd seen my blood that formed a trail across the grass.

"I think we can stop the bleeding. Should I call the vet?" Mom said. But he was already over the gate walking in between the trailers following my bloody trail.

Mom took me into the house and placed me in the kitchen sink. She washed me down with warm water. Then she doused me with apple-scented dish soap. I would smell like apples for days. Normally I hate baths, but I was too exhausted to care what she did to me.

Her fingers worked gently over my body to get as much dirt and grime off of me as possible. All the while, she cooed in my ear as only my mom can do.

When she finished, she pummeled me with towels, vigorously drying my damp fur. I said not a word. I just let her fuss over me. In a couple of minutes, Dad came back into the kitchen. His face wore a look of astonishment.

Mom had applied pressure with a paper towel on my cut paw to stop the bleeding. She turned me over and cradled me like a baby in her arms.

"Well, what did you find out?"

Clearing his throat, Dad said, "You are not going to believe where his bloody trail led me." He paused for a second then he continued, "I was talking to a couple of workers that are tearing down that old single-wide and they said...."

Through half-closed eyelids I looked at my Dad. His mouth moved excitedly, but I didn't hear a word he said. Instead, I thought of the workers and the yellow monster.

I think I'll pass on chasing grasshoppers for a while. Maybe tomorrow I'll even take the day off. Then in the depths of my aching body, fatigue found me. I lay my head on my mom's chest. With the scent of apples filling my nostrils, I fell asleep in my mom's arms knowing that I was finally safe.

ZZZZZ...

17 NOSTALGIA

Oh boy, she was getting close. I'd better run because Mom was chasing me. At the end of the hallway, I would slow down so she could catch up to me. I love to do this over and over, it drives her nuts. That's part one of my big plan.

I'd been out earlier and had brought home this really neat piece of yellow tape that someone had placed across Miss Thornton's driveway. It was tied between two of those orange cones that Maintenance Man puts up around the park. It wasn't a long piece, but I liked it so I brought it home and ran through the house with it wrapped around my rear leg. In the process of trying to remove it, Mom had gotten the tape fouled around my tail. At first it was a serious thing, but now it had turned into a game that came to an end when I ducked behind the couch. I slipped in and hid against the wall. But the yellow tape was sticking out into the front room and gave Mom a big clue where to find me. Instead of grabbing me from over the couch, she flopped down onto the cushions. Letting out a big breath she said, "Oh boy, Max, you can really tire me out." Followed by, "I wonder where he has gone, hmmm."

I thought, *Hey, maybe I fooled her.* Just then, my unruly tail started to switch back and forth as if it had a mind of its own. There was an oversight in my plan. At that exact moment, I realized my yellow prize had given me and my secret hiding spot away. Mom bent over and took hold of the exposed tape then pulled hard. She snapped the tape in two, leaving part of it under the couch.

I was not going to give up this easily. Standing quickly, I came around the end of the couch and flung myself out into the front room at Mom's feet. I began swatting furiously with both paws at the tape in a feline frenzy that made her smile, that Mom smile that I love so much.

In a second, my madness was dispelled. I sat up on the rug and rubbed my cheeks along her long fingers. She scooped me up and set me on her lap. "What am I to do with you, and the things you bring home, Mister? You know what the people in the office think of you and your mischievous ways?"

With that, Mom went to the floor on her hands and knees and started to pull what was left of the tape out from behind the couch. For some reason, it wouldn't give. She pulled and pulled but to no avail. Lying on her side, she was reaching in back of the couch to extract the last little bit of the tape, when she said. "What's this?"

Pushing the small table next to the couch to one side, she maneuvered under it and came out with a small dark-colored book in her hand. Utter astonishment was written on her face. She sat up immediately. I looked around her for my tape that I had brought home…but all I could see was this dusty old book looking thing. She opened it ever so gingerly; her eyes widened in excitement.

When she spoke her words were in fact directed at me. "Oh Max, you wonderful little man! Look what you have found."

Not wanting to be left out of something that I was wonderful at doing, I crept forward and sat on my rabbit's footies and inched towards her. It was a kind of sideways movement that only I can do, as far as I know. By this time Mom had drawn her knees up with the book on her thighs. She smiled as she turned the thick pages.

I was so close, she reached out to scratch me around my ears. "Would you look at this one," she said. I could now see over her arm at the page and gazed at a picture of her and my dad embracing each other, big smiles all over their faces. I knew it was them, but they looked so much younger. She was dressed in white head to toe, a long filmy headpiece flowing off her shoulder and down her side. Dad looked happy. But why was his leg in a cast I wondered? Laughing out loud, Mom threw a hand over her mouth then she winked at me, saying, "Well maybe some day I'll tell you the story of your crazy Dad on our wedding day and how he broke his leg."

As she continued to turn the pages, she stopped and pointed and told me that this photograph was taken years before when we all lived at the beach. "You remember, Max, by the ocean? It was the house where we first met you."

Not wishing to break the spell of her nostalgia, I opened my mouth and gave her my bestest T-rex smile. As she turned the pages the years with Dad flitted past. Finally, she stopped and looked at a small photo. "Look, sweetie, here is our first visit to the vet. You must remember that day…I wonder why your father took this picture, he does do some strange things at times."

Remember? Sure I remember! What a day that was.

"You were so scared when we left the house; you'd never been in a car before. Oh geez, sweetie… I hope you've forgiven us. You know that was a long time ago. Maybe you've forgotten?"

Not likely, Mom. I still have chills and panic attacks whenever I go to the vet. But I don't blame you anymore.

I placed my paw on the book and gave her a super nice snork just to let her know everything was all right. She smiled.

Turning the page, we saw one picture at the same moment. She touched it lovingly with the tips fingers. "Oh my, I had almost forgotten… it's been so long."

The photograph wasn't special in any way that I could see. It was just an outside shot of our old house by the ocean. There was a lawn, not too large, but with lots of water sprinklers. Immediately, memories flooded into me of my life as a stray on the streets. Then it came to me. At this very spot, I had first met my mom.

As if to confirm that thought, Mom said, "Look, Max, this is where I first saw you, where you came into our lives. You were so small." She bent over and kissed me on my head bone. "Those were happier times for us all; your dad's business was making money and I had gotten a clean bill of health. Hmm. Yes, happier days." Her pause seemed to lighten her spirit.

With that, she started to turn to the next page. The phone on the desk rang. As Mom got up to answer it, the book slipped off her lap. She stood and the page sort of waved back and forth. Without thinking, I put my paw on it like my mom had done to the other pages. It fell open. I found myself looking into the eyes of my older stepbrother. He stood tall, much taller than I had remembered and was fully-grown and as orange as any tabby cat could be. But where was he? What had happened to him? Why was he gone?

Memory brought a vivid recollection of that night outside of the house in the back where that black figure stepped out of the shadows and took him. I should have seen that bad man coming, should have done something about it, after all I was the one with all the street smarts. It should have been me that was taken …not my brother. Staggered for a second by these thoughts, feelings of guilt came to me in a rush. I quickly looked over my shoulder at my mom who was just then putting down the phone. I had to act fast and try to hide his image from her. I attempted to flip the next page over with my claw. I stood over it and pulled it up. Slowly the page swung to its apex only to have it balance there just as Mom sat down. She positioned herself on the floor, her back against the couch, and said, "Where were we, sweetie?"

I thought maybe if I were to crawl onto the page with my body, Mom wouldn't be able to see this photo and we could look at the other pics that were not so horrible. You know more entertaining and fun.

Unfortunately, when she sat down she looked directly at the picture in front of her. I let out a slight 'Meuur' and hoped for the best. She cleared her throat. I looked up into her eyes…by far the bluest eyes I'd ever seen. She tried to smile, as the corners of her mouth rose slightly. I nodded up at her and brought my paw to her arm to comfort her. Whether it was for her or me or both of us, I don't truly know.

Haltingly she said, "Well, it's been a long time since I've seen him." I nudged her with my head softly then I gave her a loving head butt followed by a huge "snork." She struggled for a bit then petted me on my head bone and said quietly, "We both miss Marty. Don't we, little buddy?"

My eyes moved across the photograph of Marty, my long lost stepbrother. His image was engraved in my brain. Frankly I hadn't expected to see this picture again. Seconds passed, finally she allowed the heavy page to fall over, where it would reside for now, in this book from the past. She began to turn the pages of the album again. As they flicked past she said, 'Well, what would you like to do, Mister?" Mom got to her feet and went to my toy basket. She looked in and announced that there weren't any new toys that she could see. 'It would have been nice if we found a new one, or better yet, what if we made our own toy? Whaddaya think?"

With that, she disappeared into the kitchen. As I followed her part way across the living room, she reappeared with her hands behind her back. I sat and waited. The tension built inside of me. All of a sudden she held out her arm. There dangling from her fingers was a length of string.

"I just got it off of your dad's UPS box…he won't mind." She lifted her arm and the string danced in midair, just above my head.

Excited and ready to play, I scooted up to her on my rabbit's footies and tried to nail the elusive string with my left paw. Before I knew what had happened she ran down the hallway. The end of the string bounced across the rug with me in hot pursuit. My claws caught in the rug's fiber and made a sticking sound as I ran after the string. A well-placed swipe from my right paw caught the end of my new toy and brought it to my mouth. To be thorough, I clinched it with my left paw, which secured the piece a few inches above me. I allowed my weight to make the string taut and pull me down onto the floor. With my mouth open and in a total cat frenzy, I swatted it over and over. Mom had stopped and now stood over me, she pointed at me, in delight at my feline antics.

The trailer filled with the sounds of my snorks and the wonderfulness of my mom's laughter.

18 STORMI

I thought I knew everyone in the park, so I was surprised when I met Stormi.

It was late in the day and I was hanging out with Dad while he talked on his cell phone.

Suddenly I picked up a scent...it gave me pause. I strained to inhale more and noticed it was getting closer. I saw that Dad had put down the phone, as he stared down the street. He is a lot taller than I am, like everyone else, so he can see farther than I can.

She came into view, trotting along, straining at her leash. A small dog, all of eight pounds. I was seriously unimpressed. When you've seen one mop-topped terrier then you've seen them all. That said, she was a strong little thing as she pulled her owner down the street. They walked up to the steps of the deck...she was a marvel to gaze upon, this dog's owner, all blonde hair and legs that went on forever, clad in denim jeans and a low cut blouse.

Dad and I made a comical sight as I tried to ignore the subminiature K-9 and Dad stood, his mouth wide open, as he stared.

The woman said her dog's name was Rebecca, and she hoped that Rebecca didn't scare me.

Dad stammered a little before he got his sea legs. At long last Mom appeared, she stepped through the sliding glass door as she wiped her hands on a towel. She held out her hand and started to say, "Hello, I'm Mrs. ..." when a loud siren came from down the street that drowned out her voice.

The stranger took Mom's hand and said, "Hey, I'm Stormi. Nice to meet you." They looked at each other with knowing eyes.

Dad stood there looking stupid, not saying a word. Mom introduced him and then pointed at me and said, "And this is Max."

Stormi smiled and bent over. Now I've got extremely good hearing along with my other attributes. And Dad was so close, that I would have been deaf not to have heard the excitement in the sigh that escaped from him. She took my paw in her hand and said, "Glad to meet you, Max." Her smile was so warm you could bask in it. I was smitten. Her dog barked and quivered like all minis do. I ignored it.

Stormi petted me on my head bone. I raised my eyes to hers and I gave her my best T-rex smile. Again she asked if her dog would bother me.

Dad finally said, "Oh, no, he's fine with dogs. He's a real little scrapper, this one."

Right, Dad.

Mom and Stormi talked a bit as both Dad and I watched in silence. Finally, Stormi said she and Rebecca had to go, and they walked down the steps and onto the street. Mom waved goodbye as they strolled away out of sight.

"Nice girl... you can breathe now, fella!" said Mom as she walked into the kitchen, leaving us standing there wondering what just happened.

That was two weeks ago. Since then Dad had been down with a cold. At least that's what we thought it was, a cold. Mom has been taking care of him night and day.

Doctor Someone had been here twice to look at him. He always left shaking his head with Mom following along softly, asking questions and looking sad.

I'd been doing my best for him too, crawling on top of him making sure he stayed in bed and got lots of sleep. It was another one of my cat's duties that felines do for their humans, when they're not feeling well.

There was a lot of stress that came through those covers. So it's at times like these that I need to vent. I have this special way of getting my aggressions out. That's when I seek out the Devil Santa who lurks in our toy basket. Baby has a few toys of her own, girly toys. You know ones with feathers and such, but mostly the basket is filled with the toys I don't like anymore. That isn't the case with my Santa. He is a villain of the first order, and it's my duty (when I'm feeling mean) to have it out with him. As a rule, I win these life and death battles. But it's the way these engagements unfold, that makes my parents heave with laughter. Little do they know the true depth of total danger in which they live.

Arriving in the living room, his eyes were upon me. I stopped in mid-stride and shifted my gaze to my right. There in the far corner, under my Dad's leather chair, was the Santa from Hell.

Usually, this happens later in the night when everyone is asleep. But every so often I'm forced to do battle with this dreaded villain during the day. At night, I have the advantage of shadows that hug the walls and corners that allow me to creep up on him for he never sleeps.

I stood so still that I almost forgot to breathe. I was seconds from either a creeping attack or nonchalantly strolling away. Of course, not attacking would signal a sign of weakness on my part and the Devil Santa would throw it up at me later.

Bloop, bloop...time passed.

I tensed for my next move, a feint. First a yawn to fake him out. Now, I have made this move so many times that I could do it in my sleep, a quick dash to the back of my mom's chest. But there was a problem. Against the wall stands a new mirror. I told myself that I'll not let this devilish thing take control of me.

Mirrors have that kind of power over some weak-minded cats, you know.

I proceeded stealthily when suddenly a paw appeared. A white and gray paw, an uncommonly attractive paw...is it mine or the mirror's? With tremendous effort, I slipped past the mirror and came out from behind the chest.

Quietly, I crept onto the ottoman, then to the leather chair. I held my breath and slowly moved over the arm of the chair as if it were an out-of-body thing. On the floor I saw the Santa peering around one of the chair legs.

Now was my time.

I dropped to the floor. He didn't move. With a mighty stroke of my front right paw, I nailed him along the side of his head. He tumbled from the basket onto the floor. I pounced on him rolled over, clenching him in my paws. I saw our reflection in the TV screen. I looked rather marvelous, even heroic, as I fought this Santa from Hell.

He was tricky, this one. I flung myself off him and took up a position a few feet away, my body low to the rug. Again I attacked. My claws ripped through his Santa suit and into his soft skin. We came to rest on my side with a thud.

He hadn't a chance of fighting back as I hit him one last time. He tumbled through space. Horrified that he might get away, I launched myself into the air, as both of us streaked toward the open front door. Inches from the screen door, I started to feel the effects of that thing called gravity.

All at once, I could see that he had made contact with the screen door, literally bouncing off it. I was so close to him that all I had to do was open my paw, extend a claw, and bingo, I snagged him. He was mine.

I felt the pressure of the screen door crushing my ear. I heard scraping as the door bowed outward. My head stopped while the rest of my body caught up with the front part of me. All the while, I couldn't stop looking at my prize ripped and torn from all of our past battles. Thankfully, Mom can fix that.

The screen door popped open and I fell out and onto the deck with a thud. My paw opened and the devil rolled out. Forward momentum carried me across the deck where I came to rest at the feet of Stormi and that dog of hers.

Towering above me, she looked down as I lay on my side wearing a stupid cat look on my furry face.

"Well, aren't you a sight?" she cooed softly with a smile that could break hearts. She glanced over at the Devil Santa, who had now reverted back into a pleasant looking Santa Claus doll. No doubt he was trying to fool her, too.

"Is your mother here, sweetie?" she asked, and stepped up to the screen door, she opened it to look in "No, I guess not."

I scampered to my feet, err paws, as she turned and descended the stairs. She glanced over her shoulder and smiled her incredible smile. "See you, Max, you little love. Tell your mom I came by." She waved, as they walked away.

I followed them down the stairs. Peering around the corner of our trailer, I watched her walk away with a graceful sway to her hips. Well, at least that's what my dad would have thought.

There wasn't a second to waste. Stormi might need me so I had to follow her. Like the expert stalker that I am, I took off down the street after her and that silly little dog.

They turned at the large field where all the kids play. She turned to her right into the spaces that are the weekly rentals all pretty and mostly new, some are empty. It's also the start of the territory that belongs to the dreaded Russian Blues. From here on, I needed to be on full alert not only for Stormi but for myself, too. That's when I got a whiff of Blues, that particular scent of oil, dirt and cat piss that only comes from alley cats. Then two of them charged me out of a low-hanging philodendron.

I sprinted toward Stormi at top speed to protect her. She stopped beside a large pickup truck as I scooted in between her legs. With a mind of its own my right paw unfolded just in time to engage the first of the Blues and snagged his cheek. A mist of blood filled the air around him. He tumbled onto his side, squealing in pain. The second one was braver…not smarter, but braver. He stood up to box me. Bad idea, Blue. I matched him blow for blow, after a short exchange of paws and claws, they both turned tail and ran for it.

Stormi gracefully sidestepped us, dancing around from foot to foot. Unfortunately, she got tangled up in her dog's leash almost falling over. All the while Rebecca barked loudly.

At a trot, I followed the Blues for a short distance. The fur on my back stood up all the way down my spine. They separated, but my feline hiss followed them as they took different routes around the trailer next to Stormi's.

A trap, I wondered?

I backed off, turned and walked towards her, pointing my front paws in this great walk that sort of makes my butt swing. I enhanced this effect by squinting my eyes into sleek slits and approached her in this most male fashion.

She bent down to scratch my ears and said, "Max, my hero."

I allowed her to pick me up in her arms. She smelled fantastic, the same scent I'd first experienced a week ago. We walked up the steps of her trailer. Stormi dropped me on the top step and unlocked the door, she opened it and I peaked inside. I gotta tell ya, this was like no other trailer I'd ever seen before. I think the correct term is "5th wheel." I hesitated at the doorway then Stormi gave me a gentle nudge on my butt with her foot to propel me into the semi-darkness. Really I wasn't scared or anything, really.

The trailer was unusually long and narrow although not as long as my Mom and Dad's doublewide. It had a long hallway, with a table and benches on one side, and a little kitchenette on the other. A foldout bed was covered with newspapers. Other boxes were stored in the overhead front-end extension where the trailer hooks up to the tow truck.

Tools were on the table as well as the floor. In the middle of the room was a chair. I walked over and jumped up on it.

Stormi opened a mini refrigerator and took out a can of soda, and popped the top. She looked down at me saying, "Okee dokee, why don't you make yourself to home, big man. I'm going to get comfy." She left the room through a skinny doorway. A yellow light came on in the other room.

Along the walls of the room were lots of pictures in small frames. I strained my neck to see who was in the photos.

I hopped off the chair, climbed up onto a bench, and, then onto the table. Face to face with this row of pictures. I looked up into the face of a young girl in a faded gold outfit. The gold outfit looked like a vintage one-piece bathing suit. She was spinning a silver bar over her head and smiled. The girl was young...maybe ten years old. I moved on to the next photo. The same young girl but a little taller, a little older in a black bathing suit stood in front of a crowd of people. With one hand on her hip as the other helped to hold a sparkly crown on her head. I followed the other pictures along the wall. Always there was the same young smiling girl wearing shiny costumes and holding trophies of one sort or another. It dawned on me that the girl was a young Stormi and this was her life in 8X10's.

Stormi returned wrapped in a white robe, her bare feet making that padding noise that my mom's make when she's barefoot. She smiled...my chest swelled and that thing in my chest thumped, bloop, bloop. "Oh, you've seen my gallery have you? Kinda hard to miss, huh? Boy you're going to know all of my secrets before this night is through, aren't you?"

She got another can from the refrigerator, popped it open. "We're back here, Max, you little cutie" She went to the last room where her bed was.

I jumped up onto the bed and sat beside her.

"You know, you are so brave and all. I should do something special for you...but what?"

Rebecca was asleep, on the floor in her dog bed gently snoring. I looked around the room. Along the wall was a corkboard covered with jewelry...necklaces, earrings, and little sticks that held rings. Along the top of the board hung rows of dark sunglasses; there were dozens of them.

She followed my gaze to her jewelry, and exclaimed, "I know, I can make you look really, really cool."

She flung herself out of bed and from a chest of drawers pulled out a pair of blue jeans. Sticking one long leg then the other into them she forced herself into the tight pants. She grabbed a T-shirt that proclaimed, 'custom shades by Stormi.' Pulling the garment up and over her head, she flipped her mass of blonde hair about in the air. Now, she was ready to make me cool.

She picked me up off the bed and we ran down the hallway. She placed me on the worktable, rummaged through a box on the floor, and pulled out a clear plastic bag filled with sunglasses marked 'Baby shades-2 years old'.

"Oh, this is going to be a blast!" she exclaimed.

She worked in a frenzy, popping the dark lenses out of the frames. Placing them off to one side of her workbench, she cut the frames in places, and added plastic pieces where needed. We went through six or seven pairs before she got her adjustments correct. They sat on my nose just fine and weren't too heavy. The problem was with the earpieces.

"You see, kid, your ears are in a totally different place than my usual customers. I'm going to have to make an extra bit of plastic that fits over your head a little on both sides and then mold the ear pieces around the back. Then, I'll add a band of elastic to keep the glasses on."

After the last of the final adjustments, she slipped the glasses onto my head. I was sleepy so it didn't bother me in the least. When she was finished, I curled up into a ball and nodded off to Z land.

When I woke, the sun was already up. I knew my mom and dad would be worried--I don't stay out over night that often. I stood up, and looked around. The smell of coffee wafted over me. I heard the soft padding of bare feet as Stormi came into the room.

"Hey, you're up. Great." She grabbed a coffee cup from an overhead cabinet and poured a cup. Rebecca came in with her leash in her mouth. Stormi sipped from her mug, and looked down at her dog, then to me. "I've got to take this one out for a fast walk before we hit the road. You wanna come with us? We have lots of room."

I sat and looked at her, not knowing exactly what she meant. A second passed, the silence was heavy. My thoughts went back down the street to my parents and my dad, sick in bed.

She bent down to Rebecca and attached the leash. She turned, slipped her angel's feet into a pair of flip-flops and opened the trailer's door. As she stepped out she said, "Well...think about it, we'd love to have you, wouldn't we, Rebecca?" Who barked in reply...stupid dog! With that they left; the door swung shut quietly by itself.

I wondered what it would be like traveling with them. What would my life be like without my mom and dad? I'd been out all night long...which, like I said, is unusual for me. I had this odd feeling that I'd done something terrible, that I shouldn't be here, especially that I was failing my dad. I've heard stories of other cats that just left their humans for someone or something else, some sort of strange bonding that whisked them away from their homes and the people that loved them. Could this be happening to me?

After a few minutes, they returned. Rebecca barked sharply at the door. Stormi shushed her, as it was still very early. The door opened as the soft morning light streaked in, filling the trailer with an unearthly atmosphere that made Stormi look more like an angel than ever before.

Stormi had hooked up her truck in a few minutes. She must have had a lot of practice, doing it all by herself over all the miles and miles that they had traveled.

She drove the truck expertly across the lot in front of her now empty rental space. The trailer followed along, slowly rocking from side to side. I felt sorry for Rebecca as she bounced around in the front seat, her nose sticking out of the shotgun side window as she barked loudly.

A hard right turn brought the truck onto the park's main street. Outside, the sun had broken through the marine layer, which covered Santee for most of the early morning. Stormi rolled down her window, leaned out and waved to me and blew me a kiss, as I sat in the middle of the street. Then they were gone, away from the park and me.

My decision made, I lifted my head up high I could hardly wait to get back home so my dad and mom could see me with my sunglasses on. I knew that my really cool look would make them smile and Dad feel better. With extreme care I walked slowly down the middle of our street.

Stormi was right. With my new glasses on, and with each step, I felt cooler than I had ever thought possible.

19 THE FIXER

I have to tell ya that I am a big, big fan of the Tony Dane show. According to my mom, this guy can truly cook. He goes off to faraway places to show us his newly discovered meals that do not come out of a can like my food does. Mom cooks a lot of his recipes and gets me to try out the fish and porky dishes.

So when we heard that Tony Dane was bringing his cooking show to Escondido, Mom went crazy and called her girlfriend Michelle. She said the "one and only" Tony Dane was coming to Escondido! They should go and see the show as it was being filmed. Maybe they could even bring one of their really fabulous recipes for Tony to sample.

Michelle was outside our trailer in fifteen minutes. In a whirl, Mom was ready and they were off on a big adventure. Almost as an afterthought, she reappeared through the back door whistling in her soft tones, "Kitties, kitties, want to go outside? Come on you two, it's nice outside."

Baby hopped off the living room couch and trotted toward the sound of Mom's voice. She then slowed down when she got to the back door that takes you to the carport. She was hesitant about taking that last step. With only one paw over the threshold, she stopped, and let out a sigh.

Mom, this may not happen. We never go out the back door....ever! I thought.

Baby cowered, then she sat down, terribly confused. Baby looked up at Mom, who petted her on the head bone. Seeing me, she asked "Well how about you, young man?" She sometimes uses that phrase even though I'm no longer a young fella.

Okay…so it's up to me. I walked slowly past the washer and dryer, to the back door and just like Baby I got confused and sat down. I looked out through the open doorway wondering just what Mom wanted me to do.

Exasperated, Mom stamped her foot. The floorboards jumped a little. She picked up Baby and let her down outside at the top of the steps. Baby walked onto the driveway.

"Well, come on. Make up your mind. We need to get going," she said. I stood, stretched, and shook my hind foot for effect and took a step outside. Mom pulled the door shut quickly behind me and rushed down the steps saying, "Cats!!! Go figure."

She walked down the carport, just as Michelle honked the car's horn.

This startled me, I took off running past my Dad's shed all the way back to the fence, which I leaped over with no effort at all and dropped into the yard behind our trailer which belongs to Mr. Neighbor.

I was instantly swallowed up by tall dead grass. It was so high that I had to rise up on my hind legs to see over it. There wasn't any kind of a path. In front of me was this large thing sitting on a trailer called a boat. It never moves, it just lies on top of its cradle.

I was a few feet away when Mr. Neighbor came around the corner of his trailer. He had something in his hand that I'd never seen before. It was long and shiny. It smelled like my Dad's truck, like gasoline. He held it firmly in one hand and pulled a rope with the other. I squatted down and waited. On the third pull, it came alive with a sort of a 'whacka dacka' popping noise. The sound was so unnerving that it made the fur stand up on my spine. To my horror, I saw a thick string whipping around at the end in a small circle. It looked like…death.

Holding his whacka-dacka machine of death, he started grinding and chewing up all the grass around him. Little rocks and bits of twigs flew everywhere. There was only one place to go…in between the trailer and that 'never-sail' boat of his. I ran at top speed hugging the trailer in the shadows, toward the sunlight and the street beyond. I wanted to be away from this whacka-dacka horror.

Taking the short distance in long strides, I entered the street. I looked back over my shoulder to see if I was safe from Mr. Neighbor and his machine. I heard the screech of a vehicle's brakes, followed by a dull thud when it hit me across the right side of my body. I found myself flying through the air...spinning around and around. The sky was so blue and the palm trees so tall. I sensed the black top and a parked car swirl past me. Unceremoniously, I landed on the pavement a few feet in front of a large old school bus.

I was belly down and splayed out on all fours. I held my head up trying to focus my eyes. I could hear well enough because I heard a lot of people all talking at once. "You should have stopped quicker…" Followed by "Oh, poor little thing…" And then my personal favorite, "He ran into me."

A lot of shoes ran toward me. I tried to get up, but the ground under me sank away in a hurry. I felt a hand around my ribs gently holding me and heard a man's voice say, "Give him to The Fixer."

I coughed, throwing up my breakfast. The blue sky turned black and hazy, the voices drifted off. I felt myself being handed to a pleasant smell, maybe a girl. I meowed once and was gone into blackness.

Some time later, I came around and found myself in a wicker basket. The haze in my mind lifted slowly. Again there was that nice girl smell I had experienced earlier. It was coming from under and around me. I was laying on a T-shirt with some writing on it. I peered up to get my bearings.

Seeing an open window I took a step toward it and leaned on the window's edge, stretching myself…now I felt some pain. A shallow but sharp ache from my shoulder let me know I wasn't going to be running out of here real soon. Slowly, I gripped the edge of the window, and rising up, got a good look at where I was.

To my relief, I was still in the park, somewhere close to the perimeter wall around the trailers with addresses in the mid-seventies. I was amazed at what I saw. In the street, there were three giant black boxes with light pouring out of them sitting on these tall stand-looking things. A man made adjustments to all of them one after the other. People walked around and talked in hushed voices. One woman held a clipboard. She was unusually animated, gesturing to a man who stood in the middle of the front yard of number 76. A white fence surrounded that trailer. It dawned on me that number 76 is the park's unofficial fish taco hangout.

Curiosity made me climb down off the seat even though it made my shoulder hurt. In the back of the bus, a man snored contently as he napped. I strolled down the aisle in-between the seats, toward the open front door of the bus just as the woman with the clipboard called out "Quiet! Quiet on the set, please."

It became so utterly silent that you could hear the wind as it rustled through the trees. A young man stood next to the woman with the clipboard, holding a camera in his hands, he stared intently into a small screen, "Rolling!" he said. Everyone's attention turned toward the older man in a white shirt, blue jeans and cowboy boots. His graying hair a bit disheveled.

"Ok, Tony, it's all yours," the clipboard woman said in a whisper.

I found myself staring at the one and only celebrity TV chef Tony Dane, and I wasn't even hungry. He started slowly, making the words up as he went along. Later I found out that their scheduled shooting in Escondido had been canceled. One of the crew, that's Manuel, suggested his sister's place. Manuel's older sister, Lupinta used to work as a chef in at a resort in Mexico and had recently retired. She was now living here in the park at number 76 and was forever putting on catered eats for local events, like birthdays and weddings. The woman just loved to cook. All of us cats know her fish tacos are simply the best.

Intrigued, Tony agreed. They must have started their trip down to our park just as my Mom and Michelle started theirs to Escondido.

Back to Mr. Dane...Tony walked over to Manuel and threw an arm around his shoulders. He began asking questions about this older sister and her experiences as a chef. Sadly, Manuel didn't know that much and his sister didn't speak a word of English. From out of the crowd, a teenaged boy yelled, "Tell him about Lupinta's fish tacos, Dude."

These people should have asked me, Max-the-gourmand. I can speak from personal experience that her fish tacos attract every cat in the park. There are fights over her trashcans whenever she cooks.

Off to the side, the cameraman's first setup shot was of Tony speaking to the teen, then back to Tony for a reaction shot. The cameraman moved the camera high then low to get different angles as the woman with the clipboard whispered instructions into his ear. Seamlessly they moved together as a unit. The crowd fell silent as Tony and his crew made their magic. Tony played to both camera and the crowd with equal skill. He only had to repeat a few of his lines, and always with a smile. With an occasional reference to a place called New York, wherever that was. What a pro, I thought to myself.

Somewhere off in the distance came the faint smell of fish. Instantly, I knew what today's goal was going to be. At this moment. I was just sitting, watching, being my untroubled self, when suddenly a humongous voice filled the bus.

"Look, everyone! Look who's up and all bushy-tailed."

With that, everyone outside stopped. They all turned in my direction. The crowd looked at me. His words had only just faded when the woman with the clipboard said, "Damn you. We were doing…" she stopped in mid-sentence, looked around searching, her gaze finally found a young twenty-something girl who sat on the white fence of number 76. "Hey you, Fixer, take care of that cat, will you?" Her attention turned back to Mr. Dane. In a less irritable voice, the woman with the clipboard said. "Okay, Tony, again from the top."

The Fixer walked over to the bus and stood in front of me. Her smell filled my cat's nose. My sense memory told me she was the same girl the T-shirt belonged to. With a soothing voice, she assured me, "Everything will be okay. You gave us quite a scare earlier, there, little man." She reached over and lifted the tag on my collar. "Max. How sweet you are!" With that, I turned my head and let her scratch my ears.

The snoring guy from the back of the bus squeezed past us. He'd not gone far when he said to The Fixer, "Hey, Wendy, the press is here."

Across the street, a van pulled up. The name of a TV channel was emblazoned on its side. A voice from somewhere said, "Must be a slow news day."

People laughed. The woman with the clipboard turned to Wendy. "Okay, see what they want. We're never going to get this shoot done."

Wendy held my paw, pointing her finger at me. "Now, you stay right here. Okay, Max?"

She walked off in the direction of the news van. Two people got out of the van as she approached. There was a lady who had her own clipboard and a microphone. Both women smiled brightly as they were joined by the driver, a thickset man who carried a large camera on his shoulder.

I watched from the bus and, as usual, I got way too curious for my own good. I stepped off the bus and walked through the shoot unmolested. No one paid any attention to me. Then I came upon a silver box sitting on the ground right in the middle of the street. A lot of black wires were plugged into it. These led to the lights shining on Mr. Dane. I started to pass this box when I noticed it was unusually warm. I stuck out my paw, feeling the heat. I touched one of the black wires, putting just a little pressure on it...all of a sudden it started to crackle and pop. I backed up, knowing this was trouble.

One of the crew saw me and yelled, "Oh no, the cat! The c-a-t!"

A worker lunged at me and in the process tripped over one of the bigger wires. The silver box on the ground sparked. The big box up on its stand flashed on and off, and then it exploded. A shower of bright sparks filled the air, which forced me to back up as quickly as I could.

When she saw me, the mean woman with the clipboard turned and screamed, "Get that cat." She threw something at me as I took off in Wendy's direction. Because of my painful shoulder I couldn't make a full run of it. A few feet from Wendy I slowed down and made contact with her shoes and slid in around her ankles. I looked up and "mah-rawwed" at her.

Wendy bent down to pick me up in her arms, just as the mean clipboard woman came up to us. Wendy introduced the woman with the clipboard and the reporter girl to each other. "Ah yes, this is Tony's producer Mary, and this is Adrienne from Channel 3 in San Diego.

Adrienne added, "And my cameraman, John."

But Producer Mary only had eyes for me. "You need to get rid of that damn cat or I will, okay?" With that, she turned on her heel and started to leave. As an afterthought, she said, "If you want to talk to Tony you can do it now while we fix the spotlight the cat screwed up." She then left in a huff.

Adrienne glanced at Wendy. "Well, that works for me. But what did the cat do to piss her off like that?"

Wendy hiked me up on her hip, fluffing me under my chin. I meowed again and they both smiled at me. "You're talent, you know what producers are like." She let me drop to the ground with a weighty plop.

The news cameraman snapped a battery belt around his waist and hoisted his camera from the ground and onto his shoulder. "I'm ready," he announced then strolled off toward number 76.

"Oh, yeah, producers and photographers, they own the world," commented Adrienne.

The girls walked off to number 76 with me following behind at a discreet distance.

The box with all the wires had been replaced, but the burned smell still hung in the air. The front door of number 76 was open. When I walked in, I was almost run down by the news cameraman as he came running out towards the van.

This trailer was different from ours. It felt like it sat on the ground and was much wider, too. Down the hall, in the back there was an enclosed Florida room with a large grill. I cautiously took a step inside. When the news cameraman came running back in, I followed after him into the Florida room. Directly in front of me was a long table stacked high with brightly colored bowls filled to the brim with different kinds of food. The smells coming from the bowls told me I had found what I was looking for.

Normally I don't care about people food, but on this day, I met my match all right, a stinky little fish called anchovy. Stealthily, I dragged myself belly down across the room. The table wasn't that high, maybe four feet. But I had two things to worry about: my injury and Producer Mary, who was lurking around somewhere. Backing up into the corner, I sat down in the shadows and waited.

The little room had filled with people all standing in a line. The news was on a TV in a corner of the room. A cheer went up at the mention of the park and Tony Dane. From the back of the line, a light stand and a light were passed hand-over-hand. The news cameraman emerged out of the tangle of people. He set up the light, bouncing it off of the ceiling. Soft light brightened the room, and in an instant my dark corner disappeared. I sat there as if I was naked.

On the patio, Tony and Lupinta were cooking up a small mountain of meat, fish, and veggies. More of Manuel's family came into the room bringing other food on trays and in bowls. Still no one noticed me. My problem was getting to that bowl of anchovies up on the table unnoticed. Tony and Lupinta, their hands loaded with big pans, left the grill and entered the room. The news cameraman, along with Tony's camera guy entered with their cameras shooting everything in sight. With all these extra people in the room, you almost couldn't move. Shoes appeared all around but still, no one noticed me.

The chefs started to dish up the meat and people were going down the table one after the other, loading up their plates. Unexpectedly, the lights in the house went out, plunging the room into semi-darkness. Someone yelled, "The fuse box!"

My time had come. This was going to be my best and maybe only chance to grab some of that heavenly, stinky fish. Instantly, my night vision turned on.

I leaped onto the table, brushing against a young girl who said, "What's that?" I sniffed the first bowl, no, the second no, the third bingo, anchovies...I was there. I was just about to dip into that utterly beautiful grilled fish when the light came back on. When that young girl, who I bumped into saw me and screamed.

Wendy rushed forward to my rescue. She stood in back of me as Tony strode up to us saying in his jovial voice, "And what do we have here?"

He leaned forward, with a dish of meat and grilled fish in his hands. The smell from the new dish got my attention. I reached out my paw, and I made contact with his hand. This brought me to an almost standing position. I let out an extremely polite "Meow" short but to the point, followed by a loud steady purr. Now you have to understand that my purrs are quite different from most cats. Not having a mother to learn from, I sort of made mine up much later in life. It turned out loud and rough.

Tony bent down. He held up his hand for quiet. I lifted my head closer to his ear and purred in my broken husky style. He exclaimed, "Now that's what I'm talking about here, a fan of your grilled fish."

He turned to Manuel's sister and hugged her. The whole room exploded in loud approval, and applause. Wendy tugged on Tony's arm saying over the din of the crowd, "Go ahead, feed him, Tony. It'll make great TV!"

He flashed his famous smile and nodded. He put down the dish on the table and picked out a piece of fish with his fingers, "Okay, here's a piece for our number one fan." With Wendy watching, he tossed the fish through the air toward me. I stood up and using my left paw (my right shoulder still hurt a bit) with a swift stroke I snagged that tidbit in mid-air. The crowd went nuts as I devoured it. Again he tossed another piece of anchovy toward me and again skillfully I caught it as it arched through the air, into my ready claw. Instantly, I tore that little stinky fish apart and consumed it.

Tony's cameraman had gotten it all, and it was "in the can" as they say. Wendy picked me up and gently put me on the floor, out of the way. She had a few bits of fish in a napkin and placed it in front of me.

Everything seemed great until I noticed those shoes. The toe pushed me away from my hard earned prize. I looked up into the eyes of Clipboard Mary, the mean producer. Wendy was still standing next to me. The producer's voice was filled with anger "You think this is some kind of joke, making me look bad? Even if it is just a Podunk town?"

Without another word, she squashed my fish under her shoe. Wendy saw this and pushed Clipboard Mary into the wall. Off balance for a second she tried to take a step towards Wendy who, in a flash, caught Clipboard Mary on the chin with a right hook sending the mean producer against the wall then to the floor in a heap, groaning. Wendy scooped me up and pushed her way past a lot of people in the direction of the front door. Finally outside, we immediately bumped into someone. That someone was my mom.

"Max, what are you?...How did you?" was all she could say.

Struggling with me, Wendy said, "Is this your cat, Ma'am?"

Mom replied, "Well, yes. I mean, he lives with us."

I reached out with my paw to touch Mom. She took me from Wendy, held me close to her chest and asked, "He didn't get into any trouble, did he?" ruffling my head bone as she talked.

Wendy was still looking around for Clipboard Mary. "Ah...no...no trouble at all, well he had a little accident earlier. But...yes, a perfect little gentleman, as a matter of fact."

They discussed the show being in town; how it came to be shot in the park and, of course, the fact that my Mom was such a huge fan of Tony's. Wendy said, "I'll get Tony to come out to say hi." She disappeared into the crowd and returned in a few minutes with Tony Dane in tow. In her hand, she carried a plastic container stuffed with fish. She presented it to my mom with the thanks of the crew. Tony told my star-struck mom how we had met, making light of the truck part. Mom said it sounded just like me. She smiled with pride as Tony told her how I became an instant media star myself when he fed me on camera.

We all laughed, thinking it had been great fun. Well, they laughed, I just hung on Mom's arm gazing at my fish.

Just before we all parted, Mom asked Wendy about her job on the show. Meanwhile, I was busy licking fish oil from in-between my pads.

Wendy replied, "I'm The Fixer."

Mom looked puzzled, "The Fixer?"

Wendy answered, "I'm local, and was hired only for the duration of this one shoot. I fix all local problems that come up on set...all shows have them."

Mom nodded, ruffling the fur on my head bone. "Problems like Max here." Suddenly she made a face and held me out from her at arms length. "Oh my! You stink like fish there, bud." They both laughed uproariously.

When we got home Baby was patiently waiting on the deck. Mom let me down and with my tail held straight up in the air, I strutted around Baby in circles showing off. I could tell she wasn't too pleased the way she sniffed at my fishy breath.

But that's okay. As Mom looked down at me she sighed and said, "Boys will be boys...huh, Baby?"

Sure, Mom, but I'm thinking...and, Maxes too...only double.

20 THAT'S ENTERTAINMENT

Baby always does this to me...and at the most inconvenient of times, too. I mean it can be terribly embarrassing.

Here, I am snoozing away on one of my most favorite places, high up on the back cushion of my dad's overstuffed chair. Normally I'm up on the couch in front of the big window, that's cat TV. But today was a slow cat TV day. So I wound up here.

I wasn't bothering anyone. Just laying here, slamming back some big ZZZs, waiting for din-din to be served, when up popped Baby, who started grooming me on my head bone right between my eyes. She could be rough, too. There have been times when my eyes have actually crossed because she licked me so hard. Have you ever touched a cat's tongue? I mean it's like sandpaper, all spiky and sharp.

Trying to be polite, I waited for her to at least get some of the day's lint off me. I have to be very still or she has issues with me later. I thought she was almost done when she reached out and bit the exact tip of my ear. I was so startled that I did a double blink to make sure it was Baby. I rose up and started to lunge at her. I had to set her straight, so my plan was to grab her by the scruff of the neck, just to let her know whom she was dealing with. But before I could put my plan into action, she quickly went right back to licking me, this time down the side of my neck.

My pique gone, I said to myself, *Well, someone has to do this and it might as well be me.* I settled into a semi-stretched out position, crossed my forelegs at my ankles, and closed my eyes.

Nothing happened.

I lifted my head a little. Sometimes, Baby needs me to participate in her grooming rituals. It's some kind of mother instinct in her, I guess. Slowly but very regally, I raised my head to her.

Nothing...Seconds ticked by...this was getting old. I opened one of my eyelids, just a slit.

Nothing...I couldn't see her at all.

Filled with anger, I opened both eyes in time to see the tip of her tail as it descended over the side of my dad's chair.

This was simply horrible! How could she do this to me, The Maxtor?

Where has she gone to? She probably thought this was funny. Was my Dad looking?

Sometimes it's just not easy being...me!

21 THE IMPORTANCE OF BEING MAX

Boy, as I've said before, it's not easy being me. Mom, my champion, sometimes makes my days tough.

I stood begging at the sliding glass door. Dad was finally going to let me out, but Mom ran up making these little "squeaky-squawky" noises. My dad even winced at the sounds she makes. She kissed me all at once, especially on my head bone, my most vulnerable place. She thinks I enjoy all of this, right!!! At last, Dad pried me from her grasp and tossed me to the floor. Quickly, he opened the door for me to escape. Just in time too, 'cause Mom was getting revved up for another go round of silly smoochie love.

I made a mad dash for the end of the deck, leaped off the top step onto the grass below. I could hear Mom's sighs close behind me. I picked my paws up and laid them down and reached the back gate in seconds. I paused for a quick look around, usually a good idea, but tonight it was unusually still. So still in fact that I could hear the sound of music as it danced close by in between the trailers. The music made its way into our backyard and flung the notes into their last little pirouettes. Those wonderful notes of delight must have traveled far because they lay down exhausted on the tips of the leaves of grass at my paws. A silver trail of beguiling notes only I could see marked a path out and away. My feline curiosity got the better of me, I just had to follow them.

I made my way down Mr. Neighbor's driveway and into the street. As I bounded along, the volume picked up, so I knew I was getting close.

In no time, I stood at the last street. Actually it's more like a service road where I saw all of the lights in the park's rec center blazing brightly. That's where the music was coming from and I had a good idea my old friend D.J. was there.

At the edge of the grass, I slunk down so low that my belly dragged. At the halfway mark, I stood and made a dash to a small shrub. There I waited and gazed at the wide-open field, looking for anything out of place. Off to my right was where the kids swing on a thing called monkey bars sat. Figure that one out. Monkeys… not in this park!

I have tried hard to understand them, but these humans don't make it easy!

A row of trees called Torrey pines lay down for the night. The young ones are not terribly tall. They run the length of the field just in front of extra parking for cars and pickup trucks. The wind rustled through these small trees, making their limbs wave at me. Even the large bushes that lived close by were at peace. As far as I could see, all was quiet around here for the night.

My caution should not be under-estimated. Sometimes, in these same bushes late at night, the Russian Blue gang might be lurking. I settled down to wait. The music faded and was replaced by the laughter of men and a strange kind of laughter, something like cackling.

A rustle in those bushes told me that someone was there. A smell drifted in from the field, not a cat thing but...Oh, no! Skunk. It was now or never. I took to my paws and ran. I redoubled my pace, my tail was bent over and the wet dew dripped from my fat sack, I came to the front door of the rec center, but it was closed.

Tick...Tick...Tick...Think, Max, think...Tick...Tick...Tick.

Across the field, I heard cats growl. The bushes shook wildly about. An explosion of cat bodies that tumbled out from the bushes followed another burst of cat growls. Blues were in there after all. Three of them took to the street with a couple of very young skunks in hot pursuit. Normally I'd sit back and watch the Blues get blasted by the young skunks and relish every bit of it. But to my alarm the Blues with the skunks behind them ran straight at me.

Fortunately I had a friend nearby, just around the corner. I spun around and made the corner in two strides. My friend was an old oak tree, bent from years of losing its battle with the building that was constructed too close to it. My friend had a terrific curve to it...but just right for a slightly overweight guy like me to scamper up on. I jumped up onto the bent trunk, claws extended. I walked paw over paw across the first lower branch, then onto the wall that is supposed to keep us critters out of the pool area. I watched the Blues who desperately searched for a quick way out of their predicament. But they had panicked and fled helter-skelter all about the yard.

With little effort, I dropped down inside the wall. The pool lights were on and the turquoise blue water looked fantastic. The temptation to lie down next to it and play in the cool liquid was great. But, I wanted to meet up with D.J. I knew whatever he was up to would be a lot more interesting.

I went around the corner of the kitchen and stood in front of a wall of glass. Halfway down, a window helped me out: its bottom panel was opened to let in the outside air. I walked up to it.

The room off the kitchen is the largest in the building. It's used mostly on Christmas and Thanksgiving though on some occasions there are these things called plays. That's why my friend D.J. was here. He is an actor who lives here in the park, all the way over on the west end. Of all the people I've met here, he is by far the most difficult to understand but the most interesting. First of all, he is extremely superstitious. For instance, tonight he'll cover the doorsill of the rec room with mint leaves, so the bad spirits can't come in to upset his rehearsal. When he goes home in the wee hours, he'll sprinkle salt over a lit candle so he can sleep in peace. Then there's always the bad dress rehearsal, good opening night superstition thing that most actors believe in. Many times I've visited him at his trailer and have fallen asleep in his make-up box. It is filled with powders of different colors like red, purple, black and yellow. Often I've come home covered in lots of different colors, making my mom wonder what I've been doing. Much to my mom's chagrin.

Tonight he was dressed as some kind of wizard. He had a long gray beard, his eyes sunk deep into his head. His hair was wavy, long and gray. A heavy, woven robe with a hood disguised his true shape. That of an older man a little plump from life...like me.

At that moment, there were only those who needed to be in this scene. They had pushed a couch into the empty room and three of them sat on the couch while the fourth stood off to one side and operated the stage lights.

At the window, I stood up trying to get D.J.'s attention, but he was on stage and deeply wrapped up in his character. He stood in front of a mural painted like an angry storm in a rugged landscape with mountains. Oh! There was a castle too. I pushed my weight against the partially opened window. It moved slowly. I brought my rear leg up onto the window frame and forced it open. After a few beats, that's actors' talk, I managed to get my shoulder in followed by a rear leg and slid onto the floor.

A spotlight came on and found me. I didn't dare move. D.J. pointed from the stage, three witches all turned to look at me.

D.J., filled with the power of his character said, "At last, a critic of worth."

A round of laughter and applause filled the room. I'd done nothing to deserve this ovation, but, okay, I was game.

"Now, now don't be too quick to judge, this stout young fellow is a friend of mine." D.J. motioned with his arm in a broad sweep, "Let's bring him up here, on stage."

He gestured to me. "Come on, Max, I could use your help." I felt ill like I would puke. I didn't know exactly what to do up there. I mean, I've seen him do this stuff many times before and it seemed pretty harmless, but never had I thought that I...could...

Seconds ticked by. The witches all waved at me, they encouraged me to take to the boards (more actor talk). I stood up and took my first steps towards my destiny.

Again, more applause followed by enthusiastic hand waving from the front row, this the witches gang of three.

Okay, I thought as I puffed out my chest. I could get used to this.

I strutted along and gave them all a good look at raw talent on the pad. D.J. stooped down on one knee with his arms wide open. His wavy gray beard twisted slightly. He opened his mouth and grinned, looking super ghoulish in his makeup. I hovered with one paw over the stage and realized this was something else and was unsure what to do. I didn't want to disappoint D.J. when he needed me, not to mention all of his friends. But I had to admit, I was a little scared.

As my paw touched the stage, D.J. gestured grandly. He signaled me to turn around, which I did. Slowly I showed them my pear shaped body, making all in the audience smile in delight. Glancing back over my shoulder I gave them a polite, "Meur."

D.J. clapped his hands together, "Now, that's what I call an entrance!"

From the couch a voice asked, "D.J., why don't you use the cat as a stand in? You're the one that's always said you can teach anyone to act!"

Another actor added, "Yes, make him your Thane of Glamis, D.J.!"

D.J. replied, "You mock me, woman, you scum. You possessor of zero talent."

Everyone on the couch erupted in a wild chorus of, "We want the cat, we want the cat," over and over again.

"Oh how I'd like to lay my hand across your skinny lip, you witch." He gestured toward one of the witches who sat closest to the stage.

Finally D.J. stood up, towering over me. He truly looked like a wizard. "If you want the cat then so be it. The cat it shall be." He turned toward offstage left and walked off. He looked directly at me and said, "Come here, Max. We've work to do."

I marched off in his direction to the witches' hoots from the couch. Backstage we entered a small room barely large enough to turn around in.

He lifted me up and placed me on a short table that sat in front of a large mirror that was covered with his makeup things. He talked about his plan for me to just follow him in his acting. His voice drifted off as I sat up nice and straight and "Zoned." I've come to master this ability to look like I'm intently listening when actually I'm far away.

At that moment, I remember him saying something about my 'cue' and a 'nod of his head.'

The next second I was back in my past. On a bright sunny morning, I had come down an alley close to the big water and wandered onto a property that didn't have any fences or walls. The grass in the back yard felt good under my worn pads. The soft blades called to me, as they always do. Out on the ocean, odd looking swells folded over onto them and ran wildly onto the biggest box of sand I'd ever seen in my life. The desire to use it, just to stand in it even, was overpowering.

Later, I stretched out on the wet grass at the edge of the cliff, my belly flattened out making me vulnerable. Small bits of rock and dirt from under my paws fell down from a great height to the beach below.

I should have heard her, but I didn't. Suddenly I felt human fingertips under my ribs. Before I could bolt I was in her grasp. Being so exhausted from my time on the street I didn't resist her. She fed me and cared for me for many days. She was young, much younger than Shoes and Socks. I stayed with her for weeks and had come to like it there, the house on the cliff with the sandbox she called a beach. She took me there often, putting me on a leash. At first I resisted the tether, but after time I gladly went along to please her.

One afternoon she asked me if I was okay, if I needed anything. Then she asked, "Where do you come from, little fella?"

I didn't know the answer to her question. The thought of not knowing bothered me. The desire to go and seek out where I had come from took hold of me.

Often she would play music and hold me close to her chest...so close I that could hear her bloop, bloop beat, just like my cat mom's.

Her house was not big, only one bedroom with a bed that sat on the floor.

The bathroom was always damp from the salt air. She liked to take baths and sometimes I'd watch her from the edge of the tub. The water and the bubbles fascinated me. Sometimes, she would place large shapes made entirely out of bubbles on my head. She'd laugh and laugh. It was the first time I remember opening my mouth and doing what became my T-rex smile...all for her. Our time alone ended when she brought home a boyfriend who had a dog. Neither of them liked me at all.

Over time, it got harder and harder for me to find safe places to hide and catch some quiet ZZZs. One day as I slept on the sill of the picture window I awoke and saw them all on the grass in the yard. They threw a ball for that stupid dog and tossed it endlessly back and forth. They looked like a family. They had even given that beast a large black collar. Attached to it was a brightly colored tag with his name emblazoned on it.

Didn't she remember that I was here first? I didn't have a collar or a tag or even a name. Oh sure, lots of cute names like "Sweetie" and "Big Man" but no special name of my own.

Over time, I'd put on weight. I had even grown a couple of inches and stood seven inches high. The dog was let in more often, which meant that I had to go to higher places on the furniture to stay out of its reach.

I had made up my mind that as soon as I could, I'd leave this place. I probably wouldn't be missed anyway.

My chance came soon enough. It happened on a wonderful sunny day. Everywhere I looked was blue--the ocean, the sky, everything. I had gotten down from the windowsill and stretched when the bedroom door opened. Out walked the boyfriend. He was smoking something. It hung from his lips burning furiously. The smoke stung my eyes and I sneezed. He grabbed me and hung me out at arms length then whistled for the dog.

He teased the dog with me, the smoking thing still hung from his lips. He laughed in his smug way. I dangled helplessly and all the while, the horrible dog jumped up at me.

I'd had enough. With a swat from my left paw, I sent that smokey thing from his mouth. The boyfriend's expression changed to hatred. At that moment, the front door opened and in she walked with an armload of plastic bags filled with stuff.

"What are you doing?" she yelled.

The boyfriend stammered something then dropped me. In a flash, I ran as fast as I could to the open front door. I was on the sidewalk, then up the alley to the busy street. I slipped in between a couple of parked cars and scurried under one. I've not had a lot of experience with cars and only knew them as large things good for hiding under and sleeping on top of. This for me was scary stuff. As one car passed me going in one direction, across the street, another passed going in the opposite. This was scary stuff for someone like me!

My decision was made for me when a pair of feet entered the street from the curb.

Whoever it was walked around the front of the car, pulled opened the door and got in. I wasn't sure what would happen next. Most of the time these car things just sit on the street all day doing nothing, but today this one rumbled to life and moved. I took my life in my paws and clawed my way out from under it and onto the blacktop. Seeing an open spot in the traffic, I sprinted across the street.

I misjudged their speed terribly, as several cars swerved around each other and me. I renewed my efforts, finally reaching an alley on the other side. Behind me, in the street a couple of cars had stopped. Two men got out and started yelling and pushing at each other. I slowed to a trot and once again found myself alone but safe. I wandered for days, continuing the search for my home, but never found it.

D.J.'s voice brought me out of the zone and back to reality, "Remember to bare your soul on stage. It is important to be yourself…no one else, just you, and that my friend is magic!" He added. "And if they don't like what we do then to Hell with them."

D.J. smiled his kindly smile and nodded his head. I nodded back, which seemed to please him to no end. He held out his hands and I scooted on my rabbit's footies towards him. He picked me up in his arms and we walked out of the little room and toward the stage. As we stood in the wings, the man his name was Tim Something who operated the lights for D.J. said, "Break a leg." Why would he want me to break my leg? Sometimes dealing with these humans is really very trying.

One of the gang of three found the controls for the footlights and turned them on. Now it was not only bright but hot, too. My tummy did flip-flops as we walked to the front of the stage. He placed me down on the boards. Then, like an old wheezy instrument, D.J. started to speak.

I tried to stand next to him. But he insisted on traveling around the stage. From time to time, he used his hands and waved his arms. I got tired of standing, so when he wasn't looking I sat down on my rabbit's footies and politely waited. One of the gang of three was wiggling her long crooked fingers at me. She whispered into the ear of the witch sitting next to her. Rudely, they would laugh, cackle and snicker. She pointed a chappy finger toward my host and said.

"He, he, he…all hail, hail to thee…MacD.J.!!! King of Cawdor!!!"

I did my best to ignore them. After a moment, I brought all my attention back to D.J.

He seemed to take forever, but this was important to him, so I waited. Remarkably his voice rose from its normal bass tone to a higher pitch. He was almost yelling. It was an old actor's trick to make our small audience settle down. D.J. used the space around him with great economy, careful not to use too much of it up all at once. He gestured to his audience, which brought more emphasis to his words. His voice seemed from another world it rasped and rattled in his throat as he neared his vocal climax. Unexpectedly he bent down and beckoned me closer. Then he stood and he spoke these words, his speech filled the room, as if he were confessing a deep dark secret to us. A matter so grave, that not to hear it would haunt you forever. Slowly, and at a much lower register. He proclaimed.

"Now…are the one half-world, tis thee nocturnal abode that I know so well, this- is- my- bane… and its nature seemed…

.…dead.…

…these lust filled wicked dreams, that I own…abuse my curtain'd sleep. Whose infamous pale witches with their naked craft celebrates these our …carnal offerings…

…could the wither'd ivory murderer, be more alarmed by his sentinel, whose howl's betray her trust, or that the bloody deed thus done, could be undone. And with his stealthy pace, might he take to flight, err this their impossible but beautiful fate…

Oh! Tarquin…such savagery might be opposed.…as with Max's ravishing strides, towards his newfound designs…

…Swiftly…he moves like…a ghost…like a ghost, like a ghost."

Upon hearing this, I knew my time had come. He was dripping in sweat and looked exhausted. No one spoke on the couch. They were all silently waiting. D.J. bent down to me, holding out his arms dramatically, grandiose even. He then gave me the ultimate compliment, he addressed me by name, my name.

"Max," is all he said.

I lifted a paw for effect, and let out a stirring, "Maaah-raaah" in response.

The room burst into applause.

I held my head bone up for D.J. to see that I, too, was in the moment. His face had a look of total exhilaration. His eyes lit up. Happiness seemed to spill from every pore of his being. Then, with reverence, he took a step back and bowed deep and long, first to me, then to his audience. Tears formed in the corners of his eyes and fell freely, running down his fleshy wizard's face. Still bent over, he jerked his head at me then toward the audience as if to tell me something. Again, he jerked his head and then it dawned on me what to do.

As a student should, I took my cue from my master and turned toward our audience. I too hung my head while my tail excitedly switched back and forth, alas, betraying my amateurs standing. I'm now a more humble feline than when I walked in earlier tonight.

Suddenly content, I smiled and realized that the magic was, to my amazement, all mine.

22 AND NO BIRDS SING

Bushes. Boy, do I love bushes. Now ask me why?
They make good cover for shade from the bright sun.
Oh, yeah!—and for birds too!

I do love to meet up with birds, all kinds of birds. The
exceptions are mockingbirds or black birds. Those are the
ones to stay away from…if you're lucky, that is.
Sometimes they find me, and that's bad. That's because
mockingbirds are just the worst, or so I thought.

After a wonderful meal of fantastically crunchy
Science Diet, it was time to go outside and put a little
nature in my day. I couldn't see either Mom or Dad, but I
managed to get the screen door partially opened. I forced
my shoulder into the skinny slit of an opening then
wiggled back and forth. In no time, I popped out onto
the deck.

I was still sitting there when my mom came into the
kitchen. She looked at me, and said to my dad, "Honey,
did you let Max out?" She came toward me, but I picked
myself up and plunged off the deck. Crouching down
between a couple of potted plants, I made my shape as
round as possible. I peeked through the twisted tangle of

branches. *Where was my tail? Dang, it's sticking out almost onto the pavers. Dad could spot me.* I pulled it in and wrapped it around my duck-like body. See, bushes are good for hiding, too.

I decided to wait there for a time to see if Dad would come out. Sometimes he tries to chase me, which is really funny to watch. I tease him by holding back. When he gets close, I dart away with my tail bent over in the wind as I go. Sometimes I reach a top sprint speed of around 30 mph.

Off to the east, I heard the mad scramble of wings…lots of wings. Hm-m-m-m birds were in the air. My day was getting a whole lot better.

I walked slowly, and scanned the whole backyard for any movement, as any good hunter does. Approaching the corner of the trailer, I heard those wings again, then the "caw-caw" of mockingbirds, followed by a higher-pitched sort of "cheep- cheep" sound. In another step I would have rounded the corner, but a shadow fell across my path. I stopped, one front paw slightly raised in case I had to change direction. I realized it was…my dad.

He burst out from around the corner and held out his hands while his fingers were twitching like a fiend. He was almost on me when I gathered my wits and took off. I sprang sideways. This move only bought me a second's reprieve. Dad saw his mistake and recalculated his next move, but he stumbled as he reached for me. With a rather big "thud" he went down on his knee, then onto the ground, knocking over a potted plant. I took this as a gift and sprinted to the back gate and slipped under it and into Mr. Neighbor's backyard where I hid behind the old wooden spool he has left here. I watched as my dad struggled to his feet. He walked away, muttering to himself. Mom appeared at the kitchen door, drying her hands on a towel. "Now what?" she asked him. He limped along and said something but. I couldn't make it out. She held her hands to her face and laughed uproariously.

"I keep telling you, you'll never outrun that cat," as she wiped tears from her cheeks.

Mom held out a hand to him. "Come on, let's get you inside where you'll be safe from mean old Max."

"Not funny," was all Dad could say as they entered the kitchen. I was finally alone.

As a rule, in the morning there are at least some birds singing or just making noise. The only ones I heard today were those mockingbirds squabbling somewhere down the street. No other birds sound like them. Beyond raccoons, mockingbirds are the biggest troublemakers in the whole of the park. That is unless you listen to Nicole, the office manager. She'll tell you that I, Max, have that honor.

I turned and took myself east down the grassy alley behind our trailer. It was the quickest way to check out what those "mockers" were up to. As I moved along, the dewy grass clung to my legs, making me smell musky--like nature. The dirt under my feet was still moist to the touch. It felt wonderful. The temptation to fall over and roll in this stuff was almost more than I could bear. I was better than halfway down the grassy alley when I realized that if I was going to get down 'n' dewy this was the place to do it.

Now there is a real talent to rolling around. You can't rush it. It's got to happen for you, sort of. I always start with a short step out, but instead of setting my right front paw down on the ground, I tuck it behind my left. Then my forward motion will take me down and over onto my right shoulder. I follow this maneuver with an easy roll.

As I descend, I thought that a flashy follow-through would be a nice addition. But there was no one to watch me, so I just plopped over and came to rest on my side.

The grass felt clean and wet. I looked up and square in my face, as if in slow motion, an extremely long blade of grass moved in an arc over me. It came to a stop just above my nostrils. A droplet of dew started to slide down the blade on a collision course with the tip of my nose. Mesmerized, there was nothing I could do but watch this happen. The dewdrop built up speed. It got bigger and bigger. My eyes seemed to cross in my head bone as it got nearer and nearer. When it happened it felt like a train wreck. Well not really. But it did have an impact...a noiseless impact. I sprang over onto my back and wiggled from side to side. This movement formed what no doubt looked like a very green and very wet grass cat angel. At times like these, being a cat is simply too good for words. I shut my eyes, and through little slits of my eyelids I saw a shadow quickly pass over me.

Two trailers down was old Mrs. Blaine's backyard. She has a really nice yard and garden. She's been planting veggies for the longest time. It was one of my most fave spots to watch for birds too because she had bird feeders and a nice birdbath for our feathered friends.

As I came into Mrs. Blaine's yard, she was bending over a row of plants, tending to some veggie.

"Max, how the hell are you, son?"

All of a sudden, her hat flew straight up into the air. Both of us were transfixed. I heard a flutter of wings as a pair of mockingbirds came around the end of her trailer. A few feet away, her hat drifted down and landed at the edge of the garden.

Suddenly Old Mrs. Blaine clapped her hands together. She pointed up at the mockingbirds and said. "Look!

Look, Max. It's those damn mockin' birds…those good-for-nothin's."

I thought they were rascals, too. Stealing an old lady's hat, really! The mockingbirds flew high into the line of trees that ran along the grassy alley, forming a windbreak. They bobbed and weaved about, they even performed cartwheels. No other birds can do them like they can. In the middle of this aerial spectacle, the sun poured through the branches, blinding me for a second.

Mrs. Blaine was still going on and on about her hat when that shadow burst out of the tree. It was much larger than the mockingbirds, who followed close behind.

I remember Mrs. Blaine's voice, though not her exact words. I remember the sun in my eyes, and how for a fraction of a second I held my head away. And forever, I'll remember the pain shooting through my body as the shadow took me down in a heap onto the ground.

A Red Tail is what someone at a zoo would call it. But out here in the county, it's a hawk. It had me by my front leg, its talons almost crushing my bone. I let out a yelp and hissed. We tumbled into Mrs. Blaine's tomatoes. The hawk's huge wings tried to cover me as it poked at me repeatedly about my neck and face. The feeling in my leg was becoming numb. I clawed at the hawk with my free paw, but all I got was a bunch of feathers.

Screaming, Mrs. Blaine came to my rescue. She threw something round at the hawk, but missed. The bird eyed her as Mrs. Blaine again grabbed at us and then backed up, getting a little farther away from her, and dragging me away in the process.

This beast had strength I'd never encountered before. We rolled over and over again, knocking down most of the plants at the end of the garden. Dirt, dust, and green leaves flew in all directions. The hawk tried to get airborne, beating its wings in a frenzy. For once, I was glad of my excess weight. I lunged at its head, but only managed to connect with its shoulder. I sank my fangs into the joint and hung on. We were eyeball to eyeball when a series of screams came from the bird. Terror gripped me when the thought passed through my mind, that if this beast could gain height… Oh, Dog poop!…no good would come from this. Then my body lengthened out and my rear paws left the ground. For a second, we were airborne. Gulp! I had to get away, now. Maxtors can't fly.

In slow motion, I saw a figure rise from just behind the hawk's head. Before I knew what it was, I was falling backward toward a row of tomatoes. I hit the ground hard. Dust obscured my vision, then my grip on the hawk's shoulder loosened as my body fell away from the bird.

The hawk slipped away. As the bird hopped past me, I caught a glimpse of a white furry something on its back. It was sprinkled with brown with some black mixed in.

It was Baby!

In that exact second, Mrs. Blaine came out of her trailer with a long black stick in her hands. She screamed so loud and fast there was no way to know what she had said, but I do remember the word, "Shoot."

I was about to launch myself onto the back of the hawk to help Baby when Mrs. Blaine pointed the black stick thing in our direction. The hawk knew a threat when it saw one. Screaming its awful hawk scream, the bird came up onto its feet. I dug my hind legs into the dirt and launched myself forward. I took a swipe at the beast with my good paw, claws extended out. I tore off some feathers, just as the hawk shook Baby off its back. In a moment of action, an excited Mrs. Blaine pointed the black stick over her head and into the sky. It exploded with a blast of fire and black smoke belching out of the end of it.

Freed of Baby's weight, the hawk leaped into the air. Its huge wings flapped once, then twice, and it was gone in a flash, the mockingbirds in hot pursuit.

My front leg hurt, but oddly there was no blood. I expected more pain, but none came. Then, I fell over into the dirt. Exhausted, I found I couldn't move. It seemed like time stood still for a minute: my head bone hurt and my eyes couldn't focus. Mrs. Blaine and Baby ran to me. Baby stood over and covered me with her body. A low mean growl emanated from her.

Mrs. Blaine, visibly shaken, took halting steps toward us. Baby leaned forward and looked like she was going to strike out at Mrs. Blaine. Baby watched every move Mrs. Blaine made. Then, Baby grabbed me by the scruff of my neck and tried to pull me away and out of the garden.

Mrs. Blaine stopped with her hand over her heart and said, "Oh my, aren't you the brave one, little girl." The old woman smiled down at my Baby, who looked up at her with those big wide cat's eyes that I love. Mrs. Blaine sat down, fanning herself with her hand. After a few minutes, she stood. Baby allowed her to pick me up, and we all went into the trailer.

Inside it was clean and neat, not a thing out of place. I lay where she placed me, not moving. My leg still throbbed and looked a little swollen, too.

I saw Baby's head pop up over the side of the table. I thought it looked really funny and I was going to snork out loud when she jumped up onto the table. I held my head down and stretched out my paw as a token of thanks for her saving me. Baby did what Baby does, she bent over me and licked my head bone.

Mrs. Blaine reappeared with a bunch of stinky stuff in her hands. With infinite care, she turned back the soft fine hairs on my leg till she found the puncture wounds in the fleshy part of my leg. "Oh, boy!" was all she said. Looking at me, she made a little gulping sound in her throat. I looked first at her, then quickly over to Baby, who was sitting very politely beside me. Her head was cocked off to one side, watching everything Mrs. Blaine was doing.

"Well, do you think he's up for this?" she asked Baby, who only stared back, her tail flicking about.

"Okay," she said and then poured the liquid out of the bottle letting it flow down my leg and into the red spot. My mind exploded and I bolted up onto my paws. I shook my leg furiously and howled mightily, but the sting wouldn't go away.

Mrs. Blaine recovered fast and wrapped a big towel around me. The evil smell of the liquid drifted away. Then, as fast as the pain came, it was gone.

Once I was all fixed up. Mrs. Blaine walked out of the front door saying, "I don't think you're going anywhere soon, Son!" She started gathering things up from the garden and placed them into a plastic tub, she turned he back to me and. Maybe I should have taken her advice. But being me, I crawled out of the towel and with some pain, scaled my way off of the kitchen table. The jolt of landing on my paws almost made me pass out. But I sucked it up and made my way over to the open door and out, where I was joined by Baby. We stayed in the shadows and headed toward the grassy alley, keeping one eye on the sky, just in case.

At the edge of our property, Baby bounded ahead as I limped along. By the time I got to the back gate, Baby was on the deck at Mom's feet, making this big figure eight in between her legs, kissing up to Mom, big time.

At that moment, Dad's truck pulled into the carport. Mom pulled the sliding glass door open. Both of us safely entered the kitchen and went into the evening's semi-darkened living room. My mom shut the door, then walked to the end of the front deck to welcome Dad home.

Painfully, I crawled up onto the couch so I could take my vantage point at cat TV. As a rule, it only takes three turns (Max's round trips) for me to settle in. Today it got done in one, as I was fading fast.

Through the open front door, I could hear my Dad's footsteps on the deck. Then I heard Mom excitedly exclaim, "Oh, oh, honey. Look up there. It's a hawk. Boy, it is a big one too!"

The fur stood up on the back of my neck for a second. I raised an eye to see Baby totally unconcerned as she rolled over on her back in the middle of the living room, trying to scratch her back. Or at least that's what it looked like to me.

Mom was still pointing up off in the distance to where the hawk had flown. All of a sudden, she turned and looked down at her feet, she held onto Dad in a panic and asked, "Where are the cats? Where's Max? That big bird could take him away, where's Max?"

Dad followed her gaze then replied, "Don't worry; Max is way too fat for that bird to carry off." He grabbed her by the arm and kissed her. Then, he said, "I almost forgot I have gossip."

Mom looked quizzical, she smiled and asked excitedly. "Really. What? Who? Tell me."

"Well, I was told this driving in, by the new security guard, you know the young guy, told me that old Mrs.

Blaine was outside in her garden this afternoon with her shotgun again…shooting at…"

His words faded off somewhere into the ether. My ZZZs found me there too, a willing victim, cradling me as an old friend would. My mind, emptied.

C'est la vie.

23 MY ANGELS GONE WILD

Where do I begin? Just the thought of having angels of my own was a big surprise to me. Then to have to interact with them left me at a loss. I mean it's not like there's a class like, Angels 101. This is definitely on the job training for me. But I've gotten ahead of myself. I was really tired from my nocturnal wanderings from the night before. Not a big surprise, I was wiped out and ready for a daylong catnap. Mom and Dad announced that they were going to be out for the day so it was "home alone" for Baby and me.

They looked so cute together all dressed up as if they were going out to someplace special like they do at night. Though it had been a long, long time since we've seen them going out anywhere, as mom tells Dad, "Money's tight you know." My mom looked wonderful in a full-length dress with an uneven hem, kind of an off-white with shoes to match. At least that's how she described her outfit to her girlfriend, Michelle over the phone. They talked all morning long about something called a wedding and a party after. They stood in the doorway. Dad didn't look bad either. Mom waved and said to me. "Okay there, Mister, you're in charge here while we're gone." Whatever that meant, but I had a pretty good idea what was expected of me. Guard-cat duty for the Maxtor. Which I really don't mind doing for my parents, from time to time.

Dad poked his head in over Mom's shoulder and added, "No parties while we're gone, okay, Max?" He waved and disappeared as Mom shut the door. I could hear their footfalls my dad's were a solid sound. Mom's were more like clomping as if she were a small pony. The family truck started up and drove off down the street leaving Baby and me alone. But not for very long as it turned out.

I sat in the middle of the living room and gazed out of our big picture window. All of a sudden a black streak appeared followed by a white one. They had burst into the street from over the Henderson's trailer and swirled around a few feet above the blacktop. Then-poof-they disappeared.

I knew this could mean only one thing; we were about to have a visit from my good and Bad Angels. They always seem to show up when I least expect them. I chased the thought from my mind and continued my way to the couch.

The morning's light filtered through the curtains filling the room with a wonderful laziness. I hopped up onto the couch and stood leaning on the back cushions to look out the window. The sky couldn't make up its mind whether to be a bright blue or just blue. A long line of white clouds stretched into exaggerated twisted wisps of themselves, drifting lazily along. I ka-binged myself on the top of the couch and after making my customary three turns I settled into a curled up Max to do my morning cat nap.

Seemed like paradise to me.

Z-land took me easily and for a long time. But it ended with a tap, tap, tapping at our front door.

It was getting dark when Baby woke me with her pesky head butts. I staggered to my paws and stretched. It took a while, but I wound up sitting on the floor, blinking. When the tapping continued it brought me up, alert. Normally, if someone drops by when Mom and Dad are gone they just go away or leave a note on the screen door. From inside, the tapping seemed to be higher than in the past, which made me suspicious. It was then I remembered the angels. Was it them? Were they laying some sort of trap for me? They must know that we can't open the door, at least not a door with a knob. Levers, now those are another story.

The house got very still. Baby and I looked at each other. Then we heard a rattling coming from the kitchen. I ran to the edge of the dining room rug and looked around. There was nothing that I could see out of the norm. The window was open over the kitchen sink and a bit of breeze picked up the windows curtains, as if out of the blue the black angel gradually appeared out of thin air, his little wings slowly fluttered as he hovered. His eyes were a brilliant green, and they seemed to sparkle at me as he slowly turned upside down. At that moment, he smiled and drifted through the wire screen that covered the kitchen window. Now inside the trailer, my Bad Angel floated across the kitchen; and descended to the floor. I watched as his wings beat slowly in turn he rose and fell. He kicked out his hind legs to grab his toes with his paws, smiled broadly and said to me. "Hey Max, whatcha doin'?"

I backed up on my rabbit's footies, knowing that we were in big trouble. I glanced over to see Baby disappear down the hallway and into Mom and Dad's bedroom. I needed her help and took off after her. I came around the corner and looked up at my mom's vanity. There was Baby sitting in front of Mom's mirror, next to the little basket where mom keeps her combs. She does keep one special comb just for us, and there it was in mid-air, brushing Baby's chin. At the other end was my Good

Angel all big eyes and bigger smiles. She stood up on her hind legs, with her white wings tucked discreetly in back of her. Good Angel waved and exclaimed "Isn't she beautiful, Max?"

Before I could answer her, the first of many crashes echoed down the hallway. It was going to be a long night.

I turned in time to see a cloud of wispy white powder explode from the kitchen and start to drift into the hallway. At a run, I was in the dining room in a flash. I hid behind the wall that held the stove and stuff. Leaning out from my hiding spot, I saw my Bad Angel standing on the kitchen counter--the one I'm forbidden to jump up on. He looked down at a large metal jar that was marked with the word "Flour." A mound of white powder had slid across the floor and into the air. I glanced up, we locked eyes. He smiled this wicked grin at me and laughed. Unable to contain his laughter, he fell over onto his butt and then rolled over onto his side. The air filled with peals of his Bad Angel laughs and giggles. Then he stood up abruptly and with his hands err paws-tucked behind him he looked at me in his kittenish manner and said, "It slipped."

The kitchen and dining room and part of the hallway were still awash in what appeared to be a white dust storm. How was I going to clean this up? I looked back, but my Bad Angel was gone.

It was getting dark and I should be up on the couch, ZZZed out, knocking down the back end of my all day catnap. Not looking for a Bad Angel run amuck! I thought.

Finding him had to be my first priority but where to start? This trailer isn't that big, and he could be anywhere. These pesky Angels move freely and fly as well, not to mention their ability to appear and disappear in a heartbeat. I hadn't had my angels very long so I didn't know them all that well. But it appeared that one of them liked to have a good time and found humor in making mischief. I heard a slight laugh and the rustle of feathers coming from the living room. I knew immediately what I needed to do…simply follow the giggles. Bad Angel would be at the end of that trail.

I entered the dining room. Crouching low I sniffed at the edges of Mom's cabinets, the ones that held all her dishes. My nose worked rapidly, searching out anything out of the norm, any little whiff of angels. But I worked at a disadvantage; I had no idea what these creatures smelled like. From behind me, I heard the flutter of wings and feathers. The soft giggle of my quarry taunted me. I turned and moved quietly to the corner of the dining room and the hallway. Peeking around the corner I saw…nothing.

I sat back on my rabbit's footies and thought about my next move. My tail switched back and forth just skimming the tops of the fibers in the rug. All of a sudden my troublesome tail stopped. Now there are times when my most extreme part of my feline body has a mind of its own. But I've never known it to stop in times of great anguish. Unable to resist I turned very slowly with my chin slipped over my shoulder. All of a sudden I gazed into the wild green eyes of my Bad Angel. He stood on the tip of my tail, his left front paw over his mouth holding back his angel laughter as the corners of his mouth turned up into a broad angelic grin. His tail, too, switched back and forth just like mine does, the germ of a plan took root in my mind.

His green eyes narrowed and he dropped his paw from his mouth. He seemed to see something grave, something important in my eyes.

Within a fraction of a second, he leaned back but he did not release my tail. What he did do was curl his tail up around his leg and then he grasped it in his paw. At that exact moment, I knew what his weakness was. Just like me it was his tail, that unruly appendage that gets me into so much trouble most of the time. My dad often calls it my "Achilles Tail." Why he says these things I do not know. If I could grab this bad boy's tail I might be able to control him. But this wasn't going to be easy. He was having far too much fun to allow me to put an end to his mischief.

We stared, eyeball to eyeball, as I slowly shifted my weight. All at once he exploded into a huge smile that lit up his black furry face. He threw out his forearms in a wide gesture as if he was going to embrace me and then poof he was gone. His angel's giggles drifted off down the hallway toward the living room.

Two huge crashes followed as I bounded into the living room to see a couple of Mom's potted houseplants that had fallen off a table and onto the floor. A mound of dirt had spread out from the foot of the table and extended some distance across the rug, on top of the table stood the bad boy himself, my adversary. He looked smug as he leaned against a third plant, which balanced precariously near the edge.

What was I to do? Holding out my front paws, I came to a stop and with my best pleading face "Meowed" at him. He only smiled and held out his paws at forearm length to admire his claws.

Out of nowhere came the streak of white. It was Good Angel to my rescue! She appeared and stopped in midair. Bad Angel gave the plant a push, and then he disappeared. She quickly caught the plant as it began to tip over, setting it back on its base. She turned as her little wings beat the air around her. She looked so stern. Then she said to me. "Oh, Max, can't you help? Do I have to do everything around here all by myself? Men! Go figure." Then she flew off across the living room. I heard them everywhere, but they went by so fast I couldn't begin to help her.

Finally from down the hallway, I heard an intense argument in my parents' bedroom. I arrived to see Good Angel as she hovered over Bad Angel, telling him off in no uncertain terms. "You know we can't interfere with our charges and you've gotten into trouble with this behavior in the past." He sat on the floor his back to me. He hung his head as she told him off. With his attention diverted, I crept up on him as quietly as I could one slow step at a time. All the while his tail, that unruly thing that all cats possess, for once lay still on the floor. Inches away, I dived at it taking the end in my mouth to lift him upside down off the rug.

She, that's Good Angel, dropped to the floor and stood in front of my prize as he swung to and fro, a look of resignation on his black furry face.

Crossing her arms, she said. "Why don't you toss him outside if you want? He is yours to command you know."

Well, no, I didn't know, but taking her word for it, I walked the best I could to the sliding glass door at the kitchen. It stood open even though I remembered my parents had shut it as they left for the day. As if by magic the light overhead came on as I deposited him onto the deck with a solid plop of his chubby body. He stalked off turned and sat in front of me.

Good Angel arrived, flitting from my left to my right side. "Okay, Mister you have to stay out there like Max told you," she told him. Then she looked down at me and asked, "You did tell him, didn't you?"

Before I could answer her that menace, my Bad Angel, was gone. She sighed then fluttered down to stand beside me on the floor.

"Oh, well, he'll not bother you tonight anymore, now that you know how to command him." She rose into the air and told me not to worry she'd clean up the plants and the flour mess before she left but for now she just had to finish Baby's comb-out. She said it was the best she's ever done.

And who am I to argue with an angel?

24 ONOMATOPOEIA

The inbox...my dad's inbox, to be precise, is wonderful. I love the thing. I get more out of it than he ever does. And if he'd just left me alone to sleep in it, which I often do, none of this would have ever happened.

My advice: stay away from the letters YU and GHJ on that thing they call a keyboard. These letters will eat you alive-- literally. So what have keys on a keyboard got to do with anything, you ask. Ok, it all came down like this.

I was knocking back some serious ZZZs in my inbox when Dad came in. The computer is in what he calls his "office." Mom was yelling from the kitchen about something. My hearing isn't so great when I'm snoozing, besides my ears are full of fur. He hollered back at her. Then he said, "Max." At the mention of my name I listened up. Again he hollered, "Max is in here. The lazy..."

I was still in the early stages of waking up when Dad walked over to the doorway. He yelled again, "Max is in here." At this point I stepped out of the inbox and took a couple of steps toward the keyboard.

That's when I met up with YU and GHJ. I looked down at the letter G. It sort of pulsated; a faint light glowed from around it. The entire area was very warm under my paws. Then I stepped over YU. Like teeth they yawned up and out, splitting the board down the middle. Suddenly they leaped out from the board and engulfed me…swallowing me whole and dragging me into the computer.

I heard my mom's voice and then Dad's reply, "He's in here…..no, he's gone."

I spun over and over and onto my back from the inside up and out. It was all very confusing. I thought my dad must have set this up as a bad joke. Bad, Dad! There I had been trapped and swallowed whole by my parents' computer. And, I was being compressed into a very skinny cat.

I tried to brake my fall…forcing my front paws out in front of me to stop. I got the sense of slowing and then my tumbling and twisting stopped. There were little twinkling lights all around me. I gathered myself up and stood in the blackness.

I could hear distant voices. I took a step and found that I was on solid ground, if you could call it ground. A streak of light bigger and broader than all the others was shining out of a tube and it was crammed with a bunch of wires. I walked over and sniffed at it. Nothing.

I forced my head into the tube and pushed with all my might. It was a tight but I made it inside. I scratched and clawed my way up. After a while I could see a soft white light overhead. All of a sudden, I came out of the tube and fell onto a curved floor with a plop. I was in a black and gray room, very tall and yes, it was very skinny.

I peered upwards, but my head was too big for this small space. Looking out of a large opening that was something like a window, I could just make out the bathroom door in my dad's office. On the other side I could see what looked like glass, a big rectangle of glass. It looked like my dad's computer monitor. What I saw next was, well…unbelievable.

Moving forward, I rose up on my tiptoes to see over the plastic that held the glass in, and there before my eyes on the other side of the glass were my mom and dad! I could hear them as well. Their voices were a little muffled, but I understood every word.

They seemed in a panic. I wondered what they were looking for. Then it occurred to me that they were looking for me, Max! As they started to turn away from the monitor I "meowed" as loud as I could. Inside the monitor my voice echoed back at me. All of the switches and blinking things went crazy. Mom and Dad looked at each other, mom exclaimed, "That's Max…I just heard him."

She ran out of the room, with Dad hollering, "Wait, I'm right behind you." Before he left he reached down and turned the computer off. My face was squashed up against the inside of the tall skinny monitor. If he had only looked up he'd have seen me. Just then I saw a cat's nose. It was Baby, staring right at me. She touched the outside of the glass and "meowed" softly at me. Concern for me filled her soft beautiful eyes.

Right then everything shut down and the monitor plunged into darkness. I felt something pull on my tail. It was a thing called RAM. In an instant I was sucked backwards into a larger tube. Then into the deepest part of the PC. If this was a dream, I really wanted it to be over.

My night vision was now fully on. The colors all around me were getting more and more agitated. The yellows raced around, while the blues literally bounced off the walls. The most terrifying were the reds. Now I don't see reds too well, but in here I could feel them. It was the first time I'd ever felt a color. Outside the color red always was a kind of gray, but not in here. These reds were very vivid and incredibly aggressive. I'd go nuts if I couldn't get away from them.

In front of me, a catwalk of sorts appeared. I looked over the side of this it and down into a dark cavern. Then I took my first tentative step out onto it. I hoped it wouldn't break under my weight. All around me and towering over me were these transparent boards, which had wires and lights in them. I promised myself that if I got out of this fix I was going on a diet for sure.

Off to my left I saw what I thought were skinny whiffs of smoke. Concerned, I stopped and looked over the side. I saw a pair of whitish gray ears, long, pointed, with little tufts at the very tips. Then they broke apart in pieces, turning into dust. As this dust fell away, multi-colored lights of yellow, blue and white flashed from the depths.

Walking along the edge of the catwalk I tripped and I plummeted straight down into the abyss. As I fell past the transparent boards I could see numbers in its little windows. FAT32, KB154 and wc_bw48 among others. There was one large window filled with viruses having a raucous party.

It wasn't a long fall, and quickly, I came to an abrupt halt with a plop on the floor. Struggling up onto my paws, I swallowed hard, popping my ears. The first thing I noticed was how quiet it was down here. I looked up to see gray clouds, like a storm. Meanwhile the multi-colored lights danced and pranced up the sides of the boards. Everything around me was covered with a coat of dust.

I had come to an intersection of the boards, from around a corner came a cloud of gray dust. It came at me very fast. As it got closer I could hear what sounded like bunch of bees doing their buzz-buzz thing. I watched mesmerized at the sight of this huge ball of buzzing, noisy dust coming straight at me. I backed up and came to the edge of the floor. I looked over my shoulder to look down into a much deeper abyss.

From somewhere came a yellow blur. It circled around and swept past me as the dust cloud arrived. I stepped back, but I was too late...the gray dust surrounded me, engulfed me then it choked me.

The yellow blur swirled around us as if it were protecting me from the choking gray dust. As it passed, I could make out these words: Norton Anti...

The dust cloud moved away. I took a swat at it. Withdrawing my paw it felt odd, it had a sort of bristly feeling. Between my pads were these small gray shapes I watched as they fell into a pile of little letters onto the floor.

The dust cloud hovered in mid-air then it went over the edge. The yellow Norton Anti pursued it and drove itself into its opponent as if it were a spear. Its job done the heroic Norton Anti turned and disappeared into the darkness.

As the cloud fell, I reached out to grab one of the letters but it was just out of reach. Leaning farther out than I should have, my claws hooked a big fat capital S in Franklin Gothic Heavy. Heavy was right, as it went over the edge I went with it. In seconds I came to an abrupt stop. Unhurt, but puzzled, I looked up. The friendlier of these letters had spelled out the word PARACHUTE and had connected me to it with the word STRAPS.

I had stopped softly with the aid of my PARACHUTE of friendly words. The dust swirled away and exposed another dark metal floor. Off in the distance I saw an orange glow where changing light lived. A crackling noise came from a black box with large round wires that ran into it.

A pair of whitish gray ears, long and pointed, incredibly came out of the dust and into focus. I was stunned. It looked like a face. An enormous gray dust bunny had walked out of the orange glow. With his bunny arms akimbo, he glared down at me. His whiskers vibrated menacingly when he growled. The whole floor jumped around as he stomped one of his huge rabbit footies.

With as much bravado as I could muster, I hissed at him.

This huge gray dust bunny threw his head back and roared with laughter. A second black dust bunny just as large as the first stood beside the first. He pointed at me. Then he, too, burst into laughter. Clouds of dust rose around their oversized feet. Immediately dust filled the room and I started to cough. With my attention diverted they snuck up on me and before I knew it they were towering over me.

The black dust bunny said. "We've heard Norton anti-virus posted a warning against you, MAX15. He thinks you'll crash this computer," his voice boomed out.

"There are patches for the likes of you, MAX15," said the other huge creature. "All of them…bad."

"Which is good for us. We are happy for the distraction from our lonely existence down here," said the gray dust bunny. Again, he roared in laughter.

I felt so small and alone and these two were so menacing. I'd no idea what to do next.

The second said, "This is going to be fun. Whenever we have fun with a virus like you, MAX15, we always crash the computers we're in, which is most excellent."

They started to argue about how to harm me. All I could think of was that if my dad's computer crashed,

crashed I'd never get out. Not to mention that he'd really be mad at me.

I thought of running...but where? I thought of fighting them, but they were made of dust...

The first dust bunny raised his footie and said, "Let's just crush him."

As I stood thinking about my dilemma, the second the black dust bunny replied, "No...just watch." Raising his bunny paw, he pointed a wispy claw at me and swirled it in the air. A huge amount of dust poured out of its tip and came straight at me. I braced for the impact.

All at once came this whirling, grinding sound. I felt a tug on my tail. Then my hind legs were pulled out from under me. I looked up to see the swirl of deadly dust that was meant for me breaking up in midair. Whatever this was, it just saved me from certain disaster. I reached out to snag some of the floor, but it was too slick. There wasn't a ripple or a flaw in it. I clawed and clawed, howling in my desperation.

My first dusty assailant took another step in an attempt to crush me with his enormous footie. I closed my eye, thinking that this was the end of "The Maxtor." Suddenly I was pulled out from underneath him, literally lifted up and into the air backwards.

All of the letters, (some of these stopped to spell out, "Bye, Max"), wires and lights passed me backwards and I went from floor to floor, then through round passages, and finally to a tray with a disk on it. I spun around, one full turn, then was thrown out of the now open tray.

I was ejected out of the computer and fell full-sized onto my back on the floor of my dad's office.

Something fibrous was over me like a shroud. I stood up. As I came to my full eleven inches, the kitchen towel that had covered me fell away. I sat back down, and looked around through my blinky eyes at my dad's office. The monitor was loading Dad's icons and the time of day. Apparently the computer had not crashed after all. I blinked again and discovered that I was still in the inbox.

I heard my Mom call me. Shaking off my slumber I jumped off the desk, and ran to the kitchen. There, outside, stood my parents. Dad said, "Well, I went on the internet to see about the microchip in his neck. The damn thing took forever to boot up…I wonder if it's got a new virus?"

A bit of an under-statement,' I thought.

Mom replied, "Well, he's around here somewhere. I heard him" She turned and looked down, and exclaimed, "Look! Here he is."

Dad opened the screen door to allow me to step out. He picked me up and then Mom took me from him and into her arms. She cooed at me, the way she likes to do. This was followed by a fast barrage of questions that she pretty much answered herself…"Where have you been, you bad boy? Asleep somewhere…right? We were looking everywhere for you! You've been gone for hours and hours! We were so worried!"

She is so lovely to look at. I gazed in wonderment and cuddled her cheek. She broke into a giggly laugh and then, as if nothing had happened, she let me down onto the deck. I strolled over to the top of the steps as they started to argue about me.

Mom: "Well, you should have been more aware."

Dad: "What am I supposed to do, follow the beastie around all day?"

Mom: "It's all about that computer, all day long the internet."

Dad: "Now don't be laying that at my feet, you use it, too."

I tuned their voices out and walked off the deck and onto the street. I sat down, and saw what looked like a dusty whirl of wind. Laughing and slightly buzzing, it came from the east where nothing but trouble lives. It touched down in the center of the blacktop, as it paused to gather strength. The whirlwind danced gracefully, then on a point of dust it tiptoed in my direction. I stepped back and watched it closely. As it got closer I swear I could see bunny ears flopping around inside. It picked up speed and grew bigger and bigger. Just in case, I crouched down. All of a sudden I could hear my dad's voice over my shoulder. He was yelling for my mom.

"You've got to see what your crazy cat is doing." He pointed at me. "Better look out, Max, that dust devil will get you."

This dust devil got closer and closer, but I knew what it was. I leaped off the deck and backed up into a small bush. I had seconds to ready myself to take this bad boy down. I couldn't understand how it had gotten out of the computer. Dirt was propelled in front of it, forming a funnel that was still getting bigger. The buzzing got louder too.

"Oh, my," was my mom's response when she got to the edge of the deck. "It's so big for a dust devil."

"And listen, it's making an odd sort of sound," Dad chimed in.

See, I knew I was right. It's the bunnies. I had only one chance. I sidestepped out of the cover of the bush and into the open. In a fraction of a second, it stood in front of me swinging and swaying...taunting me.

Its floppy rabbit ears were moving in all directions as if possessed. At that instant, I got a wiggle butt going for strength and sprung out with my claws out. I flung myself at this devil. With an agility like no other, it easily bent out of my reach, throwing dust in my face. I blinked, shook my head around then sneezed aloud.

Peals of laughter came from the deck.

Undaunted, I ran toward the devil again and took a swipe at it with my left paw. He'd never experienced a southpaw before, I could tell. As my large mitt passed through him, dust caught in my pads, the whirling devil bent some and for a moment it looked like he was a goner.

But, nope, it was not to be! With that slightly bent smile he glared me. I could see those floppy ears and his long whiskers as he hovered inside this dirty gray funnel. I had the feeling he was laughing at me.

Then, with a burst of speed, he flicked away down the road.

The last I saw of him he'd leaped up and over a truck, a trailer, and the highest point of the north wall. Every so often I could see the top of his dusty head as it reappeared, only to disappear a moment later.

The sun started to drop over S mountain just west of the trailer park. I sat and watched for some time, just to make sure that this devil or bunny or whatever it was, was really gone, gone.

25 I'M ALL SHOOK UP

How can I describe what took place on that day? So much happened and it had come about so innocently. Everything started when I came home with my surprise bow around my neck. Looking good I was, so good in fact that I had to show off for my mom and dad. But then J.P. thought of me as a good neighbor rather than a bad one.

The walk home was a treat; so many people saw me and admired my prize. At the corner of Thatch and the little service road in front of the rec center, I caused a small traffic jam. Lots of people had slowed their golf carts to smile and some to applaud me. Then I saw park's Maintenance Man with Nicole (the park manager) they stopped their golf cart, in front of number 164. That's where my friend J.P. lives and to think that I'd had just walked out of there moments before. Seconds later a Sheriff's squad car arrived. I'd seen these official pow-wows before and it made me a bit uneasy, especially when they talked to one another in the street. They even pointed at me and Nicole declared me to be "evidence" whatever that meant.

It has always been my practice to run whenever Maintenance Man comes around and I saw no reason to break my habit today. Off I went with my prize still fresh and secure around my neck. I glanced over my shoulder to see J.P. being put in the back of the squad car. I ducked under a bush between two trailers, which took me to Mrs. Blaine's and the grassy alley just beyond her veggie garden. In no time, I sat on our deck listening to my parents through the partially opened sliding glass door.

Dad sat at the dining room table a cup of Joe in front of him. He always drinks this stuff, mostly in the mornings. He calls it by a lot of different names; like coffee, or a cup java, or even just Joe. My friend's name is Joe too. We call him J.P., but let's not confuse him with a cup of, you know. Mom had been out earlier and talked to our neighbors up and down the street about all of the gifts in the past few weeks. No one knew who was leaving the rolls and rolls of tissue on all the decks and doorsteps…but I did. Then the Sheriffs Deputies walked up our steps and knocked on the front door.

I remember clearly the first time I met my skinny friend in his backyard, amongst the large brown boxes stacked two and three high. J.P.'s boxes filled the yard to the point that he had to walk sideways to get to his back door. The backyard fence was tall enough to hide his stash from prying eyes. Sadly, J.P. only had the occasional friend drop by, and no one had come around for a long time.

It was a dark rainy morning when I went for a walk just to check everything out in our part of the park. I had come to the far corner of Thatch Street when I heard this noise coming from number 164. A sort of slow music played along with a swishing sound. I liked the music immediately and knew what it was. The swishing piqued my curiosity and needed my expert investigation now. I approached the backyard from the driveway where a car was parked. All the while the song repeated over and over again. "Please don't ask me what's on my mind, I'm a little mixed up but I'm feelin' fine."

I leaped up onto the fence and was met by the tops of a bunch of brown boxes. I could see a black iron and wood lounge chair in the middle of the yard that looked good to shelter under. The drizzle had slowed, but everything was very wet. All of a sudden, a heavy blue fabric flew from one side of the far row of boxes. A tall, skinny man, with the blackest hair, I'd ever seen appeared. Clad in black jeans and a shiny shirt, he set himself to work frantically trying to cover the boxes. As he pulled on the fabric to fit it, it made that swishy sound as he drug it across the top of the boxes. The row now covered, he turned his attention toward the next one and me. In my curious state, I had moved quietly to the very edge of the boxes and came face to face with J.P.

He looked up and I said, "Hello." Well, actually, I "Merr-rawed."

He smiled and dropped the tarp. Then he put out his hands and offered to help me down. Being the polite creature that I am, how could I refuse? We went into the trailer, which was almost empty and he dropped me to the floor.

"Its way too cold and wet out there for the both of us, so you stay right here and I'll be back soon." He, in fact, was soaked to the bone. "I need to finish with my boxes, okay?" With that, he left the room as the door closed in behind him. The room was dark, a few lights were on but there were so many boxes it was hard to tell where these lights were. All around me were more boxes and on top of those were these little round cylinders. Some were all white while others were wrapped in this paper that smelled like my mom's bathroom. One overstuffed chair sat in a corner, off to one side stood a tall silver pole a sort of stand. On top of it was what looked like a silver potato? On the base of the stand were these words Old Sure Fat Elvis Microphone and Electro Voice Stand.

The kitchen was in the middle of the trailer. It too looked empty. On a counter was a little shiny oven like my mom has but nothing else. The hallway beckoned me, and I was about to go investigate that hallway and the rooms beyond. From the top shelf of a built-in cabinet, a couple of speakers like my dad has put out that song whose notes flowed like a river. It called to me.

"When I'm near that girl that I love the best, my heart beats, so it scares me to death."

I immediately thought of my cat mom and an image from out of my past projected itself onto the roll of 2 ply in front of me. I could see that German Shepherd's face, with its black muzzle and its cold dark eyes. From this little roll of Georgia Pacific Preference 2-ply Embossed White Bath Tissue and those years past, the beast growled at me. As if on cue, it rolled toward me showing a gaping hole in the middle. "Enough," I told myself. I had come to the end of my self-control, and I lunged at it. I took it down in a mighty sweep of my left paw and sent it rolling back across the floor. It bounced off the leg of a table and spun around and around, taunting me.

Still in my cat frenzy I could see the dog's face in the paper. I grasped it and wrapped my forelegs and paws around it. Finally, I sank my fangs into the beige wrapper and tore at it as hard as I could. To my utter astonishment, it started to shred in my mouth. I clawed it to the brown bone in the middle, searching for its foul blood. Alas, it had none to give. Standing over it, I used my claws on both paws to dig into it as much as I could, all the while seeing the dog's face as it tried to take down my cat mother.

The shrieks and cries she made in our defense filled my kitten's ears and my brain. She fought him valiantly, working her claws into his muzzle just as I was doing now years later in my vain attempt to help her, to protect her. I could see them clearly as they rolled over onto themselves in the short green grass as his red blood sprayed onto my kitten's little legs and my white undercoat.

I too rolled over onto my side and took the roll of Georgia Pacific Toilet Paper in my front paws and held it close to my chest. With my rear rabbit's footies, I dug into its soft white flesh and clawed it over and over again. Just as years before my cat mom had the German Shepherd by his throat doing the exact same maneuver. Then both of them fell off the shallow wall where so long ago all my siblings and I had played. Quickly, they disengaged themselves.

The dog in his dog's anger swept past me, then stopped and leaned forward with his large terrible teeth bared as saliva dripped from his mouth. I stood up as tall as I could (being so young I wasn't that tall) and swatted at him, but missed. He gulped and sidestepped away from me when my cat mom, her back arched stepped in front of me a deep growl let him know that this fight had only just begun. She had more pain for him if he wanted it. From over the wooden fence a voice called a name. This beast's ears flipped up and swiveled toward the sound and with a slight assist from his rear legs, he ran to the fence which he leaped over effortlessly.

I lay back against one of the perfumed brown boxes, exhausted from my fight with the 2 ply, and the memory from out of my past.

All around me it rained shredded white tissue paper, at that exact moment my skinny host came back into the room, he saw me in the middle of all of that shredded paper and said, "Got something against toilet paper there. Sport?" He smiled and sat down. That's when he grabbed the piece that he tied around my neck, looping it into a bow for the very first time. "I guess both of us have some special hang-ups." He added, "Mine are just crazier than yours and better documented, no doubt." He said this with a sheepish smile. This made me grin back at him.

We spent the rest of the day together; I watched the drizzle and the big drops of water as they fell from the big boxes to the ground. There they would meet up in shiny puddles that reflected the gray clouds in the dark sky above. In the middle of the room was J.P. dressed in a black leather jacket over a stark white shirt, his black hair slicked back. Like a wild man he sang along with that song. He'd lean into that silver potato thing and caress it like my mom and dad do to each other. Always at the end of the song he did these bumps and grinds. Oh, and he'd shake one leg around wildly. All for me I assumed?

As the weeks passed, I dropped by many times to see him at work in the backyard moving his boxes around. Sometimes he'd open them and pull out smaller boxes. Then we'd go off for a walk, always at night. We would move through the park as he left his special presents on the good neighbor's decks or by their front doors. All of them had these little white paper bows on them. The bad neighbors would get their bushes covered in TP. Before I'd leave, around dawn, he would always put a bow on me, a kind of reward for my help.

The voice of the Sheriff drifted through the screen door. He told Mom and Dad they were looking for more of J.P.'s boxes. That's when Nicole remembered that I had been seen in J.P.'s company. So they figured to come here and look around. Then the Sheriff remarked that some weeks earlier J.P. had stood up at his probation hearing and in defense of all of his transgressions told the judge, "A well a, bless…"

All at once that song filled my felines mind. I knew what he said…what he told the judge.

The officer went on, that with these new rounds of gifts; J.P.'s bail had been revoked. This meant that they, the Sheriff's Deputies, had come to take charge of him.

I could see him in my mind's eye, J.P. standing before this Judge person. As my skinny friend defiantly declared his reasons why he had taken all the TP. Followed by an even bigger admission of what he had done with the contents of all those boxes over the weeks and months, maybe even years, while he had worked at the store. To his credit, he offered to return all of it, if his friends had saved any. The judge declined his offer or so said the Sheriff.

It was all too much for me, with a sigh and a heavy heart. I caught the very end of my prize that little wavy white bow that J.P. had tied around my neck on a large sharp twig from one of Mom's plants. I leaned back and pulled it taut until it unraveled and fell softly onto the deck. I gazed down at it and wondered if I should have done this. Maybe I could save it somewhere, like in a special hiding place only I knew, a secret of the Maxtor that would be profound in my life. Like my efforts to save my cat mom, and the guilt I felt that it was probably me who was the cause of the dog's attack so long ago. But a friendly gust of wind kindly solved my dilemma as it came down the street and found my un-bow and lifted it up with a gentleness that is hard to find around here. With a swift caress, it carried its charge away as if they knew one another and had done this before. They swirled around and around, glad to spend this time in each other's company. I marveled at this, the most cavalier thing for a wind to do.

Oh! Dog poop, I thought to myself as I sat and waited for the inevitable. That being the sound of the sliding glass door as it opened. Followed by my dad's voice, "Max, Oh! There you are." He exclaimed. In the blink of an eye, Nicole's face popped out next to Dad and then the Sheriff appeared on her right.

They glared down at me when Dad spoke.

"Look, I told you there's no TP on my cat; he's clean as a whistle."

Dad smiled while the others frowned, and then in a rush, they were gone. I could hear a car start up and a radio came on as its tires squealed. This was followed by the voices of Maintenance Man and my nemesis, Nicole, whose arguing seemed to die away, as they no doubt traveled down the street.

Mom appeared at the kitchen door, quietly she stood next to Dad. Her arms were crossed at her chest. I silently watched as her sneaky mom smile crept to the corners of her mouth. Dad grinned and nodded at me. Without turning she said, "Don't you wish he could talk to us?"

"Hmm…how would that be a good thing? You might want to know what he has to say, but I think I could take a pass," he replied.

I looked up at these two humans, my parents, and thought myself lucky. Gamely, I put on my happy face…that's my very bestest T-rex smile. But the whole event had, in fact, left me…All Shook Up.

"Mmmm, oooh, yeah, yeah….I'm all shook up."

26 AMANDA

Her name was Amanda and this is how I met her. If she had moved on with her humans, we would have never met. But that's only if she could have kept up with the pack. It was the fact that she was so small and the total indifference of the Russian Blues as a whole that made her an orphan. It was what happened later, that led me to believe that sometimes it just doesn't pay to get off my couch in the morning. Her name became Amanda and this is how I met her.

The night's sky was filled with clouds. A high wind carried them along at a brisk pace against a black backdrop. Where high in the sky a full moon shone down, and I swear it seemed to call out to me. I had wandered far from #248. That's the trailer where I live with my mom and dad and of course Baby. My wandering aside, that night everything could be blamed on one low and slow-moving cloud that captured my attention as it made its way across the park to the moon. I was coming to a part of the park that I don't travel to very often. At the outside perimeter wall, I had gone as far as I dare. That point marked the very edge of the park. I should have turned back because on the other side of the wall was the wild wood, a place that most of us cats never go to. But that hardly included me. Close by was a small yard filled with Maintenance Man's stuff. There he had a couple of golf carts, a devilish contraption that he cleans the streets with and a few sheds. There was one large tall trailer that he filled with trash, mostly branches, leaves and things. He always parked this trailer right up against the inside of the wall where it acted like a ladder for cats like me to climb up on. From there you could safely check out what was happening in the wild wood in three directions.

On the outside was a vacant lot where a couple of old abandoned cars resided. Both had been stripped of parts and stretched out like they were too lazy to stand up and leave. Not far from them, a thick line of shrubs acted like a barrier of leaves so the outside world wouldn't bother them. When it rained these two metal monsters kindly gave refuge to an abundance of four legged creatures. In the opposite direction, more to the northeast was where the woods seriously started. At the edge was a short narrow path that meandered from the cars through to the woods, plunging into utter darkness even during the day.

As usual, I made the climb up from the trailer to the top of the wall easily enough. I was just in time to see my slow cloud meet the tops of the tall trees and be gobbled up by them. A mist swirled around the treetops that whipped them back and forth for a short time before they disappeared altogether.

Just then a black shadow passed by. It ran full tilt along the base of the wall until it came to the two cars. I could see it was one of the parks infamous Russian Blues. With the wind coming from behind him, I realized that he didn't know I was here. However, now that he had come to a stop in front of me it was a different story. He sat, his nose reached up into the breeze where a part of my scent wafted. I tensed, and waited for the inevitable, but he did nothing. It had to have been the excitement either from his run or just being here that made him commit such an error. This gave me an advantage over this Blue, my sworn enemy.

He lifted his head and this time all his attention was on the abandoned cars. His howl came from deep in his soul, from some black place that only Blues have and only their kind can speak to. As the howl built in volume, it carried far and away. In no time, the wood was alive with green, and yellow eyes. These creatures came out of the darkness by ones, and twos then they swarmed across the vacant lot to form up in back of the first Blue.

I lay in total silence and for once wrapped my wayward tail around me. Feeling secure I watched silently as they waited in the darkness. Even the wind had ceased its nocturnal errands of taking clouds somewhere else. One large cloud stalled overhead and with the lack of moonlight the vacant lot darkened. A noise came from the interior of the first burned out car. Two unusually large cats came through the glassless windshield. The pair took up position on either side of the wreck on top of the fenders. A few howls could be heard from the large following spread out in front of the wrecks, that now I guessed numbered twenty plus felines, all of them Blues. I could hear a lot of shuffling from the crowd and then a fight broke out. This was quickly silenced by serious snarls from the two large Blues on the car fenders. An uneasy silence came over the horde, for that's what it was: a horde of Russian Blues.

As if on cue, that cloud broke and the moon shone down on the gang to reveal an even larger Blue that slinked out onto the hood. On the ground, a lowly soldier jumped onto the car but was cuffed by this big beast. I was about to make a hasty retreat myself when I saw the head of simply the biggest cat I'd ever laid my eyes on. He ducked under the roofline and stepped out of the windshield; he turned and hopped up to the roof. His eyes flashed as a moonbeam traveled over this impromptu stage. He let his jaw go slack, showing enormous teeth, and a pair of deadly fangs. He must have weighed thirty pounds and had to stand sixteen inches at the shoulder. He was some sort of throwback to the Russian steppes before we felines became civilized.

I was in the presence of "Ivan," leader of the Russian Blues, a living legend in this part of the river basin. No one that I knew had ever seen him. Most of us thought of him as a myth, dreamed up by the gang of Blues here in the park, just to scare us, an easy way to keep us in line.

The crowd settled down as Ivan paced back and forth. He finally came to a complete stop and raised his voice, issuing a series of angry commands in a language I'd never heard before. I caught only a few words here and there. I was sure this meeting meant someone somewhere was going to suffer. Every so often he let out a couple of sharp howls; these would be answered by a cat or two who then ran off toward the wild wood. All the while more Blues had gathered filling up the lot and surrounding the cars. Now it was impossible for me to leave. Ivan's lieutenants had their paws filled keeping these groupies away from their master. Just in time, a cadre of big Blues had forced their way through the crowd to give a form of feline security for Ivan.

It was amazing to watch him as he filled the air with his orders. Many cats were dazed and milling around, but most held their ground until their leader had built to a climax in his oratory. He came down off the roof then leaped to the ground, his security and lieutenants formed up in back of him...the Emperor and his Praetorian Guard if you will. The sea of cats in front of him parted as he walked forward. That's when his slinky favorite galloped up, and whispered something in his ear…these two, Ivan and Mr. Slinky, burst into a run. They seemed to tower over the crowd around them. In seconds the entire gathering turned and followed, moving as one. They plunged into the wild wood and in seconds the horde had disappeared.

Or that's what I thought.

A few stragglers hovered over a small clump of grass. They seemed concerned about something. Without looking back one left followed by the other two, in a second they were enveloped by the wild wood.

Which left me up on the wall…alone.

Now you have to remember that cats are filled with curiosity and Maxes are more inquisitive than the average feline. I needed to find out what was so interesting to those stragglers. I made my way to the ground by simply going to the end of the wall and navigating down one of the bushes. From there it was a short trot to the cars. The moon had snuck away again, which thrust the vacant lot back into darkness. I sprinted toward the clump of grass and brush where the stragglers had been. I dropped down on my belly, and stealthily crawled the rest of the way. Being downwind, I was safe from discovery by anyone in this minuscule hiding place. The tops of the brush vibrated as a bit of wind swept in from the North. It grew in intensity and laid the tufts of grass over at a severe angle. I couldn't see how anyone could hide in this dinky place. The wind brought another thing to me; a scent, terribly faint, not quite a full cat scent…but there it was. I lifted my head and looked straight into a pair of green eyes, big green cat eyes. From the depths of that brush, a clear voice lifted up to me.

Not a big voice and not dainty, but a shrill, "Meow" emanated from the grass. We stared at each other for a few moments. Then off toward the wild wood I heard a scrambling in the undergrowth. A nasty scent filled my nostrils. Trouble was close and coming my way. I had to leave, now.

Without a second thought, I reared up, spun on my rabbit footies and took to my paws across the same ground I'd covered just moments earlier. At the bushes by the wall, I jumped as high as I could then stopped to look back. Suddenly I was bumped from underneath by a ball of gray fur with a tail at one end and those big green eyes at the other. For the first time, I got a good look at her. She was scrawny like most young Blues are, at the same time she was sleek with long thin legs and she possessed a head bigger than most kittens her age. I was guessing she had to be around five months old. Much too young for a female to be out with the pack, but the Russian Blues were different in the way they handled themselves. Ivan had shaped them into a warrior class where only the strong survived.

A vision went through my mind of myself when I was young, alone and on the streets. I was fighting back a choking feeling in my throat when up from the ground came a Blue who took Amanda by one of her hind legs. She screamed as they fell to the ground. A split second later another Blue grabbed Amanda and pulled her off toward the wild wood. I had a decision to make and not a lot of time to do it. Leave her to her own kind and make my getaway unmolested or jump in and take her back from these gangsters. Her pitiful little voice carried across the vacant lot. I dropped to the ground and dashed to the sound of her plaintive "Meows."

At the far edge of the vacant lot, the wood started in earnest. These tall trees and all the other old growth would not yield passage to me easily, but I had to find a way through. I felt that to take another step would bring me to the point of no return. Eerily a spotted owl flew over and landed in one of the low branches of a tree, a dead rodent clenched in his talons. He looked over at me and shook his head. Was he telling me not to go in? Ahead I could hear twigs and leaves crackling. Could these be sounds from Amanda and her catnappers? Without a second, thought I followed and moved as quietly as possible. Much earlier my night vision had come on which allowed me to pick up my pace as I wove in and out of the dense brush. At times barely making it around the dark wet trunks of the trees. I pushed on while overhead my friend the moon excitedly lit my way. The Blues that took her weren't terribly big so I knew it might take them some time to get wherever they had to go. I bounded ahead with my nose in the air searching for her scent, which was fading fast with the smell of all the other creatures that lived in this foul dark place. The thought passed through my mind that she was a Blue herself and smelled like them. Boy, this wasn't going to be easy.

I moved along in-between the lushness of the woods long green ferns when a sort of trail revealed itself. My friend the moon helped to light this new promising path. A gust of wind whipped the tops of the younger trees back and forth moonbeams danced franticly ahead of me. I slowed and to my amazement what the beams exposed were skeletons of small birds and other animals. One would expect to see such things in a place like this, but the sheer volume of bones brought me up short. I was standing in a killing ground for the horde. Fear renewed my efforts and driving me on was the thought that Ivan might make an example of Amanda. That this could be her fate was too horrible to contemplate.

The trail narrowed and came to a precipice. I could hear sounds like from a nightmare, cat howls mixed in with birds and men screaming. Getting closer, I saw an orange glow that came from what looked like a pit. I slowed to a stop and stood at the edge of a cliff that looked down on a clearing, and what was left of a hobo camp where local travelers often took refuge. The scene that awaited me was beyond belief… even for me and my imagination. With my belly dragging on the ground, I crept up to the edge, keeping under a large low hanging fern to watch the gang of Blues as they plundered the camp of two men. Both were in terrible distress. One tried to get away from a bunch of Blues that were scratching and biting his ankles and legs. A few feet away the other "hobo" with a stick in hand swung wildly at any cats that he could. But more and more of these sleek tormenters had leaped onto his back while others bit his legs and tore at his arms. He stumbled and fell back onto his tent tearing it apart. A group of Blues chased a fleeing chicken as others devoured the remains of yet another bird, their faces dripped in blood and gore. At that point, both men somehow got to their feet and fled their camp with a mob of Blues in pursuit. I could hear their screams echoing in the night's air. Feeling secure these Blues returned to the destroyed camp to mill around and wait.

In the middle of this mass chaos beside the dying fire stood Ivan, a bloody chicken leg lay on the ground. Ivan gave his commands in the language of the Blues and he was obeyed immediately. Only then did he consume his meal. Leisurely, he tore it apart, leaving only the bones.

At that moment off to my left I heard the rustle of branches as the bushes exploded in a shower of leaves. It was the two catnapper Blues. They pulled Amanda by her neck to the edge of the cliff. She resisted mightily and hissed at her abductors. I admired her bravado then again I reminded myself that she too was a Blue.

I steadied myself unsure of what I was going to do next.

In between the ticks of the bloop, bloop in my chest my automatic bravery kicked in and I sprang toward the catnappers. I body slammed the closest one as the other looked at me as if in a dumb stupor. As I got nearer to him the bloop, bloop, bloops pounded in my ears. Incredibly I saw my reflection charging him in his eyes. We collided. The impact knocked the breath out of me. As for the Blue, he tumbled over and over then slid to the cliff's edge. Before he disappeared over it, he let loose with a terror filled scream. All the Blues below in the clearing stopped in their tracks and looked up. Time stood still then Ivan howled his displeasure. Amanda opened her mouth and let out a shrill screech that caught in her throat. The broken syllables drifted in the air but not one of us moved. Well, in fact, one of us did and quickly too. Amanda turned on her paws and fled back the way she had come into the dark lushness of the ferns and the supposed safety of the woods. It was then that I locked eyes with Ivan. With more bravado than good sense, I added a personal note. I leaned forward and chuffed at him, then I followed Amanda as fast as my legs could carry me.

I caught up with her in no time, nudging her along as best as I could. I turned my head to see if we were being pursued. The wood behind us looked still…peaceful even. The orange glow had faded some. The thought that maybe we'd gotten lucky entered my mind. This calm was dashed when scores of feline gangsters burst through the undergrowth. Large and small they came on, closing the distance at a disturbing rate. Then the horde split in two. The majority moved off to the right toward the park and away from us. I could hear more of them to my left, as a few of the biggest ones rapidly charged from behind us, keeping the pressure on, keeping us moving towards the vacant lot and the cars.

Breathlessly, we ran on, flinging ourselves through the low bushes that whipped our bodies and faces. Suddenly, Amanda veered off the trail and crossed toward open ground on our right. Immediately the wood thinned from large trees to forest ferns and bushes. Too quickly we were leaving the dark safety of the thick wood for the starkness of the vacant lot.

What appeared to be a colossal mistake was nothing of the sort. Amanda, having more knowledge of the wild wood than myself, showed me that a slight change in our course put us on a new heading that took us unnoticed downhill for a short distance. This allowed us to skirt the vacant lot, the cars…and possibly the Blues. It took us straight to the park's perimeter wall and safety.

I glanced uphill and could see that the horde had collected at the burned out cars. As we closed the distance to the wall off to our left I could see Ivan's favorite, Mr. Slinky. He ran flat out on an intersecting course. He had the advantage of being uphill from us, so we had to make it to the wall first or else. Amanda spotted him also and knew only too well that this could mean her capture. She glanced back at me, a pleading look in her big green eyes, as her hind legs faltered and caused her to slow down. I reached down into my power reserve and poured on a burst of super speed from the Maxtor. I passed her and took dead aim on Mr. Slinky as he slowed along the base of the wall. He was much older than I had thought. For some reason he hesitated. This pause caused me to look to my right.

Coming uphill were the two beefy lieutenants that I had seen earlier guarding Ivan. In an instant I puffed out the hairs on my tail and the fur on my back ruffled all along my spine. My mouth opened and I let out a shriek, something I don't do a lot. Stealthiness is always the best offence. Being only a few feet away from this sneaky cowardly beast, I lowered my head and drove my welterweight fighter's body straight into his ribcage directly behind his front legs. He buckled and went down in a heap. He then rolled away but not before he screamed out a warning. In response, a howl went up from the horde and for the second time that night we were being pursued by the Blues en masse. Amanda came to my rescue and nudged me forward. Then inexplicably, she trotted down the hill toward the two beefy lieutenants that were closing on us. I was about to grab her by the tail when she turned and disappeared into a hole in the wall that I'd never seen before, not a large one but just wide enough for me to squeeze my ample body through.

The backyard we popped into was actually a large garden full of rose bushes. Amanda obviously knew where she was going. As she avoided the biggest bushes and their deadly thorns, we slipped past the roses and ran down the side of the trailer beside a long fence. At the very end of the fence were some boxes. We used them like steps, and went up and over the fence and came down on the other side. I sensed that we were not far from home, but nothing looked familiar. At that moment, the thought crossed my mind that this had been too easy. These tricky beasts could have taken us at any time in the wood. Why didn't they?

That sickening feeling came back over me as I pushed Amanda aside and took the lead.

At this late hour, the street was drenched in the
moon's light. A quiet trail of moonbeams lay down before
of me. The blacktop looked like a mirror reflecting the
sky, the clouds and the tops of the trees in the park.
Along the side of the street, I could see black shadows
with eyes, yellow and green. Every so often one of these
shadows moved. We started down the street as more and
more shadows came alive in a ballet of movement, cat
style.

How did they know where to go? Not only were they in
back of us but now they were all around. *Why don't they
attack?* We were quite literally out in the open surrounded
by them. Talk about easy meat.

I walked a bit faster. The street started to bend around
the corner that would bring us to the intersection at
Thatch Street that splits in two.

Here I thought we could make a mad dash up the
grassy alleyway past Mrs. Blaine's and into my parent's
backyard. It was the only thing to do.

A large cloud made up my mind for me as it played tag
with the moonlight. The street, being discreet plunged
itself into darkness. Amanda seemed to read my mind.
Both of us sprang forward and ran toward the grassy
path. We only had seconds to close the distance, because
clouds are fickle friends at best and they are hard to trust.

We made it to the alley before the horde realized that
we had gone. As I glanced back over my shoulder the
street was indeed empty, not one of the Blues followed
us...Why?

The grass felt good under my pads, still wet from the
evening dew. We were halfway down the alley and I could
see the glow of the light over our front door streaming
through the small fruit trees. Just then a couple of Blues
sprang out of the shadows and charged us. I picked up

the pace, but Amanda stopped in the middle of the alley to scratch her ears. *Incredible,* I thought. When she did, the charging Blues fell over her. They got up quickly and immediately a catfight ensued between them. I scampered back and pulled her to her paws and we continued to run. On either side of us more and more Blues had joined the chase but still they didn't attack. Quickly, I managed to shove her under our back gate. When her tail disappeared, only then did I leap onto Mr. Neighbor's wooden spool then to the shelf on the top of the gate and down into our backyard. We were home free.

In a second that feeling changed back to fear and dread.

It was incredible, but our small backyard was filled with Blues. I never knew so many of the breed lived in the river basin. As I walked toward the rear steps of our deck, a couple of the more feisty ones ran out to swat at my hind legs. A giant Blue body-slammed me then ran off as the others had.

I got to the steps and pushed Amanda along in front of me. Halfway up she stopped in her tracks. She turned her head toward me. Her eyes were pleading and a fearful "meur" escaped from her throat. She stepped aside that allowed me to move past her. The deck was alive with Blues. They paced on the railings. Some sat on my mom's furniture. The two big lieutenants were pacing back and forth in the middle of the deck. Directly in back of them under the stark light of the front door, stood Ivan.

I now knew why they had not attacked earlier. We were to be his and his alone. Amanda huddled behind me. When we got onto the deck she sprang toward this devil. She hissed her hatred and swatted at him, but he just threw back his massive head and smiled. Placing my body in front of her calmed her for a time. From behind us, dozens of Blues came up the steps, cutting off any possible escape.

Ivan stood and crossed the deck in one big stride and was upon me. I didn't have a chance as he quite literally picked me up by the scruff of my neck and flung me down on the deck. He stood over me and growled at his crew. They all backed off. I tried to raise up a paw in my defense, but he swatted it aside with no effort. He then grabbed and threw me into the air. He repeated this over and over again. At this rate I guessed he might get tired or bored with me soon.

A few of his gang became unruly and the lieutenants had to scramble to keep control. Ivan held me down with one massive paw on my upper body. It was getting harder to breathe. His eyes flashed when he turned his head toward me. He opened his mouth and bared his giant fangs. From behind him, Amanda jumped onto his back and drove her teeth into his side. He howled and shook her off. I watched as she landed against the sliding glass door.

She got back up onto her paws and growled. When she stepped out, the floor seemed to jump under us. The deck became a mass of gray bodies as the gangsters flung themselves in all directions, trying to beat a hasty retreat as best they could. In a matter of seconds only Amanda, Ivan, his two lieutenants and I were left on the deck. I had double vision, but I could see that the kitchen light had come on. The door's lock unlatched and a whoosh of hot air ruffled Amanda's fur. Unnerved Ivan's lieutenants growled in that guttural foreign tongue of theirs. He moved and the pressure on my shoulder let up enough for me to pull myself out from under his big paw. Free, I backed up, which forced Amanda against the sliding glass door. The vertical blinds slapped wildly back and forth as the light threw itself and its shadows across the deck as my mom appeared over us.

Spooked, the lieutenants backed away, almost falling off the front steps finally Ivan turned and then slowly almost casually he walked down the steps.

I heard Mom's voice, "Max, who's your little friend there…honey?" How she missed seeing my tormenter I could only guess. My dad appeared, his head sticking out into the cold.

"I thought I heard something! What is Max doing outside and who is this?" He asked, pointing at my young charge.

Mom scooped up Amanda, as a smile crossed her face. Dad grinned, too, as both of my parents petted her.

I just managed to drag myself into the kitchen. My whole body was one massive ache as Dad shut and locked the door behind me.

Epilogue

Well! I've never tried this before! As a rule when I end a story, it's done. However so much more happened with Amanda that I wanted to tell all of you.

When we woke in the morning Amanda was up and bouncing off the walls. Well not the walls, but me and my mom. She was everywhere and all at once. There was only one spot I could get away from her…on top of the couch watching cat TV. It was midmorning and Mom was talking to Dad at the dining room table. They talked and talked about keeping Amanda who Mom was calling, "Max's new girlfriend." After much debate, they agreed to find her a home. Mom made only one call to her friend, Michelle, who said she'd be delighted to come over and meet Amanda.

A little while later Michelle did show up with her young daughter Joanie in tow. Michelle's one condition was that Joanie like Amanda, only then could she in good conscience take the kitten. The two bonded in seconds. The moment Joanie walked in, her face lit up with the biggest, broadest smile ever. Amanda was playing with Baby on the floor. She took one look at the young girl and ran over to her, and leaped into her open arms. Our front room was awash in warmth. Even the sun came out making the entire scene seem perfect. As our guests left Joanie who still held Amanda in her arms, stopped in the doorway. She turned and gazed straight at me, she then looked at my mom and said, "Amanda wants me to tell Max something very important." Mom was a bit taken back she just shrugged her shoulders and simply smiled at Joanie.

I got down off of the couch and walked over to the middle of the room.

"Okay, should we leave or…" Mom replied.

"Oh no, you can hear too," Joanie said, and then she bent down towards me. "Amanda wants…"

"Who's Amanda?" asked Michelle, winking over at my mom.

"This is Amanda," Joanie said with a smile, holding up the kitten. "Amanda wants me to tell you that she's thankful to you for rescuing her and saving her life last night and that she loves you always. Oh, and you shouldn't worry, they won't come back." With that, she walked out of the trailer. Michelle, her mouth hanging open, followed.

Imagine…out of mouths of babes! Boy, I was impressed.

Later that day the park's manager, Nicole, showed up and threatened Mom with eviction if she could ever prove that I was responsible for all of the damage to a certain resident's rose garden, and the shredding of Maintenance Man's golf cart seats and some other damaged things in his yard.

Amanda was right about one thing…the Blues didn't come back, at least not right away. But a few days later I awoke from a fantastic forty winks on my couch. After a good stretch and a hefty yawn, I glanced out the window and found myself looking directly into the eyes of Ivan. His oversized head filled my vision. I shook my head bone to clear it and when I opened my eyes, Ivan was gone.

27 SLIPPERY WHEN WET

It was hot. The normally mild San Diego summer had turned blazingly hot and here I was stuck in this fur coat. Yuck!

As a rule, I've got no problem with the heat…as a matter of fact, most of the time I quite enjoy it. I'll lie out in the afternoon sun, letting its rays soothe my old bones, submitting to a thing much bigger than myself. On this day, the temperature had climbed into the nineties and beyond. My mom had already shut up the house. On the roof the AC was whirling away, filling our abode with cool air and making life in the east county livable. It was about ten o'clock in the morning when I heard my mom's voice call out my name.

"Max, honey, you'd better come in…you know it's too hot for you." Mom seemed to think high temperatures are unhealthy for me. She waited, and leaned out from the door…then in a few seconds I heard the glass door shut. 'No doubt she'll be back,' I thought.

I must admit the AC beckoned, but the simple explanation for ignoring her was that I was dozing on my special perch. That's the wooden shelf atop the back gate that Dad had built for me to lay on. From here, not only could I nail down some truly great ZZZs, but I could see everything in our backyard. Along with the physical delights, height makes all of us felines feel safe and secure.

The summer sky was bright blue speckled with white clouds. The heat seemed to be everywhere as if you were in an oven. Every so often a bit of wind brought some relief, but even those breezes were hot.

My eyes closed into little slits. I yawned twice, as was my habit, and then shook my head bone around. Feeling much better, I stretched my front legs and reached out to lick my left front paw. That's when I heard the crunch of leaves on the ground. Something was below me. It was brown color blended in with the leaves to the point of disappearing. A fat medium sized rodent had crawled under and through the rear gate beneath my perch.

The thought of nailing this fat morsel entered my mind and left just as fast. The heat saved him, it was just too damned hot. I watched as the animal slowly crawled away, down the rock-strewn path behind our trailer. It came to the end of the path, looked around the corner, he made a right turn past my dad's metal tool shed, and disappeared from view.

I rolled over to reposition myself. The heat beat into me...draining away what little strength I had left. Maybe I'd catch him on his way back. Or maybe not? Then I heard a second noise. It was a soft thud that came from the direction of Melisa's backyard next door. A brightly colored solid mass of fur came to a stop under me. He was right beside the wooden electrical spool that Mr. Neighbor had left in his yard to sit on when he smokes his sleepy cigarettes.

I'd seen this feline interloper before and knew he was living under Melisa's trailer. He often slept on her patio swing. Until now he'd always kept his distance. Enviously I watched as his muscles rippled under his coat when he readjusted himself. He shook a dusty front paw as if it were wet then slowly took a step out, halted and looked up at me. Our eyes locked. For a second nothing existed in my world but the two of us. Time slipped by...neither of us moved a muscle.

Max, I said to myself, it's just too hot to cop an attitude. Besides, he was tall and must have weighed in at eighteen-plus muscle-bound pounds against my fifteen. His head was big like mine and his eyes were set far apart like mine. But there the similarities ended. He was mottled orange and white...slim at the hips and had almost no fat sack. He was lean and when he walked he hung his head like he was sulking. He clearly had the look of the street about him, which made me feel sad because he was so young, no more than three or four years old. Even at that youthful age, clearly this fella was a survivor.

He looked up at me almost reverently, then he filled his nostrils with my scent. I yawned again, blinked, and lowered my head to my folded paws and let him pass.

Quickly he slipped into the shrubs that filled Mr. Neighbor's backyard. There along the fence were some dainty bushes with little green needles sticking out from long slender green stalks. My mom was forever sneaking over the back gate, and stealthily she would grab handfuls of these green needles, to use them in her salads.

Humans...go figure.

I glanced around the wooden post to watch this feline's progress and see what he was after. Hmmm...then it dawned on me, he was after that fat morsel that just passed by. And in MY yard...this could be trouble.

Moving to the opposite side of my perch for a better view, I waited. It didn't take long before I saw a white paw pop out from the fence and onto the rocky path at the end of our trailer. A few small stones were disturbed, but he made absolutely no sound. He was good, this youngster. Like a ghost, he slipped out from a broken part of the fence that I had used many times myself, ages ago. Well, at least before I got bigger and fatter.

In the heat, he seemed to move in slow motion, coming out in stages. First, that long front leg, then his oversized head followed by the rest of his muscular body. He stared straight ahead with intense focus. His ear closest to me switched back and forth. He was checking my movements no doubt. Smart guy! The other ear was pinned forward. He was a classic picture of stalking. At this point, he resembled a lion, like those I'd seen on my parents' TV. He had a flat chin, a narrow muzzle, and a long nose. His entire frame vibrated and twitched in the waves of dry heat. With one easy motion, he brought the rest of his body out and through the broken fence. His hind-leg muscles bulged as he took the width of the path in a single stride, which brought him to the corner of the trailer.

He looked around the corner, bending his body almost in half. His tail trailed behind him...someday he'd learn to tuck it in, but that's not for me to teach him, not at my age. You see, just before a strike you do get a little excited and it's easy to make mistakes. For strays like him, it's all about instinct and teaching yourself discipline. Most of the time you learn the hard way. I know about that, too.

Skyward, a cry momentarily demanded my attention. Two mockingbirds tumbled and twisted, fighting in midair. They were fought each other in a boiling black mass, then they broke, flying off in separate directions.

When I looked back down, the ghost was gone.

On my shelf, I leaned farther out with my ears up tuned in, alert. I heard a hollow metallic scraping noise and guessed he'd found his quarry. He probably had to scramble through the trailer's metal skirt to get at it. A second passed and then another, but no more sound came from around the corner. I focused on the point where the trailer and the rocky path came together. In an instant, he filled my vision as he trotted around the corner, his mouth filled with his prey.

Triumphantly, he came down the path toward me. The dead rodent's tail and short little legs hung down lifeless and limp. With his cat eyes flashing and his neck muscles popped out, this ghost held his head up high. Only once did he glance over his shoulder just to make sure he was alone and safe. I watched him intently from my perch. I sat up and hunched my shoulders forward with a paw draped over the edge of my wooden shelf. I'm sure he saw my claws when they gripped the edge just for effect.

From deep inside of me a growl built up as I glared down at him. But even forewarned, he didn't slow down until he was almost under me. At that point, he dropped his kill to the ground and looked up. Nervously licking his lips, he waited. I know fealty when I see it and I was impressed with this youngster.

I could smell the sweet scent of blood as it wafted up to me in the hot air. Even though this was his kill, and me being me, I made him wait for it. For, what you ask? Why…my approval of course. As a poacher, he needed permission from me, the yardmaster. While he anxiously watched, I lay down on my side. Hesitantly he licked his whiskers that were matted with the dead rodent's blood.

Droplets of red, red blood dripped off his lion's chin. All I could think of was how slippery fur feels when it's soaked wet with blood.

Slippery when wet, my grim little joke!

Staring off into the distance I struck my best I-don't-give-a-shit pose. In my peripheral vision, I could see him nervously pick up his prize and slowly walk to the cat-sized hole in the back gate directly underneath me. As I said, he was tall...this ghost. He had to duck under the broken lath to get through it. He then vanished around the corner of Mr. Neighbor's trailer, the waves of heat hiding him from me.

An up-and-comer, this one, I thought. ...this interloper, this ghost.

He bears watching, but not today. It's just too damned hot.

28 RAIN, RAIN GO AWAY

It was wet outside and had been all day long. I, on the other hand, was warm and dry inside our trailer. Snug in the cushions on the couch, I was settling in for a continuous rainy day nap.

I could just hear my mom's voice between cloudbursts. My mind filled with her words, "Oh geez, rain, rain go away," she said.

From down the hallway came the sound of my dad's footsteps. His voice started strong but trailed off as I was taken over with ZZZs. "Well, at least we're not outside," he said. The rain beat down on our roof...the sound grew louder and louder, waking me up.

"Where are the cats?" asked Mom as she walked over to Dad.

"Baby's asleep on our bed," he replied.

"Then where's Max?" said Mom, her voice now bordering on hysteria.

"Did you let him out?" asked Dad. "You are forever letting him have his way...you know that, don't you?"

I was in the middle of rolling over in the cushions when I heard the sliding glass door open. This was accompanied by a blast of cold air.

Mom ran down the hallway shouting, "Let's look in the front room again."

To which Dad replied. "I've already looked out there, he isn't there!" Dad went outside onto the deck. I could feel it vibrate as he ran from one end to the other looking for me.

Mom was at the sliding glass door and handed him the flashlight saying. "Here, you better take this with you. It's so dark out there now."

The cushions I was lying on had dropped way down into the sofa, hiding me from view. This made me feel so protected. I stood up, and took my usual three turns to get comfortable what Mom calls 'Max's round trips.' While I arched my back and stretched, I was in the midst of a good yawn when I locked eyes with my mom. She was standing in the dining room a look of grave concern swept over her face.

"Oh, no!" was all she said.

A streak of lightning flashed through the front windows, revealing Dad as he ran past it in the driving rain. His head disappeared I guessed he slipped on the wet blacktop. When he got to his feet, a peel of thunder chased him from the driveway to the protection of the carport cover.

From outside, I heard Dad's voice. "Max, Max..." he yelled out.

Mom turned around and dashed to the back door. I heard it open...my parents' voices were barely audible over the massive din of the rain coming down on the trailer's metal roof.

"Honey..." Mom started, "...he's in here. Yes, he's been inside all along!"

From the warmth of my hiding place I looked up to see Dad walk into the room dripping wet...He didn't look very happy.

29 MORE THAN THIS, PART 1

Everyone has to grow up sometime. In my case, I was thrust into this mean old world way too young and on my own. My education was from the street. Nothing fancy here, just lots of bad days followed by cold and lonely miserable nights.

However, on this day my one and only issue was trying to avoid my dad. He seemed to think that he was going to take me to an upcoming cat show. Why? You got me! I wasn't born with a pedigree.

One place I could escape to was, Glenn's. He is my friend over on Granada Street. No one dropped in on him much, which made my visits always special, and he always gives me "catnip." But first I had to get out of here. If I stayed inside my dad would catch me and take me to the cat groomer.

The day dawned a little gray, odd for late August. I was standing in front of the sliding glass door when I thought it might rain. Mom was in the kitchen washing dishes from breakfast. I knew if I was to get out on the QT. I'd have to fake Mom out, and make her open the door for me.

Dad yelled from the back bedroom. We heard him slam one of the closet doors, sending a shiver through the trailers thin walls. The noise startled Mom, who turned off the running water. How does water run anyway? Wiping her hands dry, she leaned over. She smiled that wonderful Mom smile, she then reached for the door handle. My whole body tensed as she started to slowly open it. I lifted my head bone up to her and opened my mouth slightly, giving her one of my best T-Rex smiles ever. She is a sucker for my T-Rex smiles, always has been.

From down the hallway, Dad's voice got louder. "Where is he? Have you seen him?" Then another closet door slammed shut. Mom bent over and scratched my head bone. I watched as the door moved another inch. Oh, come on, Mom! Just slide it open three more inches and I'll be in the wind.

I could hear my dad's footsteps as he came down the hallway. First his shoe appeared then his leg. "Where is Max? I want..." His last word hung in the air. Then Mom realized what I was up too. Dad pointed at me as the door moved that last inch. I then made my move straight out the doorway, with my head and my shoulders out, I felt the door stop. Mom had betrayed me. With a big push from my hind legs, I burst through the opening and onto the deck and freedom. I made a quick right turn and flew down the steps, my ears pinned back under the force of my run.

I was on the grass in the backyard when I heard Dad say something and then mom's reply, "Oh, honestly, he'll be back to eat soon enough. You can hide in a bush and grab him then." The door slid shut. In another second I was at the gate, then under it, and gone!

I didn't stop running until I was down the grassy alley, past three trailers and headed toward the big intersection at Granada and Thatch. That's where Glenn's trailer was located. I slowed my run to an easy lope, letting my gait carry me along effortlessly. At the intersection, I stopped and slipped under a row of large philodendron. Its long leaves arched out touching the blacktop of the street, they are perfect to hide under. Dark clouds had filled the sky. The bottom half of these were gray from being filled with water. I sat on the dirty curb, my fat frame settled down into my duck position, quietly curling my tail around me.

Patiently I waited.

I almost laughed out loud at the thought of my dad trying to catch me. Good luck there, Dad.

The sky had gotten even cloudier and it certainly looked like rain. As a rule, water falling from the sky is a favorite thing of mine. I love to sit and watch it drip down, forming puddles in the backyard. With a quick glance around, I slipped out from under my friendly cover and stepped into the street. Before I'd taken another step the first raindrops hit the ground and made perfect round islands of water on the blacktop. They looked like wet black worlds all their own. I stopped and gazed into one these little worlds of water. They got closer and closer to each other like they wanted to join together. In no time, a small puddle had formed and I was hypnotized.

I had no idea how much time had passed, but the puddle had grown large enough that when I rose up I could see myself mirrored in its depths. My ears twitched as some air pushed its way past me. Something was close and behind me. Before I could turn I saw the top of my dad's head reflected in the puddle. His hands reached out. It took all my willpower to pry myself away from the puddle and dash to the other side of the street and safety.

After a distance, I stopped and took refuge under an old car in Glenn's driveway. The rain had slackened and for the moment.

I climbed the porch steps of Glenn's trailer. There I shook the water off my body. Glenn's back door opened and he stepped out. He carried a brown bag which he took over to the trash can and dropped it in.

Seeing me, he bent over, and smiled, "Max, you old dog you, come to visit or just wanna get out of the rain?" With this remark he stooped over and patted my wet head bone. Slipping his hand under my chest he picked me up in one easy movement.

"I think your parents should change your name. You're not like any cat I know of. Let's see, hmm…I got it! You're really a catfish, right?" His breath smelled of something awful, more than stinky. I reeled back as he laughed at his joke.

There aren't a lot of people that I allow to pick me up, but I trust Glenn in a way that I don't with other people. Maybe it's the artist in him. It could also be that he feeds me by hand; bunches of treats that my mom would never give me. Dad says my weight gain is evidence that I've got another family somewhere in the park I'm not telling them about. Actually, it's only Glenn. You see, Glenn is a chef. Well, these days he is actually a cook and a really good one too. Lately, he's been doing pastry and desserts out of his trailer. He has a one-of-a-kind setup inside his kitchen. He gave me the big tour one day and told me all about his many gadgets. He is extremely proud of his working space.

I am just glad that the place is so warm all the time. Today was different, though. When we walked in I noticed that the windows in his prep station were all open, letting the cold in. The extra wide vinyl curtains dividing the workstation from the rest of the trailer were open as well.

He put me down on the floor and stroked me from head to tail. I arched up and closed my eyes, squinting at him. My loud, rough purr filled the room. He genuinely likes it, so I laid it on pretty thick, if you know what I mean, it always gets me catnip.

Glenn wandered off, so I gave myself another hard shake to get the very last of the water off of my undercoat. White dust covered the floor and I left many Max sized paw prints everywhere I wandered. Next to the worktable was a metal holder that held a couple of tall round tubes. One had the word "white" written on it the other "milk." There were hoses running out of the tops of both that led to a kind of brass colored handle. An intensely sweet smell came from the tip of this thing.

Being so curious, I needed to know what was up with this equipment. I reached out with my paw and hooked a claw into the tip. I was quite surprised when a trickle of brown fluid dripped down onto my claw, then into my paw pad to fill the curves and contours. I was mesmerized by the stuff. Did I mention how incredible it smelled?

The underside of my paw was wet and gooey; the brown color was deep and rich. I could not resist, ever so lightly I sampled a small amount with the tip of my tongue. The first sensation happened at my lower jaw where it hinges to my skull. An almost divine pain swept through me. It filled my senses with a pleasure I'd never experienced before. My eyes swelled in their sockets and my ears rang for a second. Just as fast as the pleasure came upon me, it passed. I sat stunned, immobile, letting my paw dangle in mid-air.

From the next room, I heard the clinking of ice cubes in a glass and noticed the toxic smell I'd encountered earlier on Glenn's breath.

My host entered, picked me up and set me on his stainless steel worktable. This was unusual; I had never been up on any of his kitchen tables before. He grabbed a paper towel, turned on the faucet and got the towel wet. He then turned back to me.

I knew what he wanted me to do so I held up my gooey paw for him. He smiled and wiped it off. I watched as all of the brown wonderfulness was washed away. A droplet clung to one claw. I eagerly licked it up before it fell.

Laughing his hearty laugh, Glenn's voice rang out, "Oh no, look what I've done! I've created a chocolate monster."

Glenn pushed his fingertip in between my pads, cleaning out what was left. The consistency of the fluid had changed. It didn't move the way it had earlier. But it was still wonderful…this stuff called chocolate. Glenn smiled at me as he took his fingertip and dabbed my nose with the stuff.

Quickly I licked at the goo but it had grown stiff. It took three good laps of my tongue to get it all off my nose.

My smiling host dried my damp, sticky paw and said, "I guess I don't have to offer you any catnip." He smiled at his comment. "Your first time? Yeah… I know… the first one is free and then it's got you." Not knowing what that meant but being polite I merely nodded my head.

He picked me up with his free hand and reached to grab a metal folding stool and put me down on it.

"Ok, this is a good vantage point to watch from. I think you'll find this interesting. Now don't you move."

I gazed across the empty space between the table and me. The span was perhaps three feet, no more. 'I can make this jump with my eyes closed' I thought. That's when I noticed the slab of that glorious stuff called chocolate.

Involuntarily I meowed. It was actually a cry of disbelief. I reached out with my paw and tried to touch the slab. This greatly amused Glenn, who took a position behind the slab where he attacked the chocolate with a metal cheese grater. In no time, he had a pile of flaked chocolate in front of him. As he worked he kept pushing the pile into the middle of the table. Finally satisfied, he took a hair dryer from a shelf under the table and turned it on. It howled and whirled, building heat that I could feel from my perch. In seconds, he had a puddle of molten chocolate running out in all directions.

Glenn picked up the glass filled with ice cubes and took a long drink. Revived, he grabbed another tool to work with. It looked like a golden bit of metal, maybe six inches across. Holding it face down in his hand and with a swirling motion, he scraped the thing over the surface of the steel table. Around and around he went until he folded the chocolate over onto itself. He piled it into a sort of round shape. Then he took the hair dryer, held it over the chocolate, which he heated for a few seconds. After that he went back to scraping again. This procedure was repeated several times before he stopped. When he was done he had several thinner, (but taller) slabs that lay on the table.

He stepped back and folded his arms around his large chest. For a moment, he looked older than his sixty plus years. He wiped his brow with his hand and smiled at me. I wondered to myself if I'd get some more of this chocolate stuff.

Leaning back, he pointed his finger at me. "I know what you want, you fur ball." With that, he brought his finger up to the side of his head and tapped it lightly. "Yep, you think you can make that jump and get my chocolate. Well, I'm way ahead of you, sport." He stacked the slabs together and from the counter top at the opposite side of the kitchen he grabbed a stack of waxed paper. Glenn deftly slipped a sheet off the top, held it at the top corners, and placed it over the slabs. He repeated this maneuver until he'd covered all the chocolate. Next to the stack was an odd looking thing he called a 'tape dispenser'. In the past, as a way of teasing me he'd often put a small piece of tape on my tail. Then he'd laugh himself sick, as I'd struggle to get the sticky thing off of my tail and then off my paws. People and their big jokes, humph!

But today he used the tape to shut the edges together, turning it into a bag, which totally covered the chocolate slabs.

"Damn, it's cold in here," Glenn said. He walked over to the nearest window to slide it shut. "That's better, best I do them all." He walked around the back end of the trailer, closing the rest of the windows.

"Okay, Max…you'll let me know when it's time for the next step, all right. This creation is going to be a thing of beauty."

I nodded up at Glenn who smiled back at me. "I'll be in the living room I'm going to catch the news." With that, he stepped through the vinyl curtains. I heard the faint clinking of those ice cubes in his glass and then the sound of the TV.

In no time, the room warmed up. Rivulets of water ran down the inside of the windows. I noticed a splatter of chocolate at the edge of the table. It had the appearance of wood, almost. I focused on it and waited. Gentle snores from the living room told me that Glenn had once again succumbed to those ice cubes that seem to overpower him from time to time.

Curiosity drove me to check out this new chocolate. With little effort, I made the three-foot jump over to the tabletop.

The question was how could I bite into such huge slabs? I looked around and using a claw, scraped up as many pieces of chocolate as I could find. It was not enough. There had to be a better way. Several minutes had gone by and I feared that Glenn might wake up. I stood up on my hind legs and studied the wrapping Glenn had done. What I needed to do had to be done from the front.

I sat down in front of the slabs, my tail switched back and forth, as if it had a mind of its own. I took one final glance towards the living room and noted that Glenn was still snoring; I attacked the wax paper in a fury with my extended claws. The wax paper didn't stand a chance... in tenths of seconds I had sliced my way through it. I had created an opening that showed the brown, rich color of this thing called chocolate. I took a step back to gaze upon it.

My next thought me baffled. How do I consume this stuff? After all, earlier when I tasted this food of the gods, the chocolate was almost liquid. I reached out with my claws and like a mini sculptor's tool I dragged them across the face of the first slab. I stared in amazement as little brown ribbons peeled off the tips. The chocolate curls rolled and rolled over themselves in four neat corkscrew rings, falling to the steel tabletop. A morsel clung to one of my claws. I watched as it changed back into a semi-molten state in the growing heat of the room. Licking at the brown goo, my cat's brain filled with pleasure. It was then that I knew what had to be done.

I started to shred the first slab over and over again. When I had built a good-sized pile of shavings, I pushed them around me. Turning so my back was against the slabs; I paused to listen for any movement from Glenn. Nope, just his gentle snoring. Now it was up to heat and time. I settled into a delightful duck position and waited. I stared at the pile, willing it to become liquid.

Some time later my eyes grew heavy but nothing had happened to my pile of wonderfulness. I wasn't going to give up now, not when I was so close.

I stretched out, and rested on an elbow, fighting a losing battle with sleep. In a few seconds, it was upon me. First it was hard to see out of both eyes. So I closed one, but it was just as hard to stay focused with the other. I switched back and forth so many times that I lost track of which one was which. I closed them together and opened quickly at the same time. Little grains of tears were drying in my eye ducts. My last thought was that the chocolate would still be there when I woke up.

'I'll only take half of a cat nap, it'll be quick…honest.' I said to myself. I stuck out my tongue for just a taste as my eyelids shut. My world turned black and I was gone, dreaming of chocolate.

In a little corner of dreamland, I was happily running through a field and stalking something. In the mist of all of this, a shadow fell over me from behind. It crept at a slow pace. All I could do was wait. My ability to run or just get out of the way was gone. I had no strength…I couldn't move a muscle as the shadow grew bigger and longer and then it engulfed me. I had the distinct feeling of it touching me.

All the while it was growing hot in the room. The cold steel table was now radiating heat. 'This is all a dream' I told myself. 'There is no reason to get excited or to wake up or even open my eyes.'

Deeper into my catnap I went. The shadow had
become heavy; it almost crushed me as I slept. Now it
had totally surrounded me. I became aware of a scent…
the aroma of heaven. Incredibly, chocolate had found its
way into my dream. Well at least the smell had. Like a
new mistress, it took me away, and to my absolute shame,
I went with her willingly.

30 MORE THAN THIS, PART 2

Time had gotten away from me…again. My mind drifted. And the dream began. Faces filled my senses and before I knew It, I was waking up, one eyeball at a time. But instead of Glenn's, I found myself under a strange house lying on dirt. Above me were large, very long pieces of wood. A sort of dirty cool atmosphere surrounded me. All at once I realized that I'd not had a drink of water all morning.

I started to get up, first stretching out my front legs; then the stretch traveled on its own, and moved past my legs up to my shoulders then down my back. Sometimes I arch my back but this morning I just let the stretch sweep down to my tailbone. I sat up and yawned, which often follows a good stretch.

Outside were a lot of loud noises. This house I had taken refuge under was vacant, and no one was going to pay any attention to me sleeping underneath it. I popped out from the crawl space to investigate the loud sound. A couple of guys were working on the roof of the house. A "remodel" is what I heard them call it.

These two fellas would sometimes give me little bits of some odd looking meat. Yuck. But I wolfed them down anyway, I was so hungry!

On this day, the sun was beating down and the guys were in the process of packing up all their tools to leave. Any chance of getting something to drink was looking slim. Before I could totally wake up, they rolled down the steep driveway and drove away. The bright sunlight hurt my eyes as I poked my nose out of the crawl space.

I had picked this spot because there was shelter under the house. The first night I had to fight for it. A couple of small skunks had taken up residence in one corner of the space. I got into a fight with one. We had a boxing match but before he could cut loose with his secret weapon, I scooted into a far corner to safety. In the morning, they were gone and never did come back.

It was the neighborhood tomcats that kept me hoppin'. Every night after the neighborhood had settled down and gone all quiet, they would show up. Both were old and mangy. I'd never seen cats so beaten up. With the exception of the occasional small gopher popping in, and leaving in a rush with me in hot pursuit, the space was all mine.

I begged from the guys working on the roof, but I never got much. To make matters worse, I had dropped weight and went to sleep hungry. During the day, I could get a little bit of water from out of the sprinklers next door, but it was always dirty and had bits of grass floating in it. The trick was to get to the sprinklers quickly before it drained into the ground. As mid-summer approached, the water was drying up in seconds, leaving a small muddy puddle behind and then just mud. Besides, the lady that watered didn't do it every day.

Today she was leisurely watering with a garden hose; I slipped out of the shadows of the house and stepped onto the driveway. The sun beat down on the concrete and waves of heat danced about. I tried my best to keep my fur standing up to vent myself, but the only thing I could do for relief was to hang out my tongue. I crept into the bushes and squeezed between two small bushes. The water made this incredible sound. To hear it better I stuck my head out from under some low-hanging branches.

She stood there, not more than eight feet away. Instinct told me to hold my position and be safe. She didn't look threatening. She was tall and seemed to tower over everything. All the while she turned slowly, letting the water fall where it may. Mustering my courage, I made a break from the flage and sprinted to the water. She had not seen me and continued to flip the hose from one spot to another. She moved it so fast that I couldn't get a taste of it. I decided on more direct action I ran straight at her and then head-butted her. She stopped and looked down. Then she lowered the water hose so I could get to it. With one paw on her hand and the other on the ground, I stuck out my tongue to lap up my first-ever cold water out of a garden hose. It was clean: It filled my mouth as I worked my tongue, gathering it up in my cat's fashion. She let me drink my fill. Then she petted my head bone. I leaned over to her, rubbing up against her leg... I felt good for the first time in a long time.

She let me have all of the water I wanted to drink until I thought I'd burst. Sitting down, I looked up at her. She smiled, picked me up and held me up to her shoulder as we walked across the yard, to the driveway, and into her backyard. It was an incredible yard, a veritable jungle of plants...lots of other stuff too. It looked like a lot of yards I'd traveled through but never stopped in for any length of time. I was perched on her shoulder as she tenderly petted me down my back. I snuggled in her neck while taking note of everything I saw.

Beyond the porch an open door beckoned. Wide-eyed, I gazed at everything in the rooms, the couches and chairs, bookshelves and that thing called TV (the first I'd ever seen). Then down a long hallway.

I was incredibly excited when we finally came to a room with a large bed in it. At the far side, through a window you could actually look out and see the front yard where I'd been minutes before. In the dim light, I saw a man sleeping. The sheets covered him at mid-length. An overhead fan twirled at an easy pace.

Holding me close to her chest, she touched him along his exposed leg. He came around, blinking his eyes at us, just like I do. I meowed softly, not wishing to appear rude, and held out a paw I tried to look presentable but also felt a little vulnerable.

The words she spoke changed my life forever…"Hey, Dad" Her tone was easy with an edge of excitement. "We're new parents," she said.

My dream slipped away from me. Somewhere beyond that delightful smell and the heavy touch of that shadow was Glenn. He was stirring. I could hear his footfalls on the floor as the trailer flexed under his weight.

I tried to open my eyes but found it difficult. There was only blackness. My eyelashes were glued shut and it took enormous effort and with some pain to move them. I tried to focus but there was only a black void. The urge to stretch came over me, but I was pinned, unable to move even a fraction of an inch. I heard Glenn in the other room and wondered why he couldn't hear me. I tried to lift my head but it wouldn't move. I pushed with all of my strength to get up onto my paws, but I was immobile as if an extremely heavy weight was on top of me. With both eyes open I could just see a streak of light at my paws.

Glenn's voice echoed inside my encasement. I was trapped.

"What the devil? How did you….?"

I'm guessing that Glenn took hold of whatever was on top of me because I could see his fingertips beside my paws and the light grew brighter. I "meowed" as loudly as I could. Then I could see the shine of the tabletop and my own fur on my legs as the weight was lifted off me. The fur on my back and shoulders went with it as Glenn lifted higher and higher. His hand came under the dark brown lip of the thing as he gently wiggled his fingers, separating my fur from what held me. In a few seconds I was almost free; he grabbed me under my chest and pulled me out from the trap. He held me out in the light. I let him have a tremendous "meow" of celebration and flicked my tail from side to side.

"How did you manage to get inside this, Max?" He pointed down at the stainless steel table. There lying on the table in the exact spot where I'd fallen asleep, was me, still curled up in a ball.

My head was bent down, my chin rested on my paws; my eyes closed looking like I was still working on the best catnap of my feline life, but I was inside out. Glenn asked me all kinds of questions, which I'd no idea how to answer. Then he set me back down on the table. I came face to face with a perfect negative relief of a chocolate Max.

Glenn's face lit up. He then sprang into action. He started by throwing open the windows, letting the hot air rush out. He quickly went to the far end of his workspace and opened the big sliding window, creating a draft of cool air. The rain had stopped and only the drip, drip, drip of water falling off of the roof could be heard.

I reached out to touch my chocolate self, but instead of the soft, almost molten feel it had earlier, the cold air allowed the chocolate surface to set-up into a thin shell. I pushed a little and it bent in. Glenn reached over. Holding my paw, he said, "Let us not be too curious there, little buddy. I've got work to do on this." He stood in front of the table, his arms flailing about, a broad smile on his face.

Laughing softly, Glenn said, "I can only guess….you fell asleep in front of the thin slab of chocolate and in the heat it fell over and molded to your ample body there, Max." Bending over me, he ruffled the fur on my head bone and said, "You're a genius, my boy…a genius. I'm going to make two of these…Dude! One for my customer and the other will become a permanent mold."

For the next hour, Glenn flew around his kitchen. He was possessed by a kind of creative frenzy. He flung open doors and drawers, pulling out his tools and working over the mass of chocolate that had formed over my body. His starting point was to pull out all of my wayward hairs still stuck in the mold. Then he grabbed a large bowl. He mixed in a sort of white chocolate paste, whipping it up to a froth. The next step was amazing: by propping the mold up with an extra slab of chocolate, Glenn could stuff the inside of the shell with the paste. At the very last moment, he slid the sculpture under a large metal plate. Then ever so carefully he lowered the sagging cat that looked like a twin of me back onto its new base. Next, he defined my features on the sleeping cat's face. He elongated the rear legs a bit and added longer claws. To be true to my look, he introduced a small amount of white chocolate and milk chocolate for color. *'Hmm, milk chocolate.'*

Almost as an after-thought, he reworked one eye (the semi-closed one) carving in an eyelid, a pupil, and iris. By adding extremely small chocolate shavings, eyelashes seemed to appear. He mixed a pile of both chocolates, adding more white, and melting it. He mixed it over and over again. He then scraped the whole mess up onto the blade and poured it into an odd looking plastic container. Glenn reached under the stainless steel table and pulled out a handle thing and screwed the plastic container onto it from the bottom. He took an electric wire that was hanging down from the handle thing and plugged it into the wall. With a wink he said, "Ok, little buddy, it's time to rock 'n' roll with my airbrush." The handle thing whirled a little. I was unprepared for what happened next.

Through his shirt, I could see his arm muscles tense. The ripple traveled down to his wrist where his finger wrapped around the handle and pulled it. At the same moment, the handle seemed to explode in his hand. It emitted a fine spray of white chocolate that spewed out into the middle of the room. Glenn held his hand out to stop me from jumping at it. I raised my paw as the plume of chocolate drifted past me and was transported back to my place of heaven as I licked it off my paw. Wearing goggles, he crouched down. I stood and leaned in as well, not wanting to miss any part of his new creation.

"Don't do this at home, Max." Glenn laughed at his own joke.

He proceeded to pull the trigger and with a small adjustment he turned the brown sleeping cat into a facsimile of me. First he painted it a thick solid white from head to toe. Then he switched containers and painted a gray cape onto my chocolate twin. Carefully he added color to the elegantly sculpted hairs around my neck. I've a marking that wraps around the back of my head, giving me what my dad calls a 'nineteen forties two-tone' color scheme. With absolute dexterity Glenn added white accents to the undercoat where needed.

Putting the spray gun down, he took up an unusually small bottle, which he dipped a Q-tip into. With that, he added silver shimmer to a few areas on my sleeping twin.

"Now to make you handsome," Glenn said.

"Could that be possible?" I asked myself? With that, he leaned over and using a small paintbrush, added white chocolate hairs to the muzzle and chin. Then he drew a wide white line up in-between my eyes ending at my brow.

With a satisfied look, he stepped back and folded his arms across his chest. I took this cue and sat back myself. That's when I noticed a small patch of white chocolate on the table. I dipped my paw in and licked it slowly. For a while, my troubles drifted away. My mind wasn't my own.

Glenn said, "One little bit of color and you're a done deal there, little buddy." With a deft hand he added just two colors; a speckled yellow for both eyes, then he dabbed in black for the pupil.

I stopped licking my paw and stared at myself that looked back at me. The sculpture had almost come alive as if it was going to "meow" in protest to Glenn's pulling and prodding.

Standing erect, the maestro announced, "*voila* you are done, complete and fini."I realized that the chocolate was gone. I had finished licking my paw and had gotten every bit of chocolate I could off of it. I dug into the little tufts of hair between my pads. There was nothing left. A depression swept over me; I thought I would cry. Then I realized that there was more chocolate to be had right in front of me.

I stalked my chocolate self. Like lightning I attacked. Looking over my shoulder I didn't see Glenn. I reached out with my paw and extended a claw. I shaved off a series of chocolate bits.

Could there be more than this? Could this be heaven? I asked myself?

I was in the process off licking these cannibalized morsels off me when I was grabbed by the scruff of my neck. Pulled high into the air, I found myself looking into Glenn's face.

"Oh no, this is not for troublemakers like you. I'm afraid you've been cut off."

I started to growl as he marched me to the back door. Glenn, who was my friend, opened the door and tossed me onto the rear stairs. He pointed off into the darkness.

"Go!!! You've been eighty-sixed."

As I walked away from the trailer, anger welled inside of me. Thankfully, the whirling feeling inside my head had subsided. The cold, wet air filled my lungs as I picked up my pace and began to run. For a few feet, the thought of going back and somehow finding a way into Glenn's trailer crossed my mind. But the effect of the chocolate had worn down, not unlike catnip.

Now I'm not prone to anger. The best way for me to work any out was to do something physical. So I continued to run and quickly found myself standing at our backyard. From there I made the jump up onto the shed next door at Melissa's. I walked across her metal carport cover and onto her roof.

When I got to the peak and straddled the crown, I saw off in the distance over the mountain they call El Capitan, dark clouds that filled the eastern sky. The wind picked up... looked like a lot of bad weather coming in. Most of my anger had passed, as the wind lifted my chocolate-scented fur. I was still a little bewildered about why being away from the chocolate made me feel so mad and then so sorry.

My heart thumped in my chest...the bloop, bloop sound rang in my ears. Just then a streak of sunlight pierced through the cold gray clouds and shone down, bringing new light.

It was then I heard my mom's voice...she was call me for Din-Din. I gotta get down from here right now...and go eat. Again I asked myself, "Could there be more than this?"

31 SOMEWHERE IN THE NIGHT

My mom says I'm just like my dad. He, too, is a little hard to wake up in the morning. As of late the whole household had been up early to see Dad off to his handyman job. Sadly that position was way too tough, so they let him go after just six weeks. So Dad is back on the job search. But because I'm a good son, I have continued to get up early to help Mom do the morning chores, like making Dad something to eat and then of course they talk about where his job search will be that day while I grab a quick bite myself. So I was surprised when my dad grabbed and carried me off to the laundry room…it was there that I saw the cat carrier (if you ask me its just another name for a portable torture chamber for felines). It was sitting on the washer. My blood turned cold and I let out a mournful, 'MEOOOW'.

From the kitchen Mom said, "You think he is going to be easy to handle at the groomers? Ha…." She walked out drying her hands on a dishtowel. "Hell, you haven't even gotten him into the carrier yet." She laughed as she walked away.

She was right, I wasn't in the carrier yet…there was still hope for me. Dad looked down at me then looked over at the carrier. It must have dawned on him…that he didn't have enough hands to do this. He turned toward Mom who stood there, her arms crossed over her chest.

The look on her face told me she wasn't going to help him either.

"Ha, ha," I said to myself.

From here on out, good old Dad was clearly on his own. He held out his free hand, she shook her head. I looked up at him and meowed again.

"Come on. You're not going to help me get him in the carrier?"

She shook her head again. Dad turned back to the carrier and held me by the scruff of my neck. He pulled on the latches of the top door of the carrier. I knew if I struggled he might drop me and I could take refuge behind the washer. But he really held me tight as he started to pull on the carrier's door. I watched in horror as a lever flipped with a metallic sound and the door swung open. My hopes of freedom were getting slimmer by the second.

He hefted me into his other hand in one swift motion. I have to admit that Dad knew his stuff when it came to handling beefy boys like me. But I have two secret weapons, and I was about to put both of them to good use.

He then brought me over the top of the carrier, I hung there, seconds away from being trapped. It was then I popped out my rear legs, and with my rear claws extended, I gripped the wire mesh that made up part of the roof. Frustrated, Dad stopped. "Max, damn it." A snicker came from my mom, as she watched from the hallway.

He quickly raised me up and then lowered me down headfirst. I popped out both of my front paws, again stopping my descent. Mom burst into laughter, slapping her thigh and shook her head as she walked down the hallway out of sight.

I felt Dad's anger build as he held me. He grabbed my hind legs, then swiftly switched his other hand from under my chest to the scruff of my neck. He gave me a shake (to let me know who was boss) then he tightened his grip. I surrendered as he slipped me upside down and at a low angle into the carrier, head first. And closed the wire door, I snarled and hissed at him but to no avail. Mom's words filled my cat's brain. *The groomer's.*

"Sorry, little buddy, but you are going."

He struck the latches hard, picked the carrier and me up and we walked out the rear door.

Most of the time I like road trips, when we go somewhere in my dad's truck, I know that I'm going to have a good time sightseeing. But not on this day…there wasn't going to be anything good about today.

The truck pulled out of the park. Dad drove with me in the back on the floor in the carrier. He was taking no chances on my getting away. Being on the floor, as a matter of fact, there wasn't much to see, so I thought I might as well meow really loud, which I did. After three or four choruses, it got to him.

"MAX!!" He hollered at me from the front seat.

I kicked it up a notch. My 'meows' turned into 'howls'…very loud 'howls'. I know this makes him mad so he sticks his finger through the wire mesh of the door over my head. He wiggles his finger in circles while he makes his click, click noises. I ignore this as well, making him even madder.

In his frustration, Dad stopped the truck. He reached over the front seat and pulled the carrier over to rest on the seat beside him. This was better. I could see the tops of the buildings as we drove down the street. Abruptly we came to a stop. Dad rolls down the window on his side. The wind filled the cab with dry, hot air. It's the kind of heat that is hard to move in, it's so dry. My tongue popped out automatically in an effort to drop my body temperature. A roaring came from behind us. I saw some humans glide by as if they were floating, then they came to a stop next to our truck. The men's heads were misshapen and all black and shiny. One even had a bristle of red hair that ran from his forehead over the top of his head then down his back. Dad said to one of the bikers that he should drag his old scooter out of the shed and dust it off. The man replied, "You should. We all need to get in the wind now and again." The men grinned held out their hands, a sort of greeting I imagine, and roared off.

In a few minutes, we were at that dreaded place, the groomers. Dad pulled into the parking lot and I thought I was going to puke. He turned off the engine, got out of the truck, and opened the door. I let out a solid 'meow' but he was having none of my protests. In seconds, we were in the waiting room.

The first thing you notice is the cold air, which is good and then the smells, which are not. There are lots of animals here, dogs and cats mostly. The smell is something like the vets office (another terrible place) but not so strong. Mingled with the unpleasant smells was the faint odor of shampoo, not unlike my mom's bathroom when she takes a shower.

Just then a door opened and a lady with a red dog came out. It was a stupid-looking dog, tall and mangy with its tongue hanging out of the side of its mouth. He was so excited to get out of this place, he was marching around and around in circles.

Dad, true to form, stuck his finger in through the wire mesh and, yep, started the 'click-click' thing. In disgust, I bit his wiggling appendage, not hard, but he did pull it out of the cage and he shook it vigorously.

The red beast sniffed the air. Geez, I'm only five feet away. Finally seeing me, he gets doubly excited as he pulled on his leash. She finally got a grip on him as my dad grabbed the dog by the collar.

The interior door again opened. A young girl with raven-colored hair called out my name, "Max."

Uhh…Why call me? This is all my Dad's idea. Maybe he should get groomed instead of me!

Dad stood up and took me over to her. She said, "Oh, I'll take him. Hi, Max…"

She smiled a sweet smile, which made Dad a little flustered. Girls and women often have that effect on him He blushed as he handed me off to this young girl; she looked down at me. Her smile widened, "Oh, aren't you sweet and so handsome, too." She stuck her finger through the wire mesh and…made her version of the click, click sound. Funny that her making the click, click noise didn't annoy me half as much as when Dad does it. Come to think of it I don't mind it when my mom does it either."

Then she looked at Dad and said, "Hi, I'm Susan, and I'll be taking care of Max today. You can come back in an hour."

Dad responded. "Sure, Uhh! Susan…yes, you'll take real good care of him?" He looked down at me, then glanced at her. "We're going to the cat show tomorrow aren't we, Max, old buddy?"

She smiled at me. "Oh isn't that wonderful. We've had a lot of purebreds in today for the show…what breed is Max?"

The question hung in the air for a while. Finally, Dad managed an answer. "Well, we don't know." He tried to get out a smile, but it didn't work.

The lady with the red dog leaned over and said, "Hmm…he looks like a short hair of some sort."

With all this human chattering and indecision, I settled into my duck position and waited for my brainiac Dad to let us in on the skinny of what kind of breed Max is.

Susan looked at me intently and said. "Do you have papers on him? He is so cute, but you have to have papers for the cat show."

"Well, I heard that this particular show does a domestic---"

Both women excitedly exclaimed, "Of course, the domestic housecat judging."

"Well, we'll have to get him all scrubbed up for his big day." Susan turned and smiled at me as the door swung away from her. It narrowed my view of the waiting room and my dad, who was still talking to the lady with that stupid red dog.

I had no idea how this grooming was done, and I gotta admit not having my dad here left me more than a little unsettled.

Susan talked to me softly as she walked me over to a long bench. Then she unlatched the top of the carrier, and she took me out giving me short rapid strokes on my head bone. She started between my ears but only going to the base of my neck. She turned me directly into her face, puckered her lips and made that irritating click, click noise all humans do. But coming from her I didn't mind it at all.

She then placed me on the bench. It was covered in a very soft fabric, and it smelled fantastic. The brush she first used pulled a little. She countered with a gentle follow-through, just like Mom does. She switched brushes to one with a harder tooth and was more forceful. It gave me a tingly sensation on my skin as she combed me from head to tail. There wasn't an inch left uncombed. At one point, I lay on my side as she took out every tangle across my belly and underside. She giggled when she saw my gray dot in the middle of my stark white tummy.

She flipped me over as I surrendered to her completely. She bent over to me. I closed my eyes and I felt her breath on my face. She whispered in my ear, "Don't you move now, Max, you little sweetheart." I did as she asked. All the while I kneaded the edge of the fabric-covered bench.

With my eyes still closed I heard her coming back to me. I knew she was close as the air around me pushed against my fur and whiskers. I could hear her garments rustle as they brushed against the side of the bench.

I felt her hand on the scruff of my neck. But her grip was different as she pulled me up in the air. Startled, I opened my eyes and saw someone dressed in a green smock, someone I'd never seen before.

What happened next shouldn't happen to anyone, let alone me!

This new person, this devil in a green smock, walked the length of the bench. She then opened a door and we entered a hot steam-filled room. We stopped in front of a white sink and she placed me in it in a sitting position, I looked up and hoped that this terrible thing wasn't about to happen to me. From behind green woman, Susan peeked over her shoulder, wiggling her fingers at me.

"Don't worry, little man, she'll be nice. I'll stand here and watch. It'll all be over real soon."

I gazed wistfully at Susan as I heard the snap of latex gloves. Green Woman held me tightly with one hand as she pushed a silver faucet thing with her elbow. Warm water cascaded down my back. For a second I didn't move, then the realization hit me...this warm water *felt good*.

However, my very next thought was to run. I tried to fly out in four directions all at once. But my efforts were all in vain, for I was in the clutches of the Green Woman and she had me pinned. She then started my very first professional bath, ever. Susan continued to smile just so I wouldn't struggle.

However, the stinky stuff she poured on me felt good to my sensitive skin. Bubbles frothed all over me. I surrendered to the suds. After a rinse, Green Woman took me to another room; it was warm, where a small enclosure sat on a table, it had see-through walls all around it. She placed me into this small box. She then closed the door to my dryer and left the room. Overhead, a stream of hot air filled the dryer. I stretched up toward the warmth and tried to touch it. The vibrations grew as more warm air poured into the box through some holes in the top of the dryer. I stretched again, this time extending my neck letting the warm air sweep over me, lifting my short furs around my muzzle and cheeks. My whiskers fluttered in the warm breeze.

I sat under the warmth of the air as Green Woman came back into the room. She held a couple of towels in her hands. She was amazed that I was already dry. Smiling for the first time, she clad me in a towel, vigorously rubbed my body from head to tail and laid me on my side and dried my belly. She too, laughed at my gray spot (what she called a cumber bund) on my tummy, just as Susan had earlier.

That's when Susan appeared back in the room, looking radiant. I got my claws clipped by her and then my wild hairs got trimmed all over with a pair of really small clippers, that's what the wonderful Susan called them. I watched her closely to make sure she didn't take too much off. After a short while she seemed satisfied. Then holding me up over her head, she exclaimed. "Well aren't you the one and so handsome, too." Nuzzling her nose behind my ear she said, "I think you're going to win tomorrow, Mr. Max."

Back in the front room she placed me on a table, where a young woman sat answering the telephone. All of the girls came out to admire me. Before too long my dad walked into the waiting room and saw me being petted by my new fans.

One of the girls asked. "Oh, you're Max's dad aren't you?"

She gave him a half-off coupon for my next grooming, which was extremely cool. Then all of the girls, including Susan and even the Green Woman, came out to wish us luck at the show. Dad beamed at me, he was so proud.

When we got home, Dad went on and on about all that was said at the groomers. Mom served an early celebratory dinner. I went to my couch to check out the last of cat TV. The sun had slipped over the backside of S Mountain, leaving the valley in darkness.

It must have been hours later…I was jarred awake by a lot of yelling. Mom was screaming in my dad's face. He looked as if he could barely contain himself. "We don't have that kind of money, and you took him to the groomers for what? So you could take him to a cat show?" She held out her hand with a slip of paper, "And you preregistered him on our credit card….for whaaaat?"

From the top of the couch I saw Mom leave the room, she slammed her bedroom door. Dad walked quickly into the laundry room.

Now that it was safe I jumped down from the couch and ran after him. I stopped at the doorway and peered around the corner. He was standing on his tiptoes and pulled a box from the top shelf of the overhead cabinet. The box tumbled down with a crash, spilling out its contents. He bent over to pick up a helmet and a pair of battered black leather gloves.

I wanted to go to him, but he seemed angry. I held back, and to my surprise I bumped into Baby. We both waited, not daring to breathe. Dad opened the back door and stepped out into the night. We heard the 'crunch, crunch' of gravel under his boots his footsteps going down the driveway. At first I didn't know where he was going, but then we heard the unmistakable metallic sound of the lock on his metal shed of the doors as they scraped the ground as they opened. I jumped up on the washer and tried to look out of the narrow window beside the door, but I couldn't see anything. What we heard was a lot of moving around in the shed. Finally, Mom came down the hallway. She looked concerned. Clutching her robe tightly around her body, she opened the door and stepped out.

We saw our chance…both of us bolted out the door and onto the steps. There beside Dad was something I'd not seen outside in a quite a while, long, lean and black as the night, it was his old motorcycle. Before they could spot me I crawled down the steps on the far side and crept along the trailer to the street.

As I made my way around the corner of the trailer Baby ran past me, I took off after her at a dead run. The sound of my parent's voices rose in a heated argument behind us. We ran non-stop to the grassy field when I finally caught up to her (boy can she pour it on) I tackled her at her hindquarters and we rolled onto the wet grass over and over again. Still moving forward we tumbled into the sand pit where the park's monkey bars are. I stood up and shook off as much of the dirt as possible when off toward our trailer I heard a motorcycle start up; the engine coughed and sputtered. Its headlight came on over the roofs of the trailers that faced the grassy field.

Was it my dad?

I could see the headlight of the motorcycle going down the street we live on, so it had to be him. In a few seconds, it would be at the first intersection, at Grainger and Vallejo streets. I burst into a sprint. Small dirt clods flew off into the air around me. I made it to Vallejo just as my dad's motorcycle sweep past me. I turned to pursue it and dug in with all my might…but the bike was too powerful. It pulled away from me with ease. Almost spent, my mouth dropped open, sucking in oxygen I slowed to a walk, barely keeping one paw in front of the other.

At the park's entrance my dad leaned the motorcycle over to the right, revved it again and, without looking back, he roared off down the street. A feeling of loneliness swept over me as I stood at the street. Then from in back of me came the soft patter of paws and the click, click of claws. I spun around quickly and was thrilled to see Baby as she trotted out of the darkness. She rubbed up against me, and quietly sat down.

Cars sped past us on the street and for the first time in my memory, I was outside the park. A bunch of white lights came toward us and red ones ran away. Scary was a good word to describe this place. Baby nudged me I knew she wanted to go back home.

Later, when we arrived at the deck, Mom was there waiting to let us in. She took one look at me and without asking what had happened; she picked me up and marched me off down the hallway. At her vanity, she put me on the tabletop, then she proceeded to comb out all of the new tangles.

"Damn it, Max… You are filthy, we just had you at the groomers today, and that costs money, Mr." She held me up. "Oh!…have you been fighting again? Did you get cut …?" She looked me over searching for a wound; luckily there was none. Mom dried me as best as she could then she started to comb me out. The brush mom chose made precise long strokes in my coat as it took out little pieces of leaves and stuff. "Ok, big guy, you had better do good tomorrow, because I gotta tell ya…well, you just got to do good that's all." She shook the brush at me as she spoke. Then she picked up one of my paws, and combed it ever so lightly and said, "Since your Dad has been out of work, we've had to cut back on a lot of things. If you haven't noticed we changed your food as well." She held back a tear and continued, "You know we love you two, and I want your Dad to…" With that she picked up my other paw and looked deep into my eyes. "You don't understand any of this do you, little buddy?" She leaned forward and kissed me on the top of my head bone. "Maybe when your dad comes back, he'll explain it all to you. That is if he's coming back."

If he's coming back, of course, he is coming back, what a thing for my mom to say.

Finally, she did my undercoat and my tail. My tail loves to be combed. Before long she declared, "You are such a handsome little man." She smiled her mom smile as she dropped me to the floor. Then she brushed out Baby.

While the girls were busy, I walked down the hallway. There in the middle of the floor was my cat carrier. I walked over and sniffed at it. I decided to wait here, so I made my usual three circles in front of it…what my mom calls, "Max's round trips." I settled in for a late night catnap and waited for my dad, who was somewhere in the night.

32 MAD MAX

The day dawned way too early for me because I had been up so late waiting for Dad to get home. When I finally did wake, I immediately got up and walked into the kitchen. There stood my dad talking on the phone. At his feet was the cat carrier. I physically felt sick at the sight of it; these portable prisons never mean anything good, it takes me away to places I never want to go to. My feelings last night about being a dutiful son were quickly going, going, gone in the full light of day.

Mom walked into the kitchen, where she sensed my trepidation; she scooped me up in her arms and told Dad that I needed a final brushing so off we went down the hall. She then shut the bedroom door. Sitting on her lap at the vanity table, I felt that at least for a while I was out of danger. She reached over and pulled my cat brush out of a small wicker basket and began to comb me out again. This was the second brushing from her in less than a day, not to mention my day at the groomers. That brush had some kind of magical power, as all of my worries drifted away. I'm putty in her hands whenever she uses it. But today the session didn't last that long. She stroked me from head to tail and made sure that I was untangled and twig free all along my belly. The morning light fell on her face as she worked the magic brush down along my back…she looked so beautiful. Her smile showed me her love and devotion.

At that moment, my Bad Angel appeared in a poof and hovered alongside me.

"Max, quick we can make for the door. I'll help you. You know you don't want to go to this cat show do ya buddy?"

I was thinking along the same lines, but my mom had gone to such great lengths to make me look so nice. Besides Dad really wanted me to go.

Dad's voice rose from behind the closed bedroom door. Mom put the brush down on the tabletop; in a second I dashed straight to it and rubbed against its teeth for one last magical stroke. The door opened, Dad stepped in. He held something behind his back. I don't care how many times he has tried to get me into that torture device; he thinks he can sneak it up on me…like I'm stupid or something. I looked up from my brush to see the cat carrier sticking out from either side of his body. Good old Dad, saving me from way too much anguish.

He placed the cat carrier down on Mom's little vanity chair. Both my angels disappeared in a poof leaving me to my fate. Then he reached over to grasp me behind my neck. He held me in the same spot where my cat mom had when I was a kitten and believe you me; I didn't like it when she did it either. With one swift motion, he swept me into the carrier. At least he was getting better at that and he wasn't wasting any effort with me this time. I snarled and growled a lot, but it didn't matter. Dad really wanted to do this thing called a cat show, and for some unknown reason I had to go, too.

Driving to the show in the truck was uneventful. I slept most of the way. Dad drove straight through on the freeway. I was in the back of the cab on the fold-down seat. I saw the sky change from an overcast gray to a light blue then a few wispy clouds rolled past. All of a sudden a tall palm tree appeared, then another and another whiz-zzed past. The truck slowed down and Dad made a wide left-hand turn. With and easy motion he flipped a switch and the driver's window rolled down. Out of nowhere, a man in sunglasses stuck his head up and held out a piece of paper in his hand.

Mr. Sunglasses said, "You pay when you leave. It's timed. You know what I'm saying, man?"

Dad smiled as he took the slip of paper and tucked it into his breast pocket.

Mr. Sunglasses continued, "That your cat, man? Kinda old, don't ya think? I've seen a lot of really great felines here today and I gotta tell ya this beast ain't got a chance, man."

Dad glared at him. Mr. Sunglasses stood up and raised his heavy black-framed specs for a second look at me. He snickered then waved Dad on.

The truck lurched forward. Dad said under his breath, "Jerk."

The truck came to a stop a few moments later. He parked and got out, opened the cargo door, reached in and took hold of the carrier. He looked down at me and said, "You're not that old are you, little buddy?" He stuck a finger in through the wire mesh, fondly touching my face and cheek. "You'll show 'em."

I nodded up to him in agreement and gave him my best T-rex smile. His finger turned over from my cheek to the underside of my jaw scratching me along the bone. My reflex was involuntary and I let out a series of snorks, making Dad smile.

Dad lifted the carrier out of the truck and placed me on the blacktop. For the first time, I got to see the enormity of where we were. The parking lot went on and on. People in all shapes and sizes walked past us…some with cat carriers. I sat up, all alert, and strained to see if I knew any of these beasts. Most of the cats hung their heads, not looking out at all.

Dad grabbed the wire handle of my carrier and started off toward the gigantic white building. It stood tall and looked like it was terribly old and had these fancy white columns in front. Dad had to climb many steps just to get to the front door. We got into a line that moved along quickly. Across from us was another line with lots of people.

When we got to the front, a young girl smiled at Dad as he handed her a slip of paper. She tore off a small piece and handed it back. Then she pointed behind her and said, "There is registration. Good luck!" She bent over to me, wiggling her finger. "Oh aren't you a handsome fella." I tilted my head and nodded up at the melodic tone of her voice.

Smiling, Dad turned and started off in the direction she had indicated. We arrived at a large table where an older woman with a glossy badge pinned to her jacket sat. Unsmilingly she handed Dad a folded pamphlet and said, "The registration fee is fifty dollars" She quizzically looked from Dad then to me, she wrinkled her nose and continued, "unless you're doing the domestic judging?" She paused and waited.

Dad stood still for a second. "Domestic?"

"Domestic, as in housecats, sir!"

Dad nodded, "And how much is the domestic judging, Ma'am?"

"That will be ten dollars, sir."

She took the money from him and handed him two nametags. Dad bent over and wrote something on them. Then he picked up the carrier from the floor; he placed it and me on the table. He stuck one tag onto the top of the carrier. I looked up and through the thin paper saw XAM

279

on it. *Was that what my name looked like written out in pen, I wondered?*

The woman leaned forward, "Looks like a shorthair of some sort. Max…hmm…not very original. Maybe he was already named when you got him at the pound or wherever?"

Dad made busy fixing the glossy badge onto his shirt. He bent over close to her ear and whispered, "You watch; he's gonna win."

The woman scoffed, "Look around you…Sir. They *all* think their cat is going to win."

On that note, Dad walked off with my carrier hanging from his hand swinging and swaying as we went deeper into the building. All around us were lots of people and lots of cats. Some were in cat carriers and some on leashes being paraded about as people stopped to talk to one another. A few owners looked at me. Some pointed and laughed politely. I did hear a few comments like, "Oh how cute he is."

A young girl, maybe five or six spotted me from across the aisle. Dad was getting instructions on what to do about the domestic judging while I just sort of hung in midair. I wasn't paying much attention to anything, but I did see the little girl. She ran across the open aisle between endless rows of folding chairs. What got my attention was the look on her face; it was all wonderment and surprise. Her hands and arms went up into the air, her mouth flew open and she squealed "Cissy" as she quickly covered the short distance. Meanwhile, her father had seen her run; he was now in pursuit of her. He got to her as her stubby fat fingers wrapped into the wire mesh and pulled the handle out of my Dad's grasp. Just then her father caught her as she tipped back and over from the combined weight of me and the carrier. All of a sudden I was weightless. Her face had filled the whole of my vision, then receded as I fell away from her and we all tumbled to the floor. I could hear a lot of voices that seemed to collide with one another. I heard my dad's voice then the little girl's as she burst into tears. Her high-pitched cries made my ears hurt.

The carrier had landed on its side and I had rolled over with it. It made a scraping sound when it hit the floor. The plastic sides bent down and bowed out. That's when it happened...the carrier's door simply popped open. Could this be my chance? The door swung open and formed a kind of ramp. Then I saw a black shadow come over me...it was time to go. Acting out of cat instinct, I released my rear legs like a coiled spring and hurled myself out of the carrier.

The overhead lights made the indoor world beyond bright. I blinked my eyes and skidded across the slick floor. All of a sudden there were hands projecting out toward me. Now for *sure* I had to get away.

I turned and bolted into the rows of folding chairs where the little girl had come from. In back of me I could hear Dad's voice yell my name, "Max-x-x-x!" Above it all, came a voice over the loudspeaker. It was calm in tone and very business-like as he directed people around the large room.

The first obstacle was an older couple. They sat with their cat, a Maine Coon, in a carrier that looked like mine. I slowed down just enough to jump on the cage, then vaulted over the couple's knees. Coming down on the other side, I hit the floor running. Seconds ticked by and then I heard a man say, "He's over here," followed by the scuffle sound of folding chairs and other distant voices.

I got down on my belly and crawled under a chair, which brought me into the next row. I repeated this again and again. Finally, I came into an empty space, a kind of arch or bend in the rows. More voices filled the air around me. That's when my Bad Angel appeared on top of one of the chairs. He looked down at me his little wings were spread and moved with a slow deliberate rhythm. He pointed over the row of chairs.

"You can't go back buddy we'll have to keep moving forward." He slipped off the chair and floated in mid-air. "Follow me," he said and disappeared over the row of chairs.

How could I follow him, I thought Max's can't fly. I took one shallow breath to get control, then a deeper one to calm myself down. The pounding in my ears had abated. In front of me I could hear more people moving through the front rows. The voice on the loudspeaker added to the din.

Loudspeaker Man said. "Attention, everyone, we've got a loose cat out there. Yep, big surprise, we got another one. His name is 'Max' he is gray on white and an American shorthair and he is hiding among the rows of chairs here in front of the stage. Please look around you on the floor and…" The noise got muffled for a second as Loudspeaker Man took a question. "Ok, I'm told that Max is alright to pick up." His voice was followed by some static-y noise.

"Let's be on the look out for a fifteen pound gray on white American Shorthair." In back of me I could hear voices getting closer. It was time to move out of here now!

They were hunting me.

I needed to know where I was, so I jumped up onto a chair in back of me. There I stood up as tall as I could and with my front paws on the back of it. I got a good look around to see what was happening. As I brought my head up, I found myself looking directly into the face of a smiling man, who sat a few rows away. He pointed his finger at me and yelled, "Here! He's over here!"

"Now you done it." Bad Angel said. "Quick this way." He flew under the chairs and this time I followed him.

The mans voice began to rise; again he yelled, "Hey, he's over here." He leaned forward and snapped his fingers at me. "Hey, Max, old boy. Come on there, fella." He was closing distance fast, but was still three rows away; he stepped through the chairs, and pushed them easily aside. I had seconds to make up my mind…On my right came another man, in a flanking maneuver. I often do this in our backyard when I'm stalking prey and this is what I am right now, prey.

My Good Angel poofed unto the floor and shook a paw at me. "You mister should go back to your cat carrier and be nice." Her little claw shook quicker and quicker. "Your Dad is worried sick!" She sounded just like my Mom. The thought of being nice and safe in my cat carrier did have a certain appeal but so did having my freedom.

Bounding to the floor I turned and ran straight back toward the older, smiling man who was now in my row. I was going to fake them out. He moved in sideways, but the bend in the seats made his progress slow. The jumble of chairs caught him off balance for a second. I allowed him to get extremely close to me then I slunk down to the concrete floor and bolted between his legs.

I picked up speed when I heard him exclaim, "Damn! He got past me. He's coming back toward you at the big aisle."

Bad Angel flew right beside me, smiling his broad kittens grin having way too much fun. "Wow that was

283

great Max, I'll look out for you." Then he zoomed off a blur of streaky black.

With no pesky humans to encumber me, I covered a lot of ground fast. The bend in the rows had straightened out a little. I slowed down and made a turn under the next row of chairs, moving carefully, keeping my tail down. I almost hit a woman's legs. She looked down at me. Her face was quite round and red, with a slender nose. The nose had a pair of green glasses perched on it. With a deft move, she scooped me up and placed me on her lap. I looked around to see if I was safe, then, not to be rude, I gave her a polite, "Meow." And nodded my head, no reason to be impolite.

She said, "You must be tired after all that running around." She jabbed the lady next to her. This woman got up and started to wave at the stage where Loudspeaker Man sat. Was this a trap? It looked like it might be. I leaped from her lap and landed on the chair in front of her. There were lots of people in this area. I hopped like a rabbit from chair to chair, row to row. At one point, I almost landed on someone's shoulder. Finally, I arrived at the first row in front of the stage. I looked over my shoulder and saw a lot of people looking back at me. Most were smiling. Some even waved at me. Cat lovers...go figure!

I turned around to look up at the stage as Loudspeaker Man gazed down at me. He spoke softly into the microphone. "If you are helping us look for Max, he is right here at the stage."

All around me they closed in, these men and women, these cat fanciers. I heard lots of clucking and clicking like my dad does and there were the ever-present smiling faces. My tail switched back and forth. Excitedly the crowd parted to allow my dad to step forward. He didn't look mad, but I sure was. Imagine me getting trapped so easily by this bunch of pesky humans!

With no place else to run, I accepted my fate and sat up straight, to wait for my Dad to make the next move. He bent down on one knee, held out his hands and wiggled his fingers. This was to let me know that everything was okay.

I had a decision to make and quick, too.

"Here we are, folks, in the very last moments of Max's run. What's it going to be, is the little guy going to give up to his owner or...?" I looked up over my shoulder and gave him a dirty look. He paused for a second. "Oh, boy! You should have seen that dirty look Max just gave me, this is one pissed off cat. Let me tell you this is one Mad Max."

Owner? This ownership thing I did not understand. Maybe that's okay for other cats. So showing my independence, I stood up, my Bad Angel poofed at my shoulder and said excitedly.

"Don't do it, Max, it's a trick. Trust me I know all about parents."

Standing at my Dad's foot was my Good Angel she had her arms folded across her chest just like my mom does when I'm in trouble. My fate was sealed. I walked into my dad's hands and ended this drama. And what did Dad do? He turned me over to an official right there and then. What a traitor!

I heard a poof noise and my Bad Angels voice say. "I told you so."

Loudspeaker Man said, "If you want a close-up look at our newest feline celeb, Mad Max, the judging of domestic house cats is about to start."

I had no idea what would happen next. At the judging ring, which held a lot of people, there were only two judges. One placed me on a large black wooden box. I was being displayed in such a degrading manner, it left me speechless.

Please, Dad, help me. I promise I'll never run away from you ever again. I'll always come to you whenever you call me; I'll stop begging you to let me in at the sliding glass door and then running away at the last moment. Honest. Please make these judges stop. But he didn't hear me.

The other judge approached, and I braced myself as he gripped me under my forelegs right in the pits. With his other hand, he had me in front of my rear legs at my belly. My fat sack hung down so everyone could see it…this was simply horrible.

He walked down the line of wide-eyed humans and smiled as he went. A stir went from one spectator to the next. I glanced across the room and in a mixture of wonder and delight I found myself looking at a white cat with a gray hood and cape being held up to the crowd at the opposite side of the circle. The two judges approached the middle of the room. The crowd pressed in, the circle getting smaller and smaller. All the while the other cat was getting closer and clearer.

It was as if I were held up to a mirror of myself. A gasp came up from the crowd. At a big show like this you'd expect to see felines that are uncommonly close in appearance, but this was spooky. This was something else. This beautiful female could be my twin.

The judges compared me to the other cat. They inspected me and my twin closely, they turned us over and over. They looked at how our markings started, where they ended, then how the fur lay and lastly our eyes and noses. After a lot of inspection, they stood in the middle of the circle and said, "As far as we can tell, these two cats are identical in every way. Will the owners of these two wonderful felines, Max and Cissy, come forward so we can take down some information?"

Smiling, Dad walked up to me and ruffled my head bone the way he always does. Meanwhile the judge bent over to make that click, click noise that all humans think we cats like. I just stared back at him and 'me-urred' indifferently. At this point, the judges held us up side by side. The similarity was beyond startling, which caused another gasp from the crowd. A faint scent from this female cat filled my nostrils and triggered a sense memory. More like an echo from out of the past, from a long, long time ago.

Beside me, I could hear my dad, who answered some questions about my age, and where we lived and had I ever been "studded out." He also asked if there are any other littermates? At this point, Dad stopped and thought about the last question. He glanced at me and said, "Max was a stray...he adopted us." That brought applause from the crowd

Good Angel appeared hovering in-between the judges, she watched intently and said, "Oh! Max they all like you." She beamed with delight.

"And where was that?" asked one of the show's officials.

Dad's answer came slowly as he took great pains to find the words, "Well, we were living on the 4600 block of Tivoli Street near the beach..." The official repeated it aloud as he wrote Dad's answer on his clipboard. When the other cat's owner turned to Dad, he asked, "You lived on the 4600 block of Tivoli? We live on the 4300 block of Grainger, one street over." A silence came over the officials. Their expressions said that they had discovered something, but what?

At that moment it made more sense to me than to

them. I looked at my look-alike, and gazed deep into her yellow eyes, the thought formed in my mind that she could be a cousin or even a half sibling. Here might be proof that my cat mom had lived through that horrible day when the dog attacked us in the backyard of the house where I was born, the house up on the hill from the cliffs above the ocean. The one I could never find my way back to. In her yellow eyes I saw my siblings. They must have lived through the attack as well. Was I the only one who had run off and gone missing and been lost all of this time?

A flood of emotion swept over me. My half-sibling's scent became more acute, more defined. Her owner pulled out his wallet and produced a photo of an older female cat that looked exactly like both of us. He said that this was my twin's mom. For the first time as an adult cat I looked at my cat mom. She stood very tall, not like me at all. But she was white with a gray hood and cape on her back. On that account we looked just alike.

Dad was relating my story to all these new people...how I'd showed up at his house that one day, when I was only a few months old. They thought that I was just a stray, lost from somewhere...maybe even abandoned. Dad said that this was almost too much to believe, and how excited Mom was going to be that I had a real cat family. The judges agreed all of this was wonderful but how were they to solve the judging problem at hand? As they spoke, a short wooden platform was brought forward by two men and laid on the floor. It stood only a foot or so high and was just big enough for two people to stand on, side by side.

The crowd was getting restless and a few people asked, "So, so?"..."What's it going to be?"..."Are they littermates?" And "You know the rules!"

Hovering in front of both of us were my angels, they both gazed from me to Cissy and back again. Their eyes were wide and a look of wonder had them for the first time ever speechless.

The judges could agree on at least one thing: I was much older than Cissy, my look-alike half sister… The judges who held us spoke in hushed voices; they nodded to each other saying, "Right we're in agreement?" With the two of us in hand they stepped up onto the platform. The judge holding me cleared his throat and said. "The winners of the 29th annual San Diego Cat Fanciers' Show for best domestic house cat are…"

The room fell silent. From somewhere in the crowd a voice called out. "It's a tie, right?"

Together the judges replied, "Yes, it's a tie."

Applause filled the room. My Bad Angel did backflips in midair, as my Good Angel hugged herself. Many people took our picture as Loudspeaker Man announced to the entire auditorium that, for the first time ever in the official annals of the unofficial best domestic housecat judging, there was a tie. Max and Cissy were the winners. The judges held us both up to the crowd, turning us around and around so everyone could get a good look at us. There was immense applause, thunderous even. People came up to shake Dad's hand and to pet Cissy and me. My angels flew in circles around and around me.

They couldn't get over how much she and I looked alike. And they all loved our story. Everyone was having such a good time! After a short while a few people left the judge's circle and the applause gradually died away. The immediate glory faded, but some of our new fans called out our names and waved goodbye as they left the room.

That's when my dad reached out to take me from the judge. Cissy's owner came up with her across his chest.

As they shook hands, he handed Dad a slip of paper with some numbers on it. He said that Dad should call, so we could all get together.

Dad and I stood there together. He cradled me in his arms fondly, this man I call my "dad." Beaming he said. "You won Max, you're the best. Well, you tied at least, but as far as I'm concerned you won, little buddy." Filled with pride, he smiled back at me. My angels looked on from a short distance away. My Good Angel smiled and waved in her petite fashion a tear in her eye while my Bad Angel grinned from ear to ear.

I know, Dad. I won a long time ago when I met you and Mom. He took his finger and playfully touched my nose. I reached out and hooked a claw in the end, letting my teeth tenderly touch down onto it, and showed him my deep affection. A tear rolled out of my eye and fell silently onto his hand. I looked up at this man that I have trusted with my life and cried to myself.

In an instant all of my pain and the years of anguish over the fate of my cat family left me. I now knew who I was, who my family really was and had always cared for me.

Just think of it…at a thing called a cat show that I didn't even want to go to. I'd won myself an unofficial title, a distant family and officially I was a member of a breed. I'd gone from being lost, to be found and then found again. Forever in my life…from this moment on…I'll never be lost or lonely again. And the angels of my better nature agreed.

My name is Max and I am an American Shorthair…

THE END

All done!

Thanks a million!
Glad you had a good time.

Oh, purrs! Thanks for taking the time to read *Tails From The Park*. If you enjoyed it, please tell your friends or post a short review. Word of mouth is an author's best friend and much appreciated. Paw pats of thanks!

I want to hear from you, gentle reader! Readers like you make me turn in circles and purr.

Send me a message at maxtails123@gmail.com
Or, leave me a message on my Author Page.
amazon.com/author/maxtails
(Just copy and paste to your browser.)

Want to know when the next book is out? Join the Max Gang.
http://eepurl.com/bomzvr (Just copy and paste to your browser.)

Head bumps!

Max

ABOUT THE AUTHOR

Meet Max, a cat who tells stories. The cat stories composed with a bit of adventure told with wry humor make *Tails From The Park* a fun read for cat lovers who know that however regal cats appear, at bottom they are very basic creatures. Get your Maxitude!

Tim Hammill was working on a crime drama film script when Max came to him and said, "Tell my stories." Max told him stories. Tim started writing. He has fun listening and writing them down. Tim is currently working on an adventure series about two fellows, Mark and Ray, who walk into trouble consistently due out in 2016. He lives in the Southwest where he serves as staff for two cats. When he's not writing, he rides a Yamaha V-star Classic bike, works out, and explores different tastes in the kitchen.

Made in the USA
Las Vegas, NV
16 November 2022